Hawke's Cove

Books by Susan Wilson

Hawke's Cove
Beauty

Hawke's Cove

SUSAN WILSON

DOUBLEDAY DIRECT LARGE PRINT EDITION

New York   London   Toronto   Sydney   Singapore

POCKET BOOKS, a division of
Simon & Schuster Inc.
1230 Avenue of the Americas,
New York, NY 10020

Copyright © 2000 by Susan Wilson

ISBN: 0-7394-1028-8

POCKET and colophon are registered trademarks of Simon & Schuster Inc.

Printed in the U.S.A.

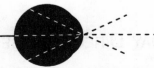

**This Large Print Book carries the
Seal of Approval of N.A.V.H.**

Dedicated with great love to my family: my husband, David, and our beautiful daughters,
Liz and Alison.

Special thanks to Andrea Cirillo for her steadfast support in the evolution of this work.

Thanks to Eulalie Regan at the *Vineyard Gazette* for introducing me to her extensive clipping file from which I learned a great deal about life on the homefront.

Love to the staff at the Oak Bluffs Library for support in ways they have no idea they provide.

The Yankee humor comes from a variety of sources, notably my grandfather, George Geer, and Peggy Scott, both of whom knew how to tell a joke.

And, in memory of Vincent Frankwitz, who fell from the sky to the sea.

Prologue

Hawke's Cove

If you asked, no one could quite remember when he first appeared in Hawke's Cove. After nearly fifty years, it seemed as though Joe Green had always been a part of the scenery, whether driving down Main Street in his beat-up old pickup truck, or sitting at the counter in Linda's Restaurant with the rest of the old men, drinking endless cups of coffee and telling Down East stories peculiar to whiskery old men wearing stained work pants and suspenders.

Heard about Lucius? Found him doubled up in the gutter, right out there, in front've the coffee shop. Asked him, Lucius, what's the matter? He says, Get me up, Joe, I'm ruptured. So I help him home like he is, bent half over like a tree in a wind storm. Next day, I see him in the hardware store, big as life and fit as a fiddle. So I says, Hey, Luke, thought you were ruptured. Well, Joe, he says, heard it snap, felt it give. But weren't no rupture. Just my galluses givin' way.

For Hawke's Cove, this was a knee slapper.

Although Joe Green had done about every kind of job, most remembered him as the milkman. Oh, like most, he'd done time scalloping. Spent a couple of seasons on Pete West's fishing boat, but never took to it. Liked working with warm-blooded animals better, he said, than handling cold fish. Now he took tickets at the movie theater they built in Hawke's Cove in the sixties. Been there long enough for most schoolkids to think he'd always stood at the white double doors of the Elm Theater in his crumpled blue seersucker jacket and white slacks in the summer and the heavy fisherman's sweater and wool trousers when the wind off the water blew in the unheated foyer.

Ask anyone about Joe Green and most would say he was a fair-dealing man, a hard-worker. A nice guy. Ask them who he was and most would shrug and say, Why, just Joe Green. Came here long ago and made a life.

And, except for one person, no one knew who he really was.

One

Charlie—1993

Charlie Worth leaned back in his ergonomically correct desk chair and shot a wad of paper at the wastebasket with an over-the-shoulder hook shot. He missed, and the crumpled memo joined a flock of others surrounding the metal can. This presidential-vacation thing was getting out of hand. Priscilla the Killer kept coming up with more and more stupid angles to write about, and this one was worse than the suggestion about interviewing people in Kennebunkport to see if they could give the people of Great Harbor any good advice *vis-à-vis* presidents on vacation.

Charlie was determined to be the only

feature writer not camping out in Great Harbor for the proposed visit. Besides, he kept pointing out to any who would listen, the Clintons would probably choose the Vineyard. Heck of a lot better golf to be had there than anywhere near this hole-in-the-wall vacation destination. Now, if the Clintons did go to the Vineyard, maybe he'd tag along. At thirty-nine, there were few places Charlie hadn't been to during his journalistic career: Beirut, Saint Petersburg when it had been Leningrad, and London as a correspondent for the *Globe.* He'd been to most every Caribbean island, Belize, and rugged Alaskan camps while he'd done a five-year stint as a travel writer. This feature-writer thing, though, was alternately fun and boring. Craving a settled existence, Charlie had given up the travel for the post, sacrificing adventure for a stable home with a garden he could enjoy through all of its seasons. After eighteen months, though, Charlie found himself daydreaming of chucking the whole security thing and following in the footsteps of the great travel writers, immersing himself in some rare culture, then writing a whiz-bang best-selling memoir.

But even as he played with the notion, Charlie knew that one thing kept him close to home. The same thing that had brought him back to the paper and a desk with a once-a-week byline. His aging parents.

Charlie got up and stretched, reaching for the ceiling. On the way down, he rubbed his hands across his middle in the hope that it had gone away. Leaning over the keyboard, he sent a quick E-mail to his buddy Dave in Sports to get a racquetball date set up. Conscience momentarily salved, he headed towards the coffeepot. As luck would have it, Priscilla St. Lorraine was on her way to his cubicle and caught him before he could take a quick right towards the men's room, which, so far, she hadn't yet invaded.

"Charlie, have I got a story for you!"

"How nice." Charlie smiled, recalling that, in the rarefied code of southern women, "How nice" meant "Fuck you."

Priscilla launched into her story idea, something about an old plane wreck discovered in the waters off Great Harbor during the routine aerial survey prior to the potential visit by the president and his family. It was only when Priscilla told him where the plane had been barged that Charlie's interest was piqued a little.

Hawke's Cove.

When Charlie was little, maybe eight or nine, he and his older sisters had found a Jumping-Jacks shoe box filled with un-catalogued photos. Most of the photos had quasi-familiar adults in them, people they called by the honorific *Aunt* or *Uncle.* Uncle Jack, who was Daddy's partner, and his wife, Aunt Joan, dressed up in party clothes, martini glasses held up to toast some New Year long ago. There were pictures of their parents, looking odd in their old-fashioned hairstyles and out-of-date clothes. Charlie couldn't reconcile his father with this boy with thick blond hair.

Three or four of the pictures had an ocean background. One, a very old sepia print, was of a young woman in a hat, a small terrier standing near her, a barn behind her, the doors half open.

"That's Gran the first year she lived at Hawke's Cove." Vangie had come upon her children, the scattered pictures surrounding them on the worn Oriental carpet. "What are you kids up to here?" Vangie sat down beside Charlie and began gathering up the photos. As she collected them, she began to tell Amanda, Julie, and Charlie who was who and what occasion each photo captured. Charlie vividly remembered the feel of her thick, still-auburn braid touching his cheek as she reached past him to pick out one photo. A thin, bearded man stood holding one end of a line of fish. A crew-cut, heavier-set man stood at the other. They both wore pleased grins.

"Who's these guys?" Charlie asked.

"Who *are* these guys." The correction purely reflexive. "That's Ernie Dubee." She tapped the crew-cut man's face. "He was our police chief in Hawke's Cove."

"Who *is* this one?" Charlie touched the face of the other man with his small forefinger.

"That's Joe. Joe Green. He worked for me on the farm in Hawke's Cove." There was something in her voice that made all three children look at her just in time to see a small, private smile tease her lips.

His mother reached into the cluster of old photos and picked up another one. Charlie leaned against her arm and looked at a picture of a man standing near the barn, a small, pleased smile on his face. "Is that Joe Green too?"

In the way of childhood memories, it was distinct in his mind that his mother only nodded and put the photo in her apron pocket.

That was the first time Charlie would hear about Hawke's Cove and the time his mother spent there during the war.

"So, Mom, what do you remember about Hawke's Cove?"

Evangeline Worth smiled spontaneously at the name. "I remember how the air smelled in the morning, the feel of the wet grass on my bare feet. I remember how brilliant . . ."

"Mom, I asked you, not Evangeline Worth, 'Poet to the People.' Just tell me."

"Tell you what? Stories? You've heard all of them."

"No. Actually, I need to know if you remember a specific incident. A plane crash."

Vangie was glad this conversation was taking place on the phone. That way the sudden shaking in her hands wouldn't frighten Charlie into thinking she'd developed a tremor. "What plane crash?"

She knew, even before Charlie began to tell her. She knew that the Hellcat had been found. As he told her about the presidential vacation and the sonar survey, she felt her mind wander back over half a century. Her mouth twitched in a little self-derisive smile. After this long, which secret needed the most safekeeping? Did it really matter anymore where Joe had come from? What mattered was only that he'd come and her life had been sweetened.

Two

Vangie

Vangie forced herself to finish doing the dishes after Charlie's call. Last dish put away, she began to pace around the house where she and John had raised their children, had lived for most of their married life in relative contentment. She touched things here and there, Amanda's wedding picture and the Mexican clay horse Julie had brought back from her foreign exchange year.

Vangie found herself in the bedroom she had shared with John. She stared at the bed, barely ever disturbed with her solitary occupation of it. Since John had gone to the nursing home following his last stroke, Vangie still found herself keeping to the same side of the bed she had slept in for fifty-seven years. She ran a finger along the edge of John's bureau, clucking at the dust she could now see only in bright daylight. John's things were still where they had been for years: the little Devonware dish where he'd placed his cuff links and change; the bone-handled brush, long since out of use; his matching shoehorn. Now there was a thing rarely put to use in these days of soft shoes. In the home he had a bedside stand with a deep drawer where she kept his shaving things and glasses. There was little else he had need for. Every day she went and shaved him, fed him his lunch, and filled his ears with news about their children and the grandchildren, or silly chat about neighbors she wasn't certain he even remembered. How much of her one-sided conversation he understood she had no idea.

At the foot of their bed was her cedar-lined hope chest. The low cherrywood Lane chest had served to hold blankets and baptismal dresses. Every day John had sat on it to put on his socks and shoes. Vangie opened the cover, releasing a faint whiff of cedar underlain by a mothball tang. Using the edge as a support, she slowly knelt in front of the chest as if at the Communion rail. She didn't need to grope to find what she wanted. Her fingers touched the hard cover of her journal, finding it exactly where she had placed it so long ago.

Pushing herself back onto her feet, Vangie closed the lid of the chest and sat on it. She held the composition book in her lap, marveling that every day John had sat on top of her most dangerous secret, blissfully unaware that hidden beneath him lay a piece of herself that he could never have imagined possible, and which would have altered their lives irrevocably had he ever known of it.

Vangie stared at the diary, at once so familiar, a memory made concrete. She hadn't opened it since the day, more than forty years ago, she had placed it in the chest. Funny, she remembered so clearly doing it, putting it in the chest, consciously thinking that it was a dangerous thing to do, she should be burning it instead. Vangie reached for her better reading glasses, remembering how she had read just the last entry before laying it to rest.

She should have ripped at least that much out of the journal, but the words were too dear. Vangie opened the book, fearing a little that it would crack, but the binding held.

Three

Hawke's Cove—1944

April 17, 1944

Yet another stormy day. It seems as though April's lyrical attempt to cleave to the nursery rhyme has been successful. I certainly hope the May flowers live up to the challenge. The rain is intermittent today, as if even the clouds are bored with it. Less prosaic, but more relevant, I need to do laundry. Ted Frick, who came to see about getting the electricity on out here, says tomorrow should be better. Ted's lived here in Hawke's Cove all his life, "so far," he says with a chuckle.

I feel as though I've lived here a whole lifetime, except that my "lifetime" has been made up of a patchwork of almost thirty summers. I grew up thinking all children were treated to summers in the country. I lived each winter in anticipation of returning to Hawke's Cove. Even as a little girl counting down the weeks, then the days, until my parents would put me on the train from Boston to Great Harbor, confident Gran would be there waiting for me.

Although I see to plumbing and electricity and make blackout curtains and sign up for my few ration coupons, I don't know if I'll see this war to the end here. If the war ever ends. No. I can't let myself think that. I should strike the thought out, but this is a journal meant for private thoughts, not edited for public consumption.

I wait, and the waiting reminds me of pregnancy without the hope, and pregnancy reminds me of death.

I found a pair of John's dungarees and a plaid work shirt in his bottom drawer. I don't know why I pulled that drawer open, but there they were, the mustiness pungent in them and damp to the touch. I'll wash them tomorrow, weather permitting. I wish they had smelled of John. I came to Hawke's Cove partly in the belief little here would remind me of him. But everything conspires to make me think of my husband, still in England, still training for the inevitable. To be sent into combat. If he knows where or when, he has been remarkably circumspect. His letters tell me little.

When I was a girl, spending summers here with Gran and the cousins, we used to put sachets of lavender in our drawers to keep away the summer musty smell. Even so, there was always that faint woody odor released when a drawer or closet was opened. A summer smell, old farmhouse and salt air. Spring odors are different, fecund and wet.

Maybe Ted is right about tomorrow. I hear a plane from the naval air station in Great Harbor overhead. The drone is mixed with the sound of spring peepers.

I went outside when I heard the plane. The sun broke through the clouds just as it passed overhead, and I shaded my eyes. I watched as the single-engined fighter plane nosed its way higher and higher, tucking itself back into the cloud cover to disappear from sight. The sun disappeared with it, and I dropped my hand.

April 18, 1944

Well, Ted was right; after last night's heavy rain and wind, the storm has blown out, and today has been partly sunny, jacket cool, but softer than any yet this spring. For a long time after coming home from the Laundromat, I stood daydreaming on the dunes. There is a little depression in the leeward (or "looward" as they say around here) side of one of the dunes, and I sit there, my thoughts like bees going from blossom to blossom—except that my blooms are not always pretty. When I am on my dune, though, the distraction of seagulls fighting over some disgusting scrap or the windup-toy movements of the sandpipers offer sufficient distraction to me, and my gloomy thoughts are chased away for a few minutes.

Maybe I should get a dog. Something slightly floppy with puzzled brown eyes and a penchant for chasing skunks. "But what would we do with a dog in the city?" I can hear John's voice clearly even if I cannot recall his scent. Poor John, he's never understood my love for this place.

He has no history here to overlie the obvious flaws. He finds the locals dull and ignorant. His words, not mine. I met Mrs. Frick today, and she's neither dull nor ignorant. Plainspoken, that's what I'd call her. Has a tale about everyone on this little peninsula. Describes herself with pride as a "lifer."

I had just put my basket of wet clothes in the backseat of the car, thinking I'd treat myself to a grilled cheese at the Rexall, when Chief Dubee walked by with a naval officer beside him. Both men tipped their hats to me, but didn't pause in their conversation. When I was spending my youthful summers here, Ernie Dubee was one of the few townies I knew. I think he dated my cousin Frances the one summer I didn't come to Hawke's Cove, the summer my father was so ill. Now when Ernie and I pass each other on the street, only in the cautious way we smile at one another is there a flicker in acknowledgment to our shared youth; our greeting is that of old friends with little left in common but a vague recollection of another time when we met on the beach. When I am ready for long conversation, I'll ask him if I am right about Frances.

The marbelized gray counter was a bit sticky, even after Sam Moore swished a damp cloth underneath my elbows. With all his teenage help in school, Sam gives off the impression he is overworked. He stood, tapping one foot against something below the counter, while I read the handwritten menu. I made him wait, then ordered what I had planned on before going in, a grilled cheese sandwich, on white, and a cup of tea, milk not lemon.

I got off the stool and loitered over the selection of magazines while I waited for my lunch. I found the saccharine-sweet cover of *The Saturday Evening Post* mildly offensive, depicting life as they think it should be. Suddenly I was bumped from behind by a woman looking over the card selection.

"Oh, I beg your pardon." The woman blushed and then touched my hand, "I'm Judy Frick. You're Florence Bailey's granddaughter, aren't you?"

"Yes, Vangie Worth. Your husband is doing the work out at my place?" I don't know why I asked; I certainly had heard Ted speak of his wife, Judy.

"Yes. That's right. I've heard you're staying on after the season."

"I don't know. Depends." I had no need to say what on. "I'm about to have lunch, join me?"

Maybe I'm simply starved for neutral conversation, but I really liked meeting Judy. She's enough older than I to take the conversational lead. We lingered over two cups of tea—long enough for me to be late getting my clothes hung, and I ended up having to leave them on the line overnight.

I'm getting better about going into town. People like Judy know who I am, in that way of small places, but not much more than that. Generally, the older year-rounders recognize me only when I mention my grandmother. They remember her having grandchildren come spend the summers, but not us in particular. Those my age are gone, doing factory work in the city, most of the men overseas like John. Besides, I don't want people to know my story—not yet. I couldn't bear it. It's enough they simply think I'm here waiting out the war. As best I can, I avoid conversations that might lead to those perfectly understandable questions about children, like, when are we going to start a family? *Start a family.* Sounds like gardening, starting seeds. I started a seed that took root and grew for a long time, almost to harvest. I think, maybe, someday, there'll be a poem filled with that metaphor. But not just yet.

Thankfully, Judy nattered on about other people. She charmed me with her smile and her observations about everyone who lives here in Hawke's Cove. There isn't a soul she doesn't know or have an opinion about. "Bart Lewis, cagey old coot, can dither a nickel out of every deal he's offered." I'm not sure what exactly she meant, but her language is so colorful I don't ask for a translation. "You want Edmund Willis to do your painting. Anyone else will take one look at you and add fifteen percent to every price they mention. Edmund's fair." Everyone she mentioned has an attribute attached. "Fair," "deliberate," "cagey," "bad news." I wonder what adjective Judy will use for me.

When we finally left the Rexall, Judy pointed down towards the harbor. "I hear they lost a flier last night." I could see the little flotilla of lobster boats heading out of the mouth of the harbor, the larger naval cutter waiting in the cove.

"I saw a plane just at sunset. I wonder if it's that one."

"Suppose it might be."

"Do you think they'll find him?"

Judy shrugged. "They'll try." There was a touch of resignation in her voice, as if she didn't expect success.

Getting home, and despite the lateness of the afternoon hour, I left my basket of wet clothes beside the clothesline and walked along the worn path to the dune overlooking the slight dip in the shoreline sometimes called Bailey's Cove and sometimes Bailey's Beach. Judy Frick's referring to me as Florence Bailey's granddaughter had brought the old woman so clearly to mind.

Gran, the daughter of well-to-do Bostonians, fell in love with Henry Bailey of Hawke's Cove. Meant for cotillions and social philanthropies, Florence defied her parents and settled here to farm. Her defiance did not exclude her from their love, and when they died, Gran inherited what was a modest fortune from them; a comfortable nest egg that enabled her to send not only her own children to good schools, but me as well. Like so many others at the beginning of this century, her children, my father among them, scattered to the greater world beyond the peninsula, in search of a living away from the farm and the sea.

Even at the height of the Depression, she was able to keep two men employed on the farm, although the trade-off was to let the farm buildings run down. Yet she willfully chose to ignore the change in Hawke's Cove from an agrarian to a tourist economy and scoffed at those who were offering rooms to rent to help keep food on the table. "It'll be a cold day you-know-where when Bailey's Farm turns into a motel. We'll keep using sticking plasters and determination to keep the roof up." She no longer ran the place as a farm a few years before she died, claiming she was too tired to keep watch over hired men anymore. The little room off the kitchen was empty for the first time in my memory the year I was eighteen. Looking back, I suppose that my education came at the expense of the hired men. When Dad died, I know she provided my mother with discreet financial help, providing my full tuition to Smith College.

So clearly is Gran in my mind that coming back along the path, I half expected to see her there as she was when we were children gamboling about her, intent on sucking dry the full summer days. Under her broad-brimmed gardener's hat, seated deep in her Adirondack chair, she watched us, drinking her bootleg scotch and smoking cigarettes with a languorous movement.

I hung out my clothes, looking up now and then at the search planes hovering about, still looking for the missing pilot. With the naval air station only a few miles away, we see so many trainees crisscrossing the sky, a noisy reminder of the war. The sad fact is that they are mostly boys now, boys with a man's duty strapped on like their parachutes. Every now and again one of them crashes. Last week one landed in Sylvester Feeney's hay lot. The plane ended up on its nose when the front wheels tripped over the stone wall half hidden by the grass. When they hauled him out of the cockpit, the kid was crying like a baby. Mr. Feeney, when he was delivering my milk, told me the boy was more afraid of being punished for losing the airplane than from nearly being killed. "They're too young to realize death is unavoidable." Mr. Feeney closed his hand around the money I handed to him. "Still wet behind the ears." I don't know what that expression means, but I imagine little boys with big ears and slicked-back hair, fresh from a bath.

We have the occasional air-raid drill here. I'm so far away from town that if the wind is out of the north, I don't hear the siren. I'm careful to draw the blackout curtain in my bedroom, although I'm not certain if the weak yellow light from my oil lamp can be seen from the water. But, why take chances? Rumors of submarines offshore percolate through Hawke's Cove all the time. In the silent dark of a cloudy April night, with the newspaper filled with casualty lists and the solitary movie house in Great Harbor showing graphic newsreels, it is easy to imagine a Nazi sub lurking beneath our shoal-infested waters—perhaps one in an endless chain of submarines aligned along our eastern seaboard waiting for some sinister signal. I keep my curtains closed.

April 19, 1944

I slept poorly last night. My grandmother would have dealt with sleeplessness with a shot of scotch. I dare not, but resolve to go soon to Great Harbor and pick up a bottle of sherry for such nights.

My thoughts dance from John—glad he's still safely tucked away on some English base—to the condition of this house until, finally, they light on my grief. Sometimes I am able to press the thought of the baby out of my mind with diligent focus on solving some problem: How big should I make the garden? Should I buy a pig, like Ted Frick suggested? Something to eat my leftovers and ultimately to provide food. Having come here to be solitary, I am cursed by being alone. Without others to think about, I am left with my own thoughts stimulated by my overactive imagination. Yet, I don't want to go home. My surroundings there are much too familiar. No, *famil-iar* isn't the word. *Reminiscent.* Reminiscent of other times. Of being pregnant. There I ate the strawberries I craved. In this store I bought a layette. Harriett was sitting on that chair when I told her I was expecting. And Boston seemed filled with pregnant women, and I wonder how that can be. All the men are gone. John is gone. He left for England so soon after we lost her, I confuse the events.

I had hoped that Hawke's Cove, Gran's farm, would remind me only of summer and youthful fun. I would plant a Victory garden and write poetry. I had forgotten that it was here, in Gran's old spool bed, that our child was conceived.

Looking for gardening tools, I went into the barn today for the first time since I've been back. I found some bits and pieces of useful tools, but scarcely anything whole. An iron rake with a broken handle, a dented hoe. The grass rake is missing more teeth than an old man. I do find a box of hand tools—hammers and wrenches, a variety of screwdrivers, and some odd things I'm not sure I recognize.

They were put away carefully by someone, neatly laid in their toolbox just waiting to be put to use.

The only other thing remotely useful in the barn is a bicycle. Two, actually. They rested against the stall wall, coupled together like two beasts. I extricated the best one, an old Schwinn, provenance unknown. I resolve to take it to the Sunderlands' for repair. In these days of gas rationing, when every decision to drive is weighed against patriotism, it will be nice to have locomotion without guilt or fear of running out of coupons.

It rained again in the night, and the clothes hang limp on the line. A patch of blue "big enough to mend a sailor's breeches" offers hope that the day will eventually be sunny. Our faithful southeasterly breeze caught the sleeve of John's plaid shirt, draping it gently over the shoulder of my blouse.

I drove down the long rutted drive to the Sunderlands'. Like ruffles on a curtain, the shoreline dips in and out, creating little coves that take their names from early settlers. Sunderlands' overlooks Dwight's

Cove. I'm told that on the maternal side the Sunderlands are "Dwights," and that family has lived on that property since the peninsula was settled. The Dwights were Loyalists, and the white-and-black-painted chimney of the tumbledown house still stands testimony to that. Chimneys painted thus were signals to British seamen of safe houses.

The antique house is surrounded by the detritus of modern life: automobile hulks; all manner of metal scrap, tires, wire, batteries, and wood. All piled according to some Sunderland boy's specification. As long as I've come to the Cove, long before the War Effort required salvage, the Sunderlands' property has looked the same. Only now they are legitimate scrap dealers and are making a tidy profit from the business. And, as long as I can remember, they could fix whatever mechanical problem you might present to them.

What a pair they are, as alike as twins. Somewhere in their middle sixties, they are always referred to as the Sunderland "boys." Born and brought up in Hawke's Cove, the only time they've ever left was to serve in the Army during the Great War.

When I got there, they were arguing about fixing a motor. Jake approached me as I got out of my car. "Darn fool, don't know nothin' about engines." He kept his voice low and out of earshot of his brother. Inseparable, they observe a legendary politeness to one another. Jake helped me get the bike out of the backseat, nodding all the while to my litany of what I thought needed to be done. "Chain, oil, wheels need straightening . . ." Howard came along, nodding in the exact same way as his brother even before he heard what I was saying.

"Dontcha worry. We'll take care a it." Jake, his pique at Howie dissipated, slapped his brother on the shoulder. "Howie here'll do it. He's got a way wi' bikes."

"Good. I don't have a phone, so just let me know when it's done when you see me." I started to get back into the car.

"Naw. We'll deliver it to ya. No chaage," Howie offered. As he stepped back to open my door, I noticed a life raft lying in the tall grass behind him. Most of the air had oozed out of it, shaping it into a lop-sided yellow pool of rubber. Jake saw my glance at it. "Found it washed up this morning. Musta belonged to the flier gone down. No sign a him, though."

"Poor guy. Wonder what happened." I left my car, leaving the door open, and walked over to where the rubber raft lay on the bent grass.

"Probably got dumped out. Seas were still rough yestahday. Woun't wanta be out in a little raft like that nohow." Jake and Howie simultaneously shook their heads in respectful regret for the anonymous pilot's end.

A shiver at the thought of being thrown into inhospitable April water made me shrug in sympathy. I'd been in Hawke's Cove too many summers not to know of drownings and to learn respect for a contentious sea. Fishermen and children drowned, and now this anonymous pilot. Three miles away from home, not three thousand. I expect that the pilot went quietly in the cold water, dead probably of cold, his life vest keeping him afloat and soon to wash up on shore.

"Any rate, the Navy's coming by to get the raft. We're hopin' they'll leave it once they've taken a look."

Something caught my eye as I turned to acknowledge Howie's remark, a slice in the side of the raft, pouted like two lips pressed together. I bent over and poked my finger into the two-inch cut. "Did you see this?"

Jake and Howie looked at each other before nodding. "Yeah. Might be he gave up."

"Gave up?"

Howie shrugged. "You know . . ." He drew a finger under his chin like a knife.

"Oh. Why?"

"Quick death's better'n a slow one."

The day was still warm by the time I got home, so I left the clothes on the line and treated myself to a cup of tea and the seed catalogue. I still haven't staked out the garden, but it seems to make sense to pick out what I'm going to grow before I do.

Immersed in my task, I have nearly left the clothes too long again. The wind has just begun to take on the evening's dampness; the ethereal wisps of fog that sometimes blow in off the water look like ghosts. I like the image and maybe I'll use it sometime in a poem. This is all well and good, but I'd better put this journal aside and bring the clothes in.

The oddest thing. John's clothes are gone.

April 20, 1944

Well! Ernest Dubee certainly was more amused than alarmed at my theft. He hasn't changed much from when we were teenagers, just a bigger version of himself. Still fair-haired, although it's cropped military short. He's either outgrown or trained himself out of his adolescent pudginess. Although his dad was the chief when we were growing up, the title more honorific than official in this one-cop town, I am a little surprised to find Ernie in the role. I suppose it's like being a farmer or a fisherman; you just follow the footsteps laid out before you and don't look side to side.

"Mrs. Worth, I expect that it's just some vagrant in need of a change of clothes who swiped your husband's things. Probably halfway to Boston by now. I don't think you need to worry." Ernie scratched a few notes on a report form, then looked up. "It's not like the old days when we were kids. Depression sent a lot of men to wandering. Usually they get to the end of the peninsula and turn around."

"Ernie. It's not that I'm worried about the vagrant. I just want the clothes back." I was seated on the other side of the large banker's table Ernie uses as a desk; piles of wanted posters and reports form a crenelated mountain range on three sides. Over this Ernie regards me as if trying to bring the current me in line with his memory of the skinny red-haired girl he wrestled with on the beach.

Ernie's mongrel eased its way out from under the table. Ernie snapped his fingers at the dog as it sniffed at me with that interrogatory snuffing peculiar to its kind. Ignoring Ernie, the animal began wagging its pointed tail in satisfaction that I was harmless.

"Pal, get over here," Ernie ordered, and the dog sighed itself back down under the table. "Maybe you should get a dog, missus."

"Only if it's a loaner. I can't have a dog back in the city."

"Pal, you wanta go live with Mrs. Worth?"

Pal raised his eyebrows but was otherwise noncommittal.

"Hey, Ernie, what's with the 'missus'? We've known each other since childhood."

Ernie didn't answer, only shrugged and smiled, and I felt a little embarrassed that I had called him Ernie.

When I left the police station, Judy Frick was just coming down the narrow sidewalk. I must have looked upset, because she stopped and grabbed my arm as if about to shake the story out of me. "What's the matter, Vangie? You look worried."

These days such a look can portend calamity, and immediately I was chastened. "Nothing important. Some son of a you know what stole John's clothes off the line."

I don't know whether it was my implied profanity or her relief it wasn't worse news, but Judy fairly strong-armed me towards the coffee shop. "Let's get a cuppa and you tell me everything."

For one instant I thought she meant about the baby. I don't know why that should pop into my head that way, but I realize thoughts of her are always so close to the surface anything can raise them. In the next instant I knew what she meant and, in my relief, blurted out, "No, come to lunch instead." And in the next heartbeat wished I hadn't. I'm really not ready for confidential chats yet, which lunch and a shared cup of tea promote. I hope she's got other things to do this afternoon. I hear her car in the drive now.

The sun had begun to descend behind the tree line by the time Judy thought to go home. We sat in the Adirondack chairs, remnants of lunch on the ground beside us. The April sun soaking us in unseasonable warmth. Judy kicked off her shoes and peeled off her mended stockings, digging her bare toes lasciviously into the new grass. I made lemonade from lemons Judy brought. I use so little of my sugar ration that I could make the batch nice and sweet. Judy is about forty-five and plump in a nice maternal way, no bones, just soft places to cry against. I don't know why I write that; I didn't have the urge to cry to-day.

I did end up doing some confiding, voicing thoughts that are not incendiary, such as plans that I keep mulling over. "I don't know how committed to get to this place, Judy. I mean, John could come home and we'd go right back to Boston."

"I don't think there's much chance of the war ending before you get a garden planted, grown, and harvested, my dear. Get at least that much done and you can justify being here."

She's placed a finger on my anxiety. I want the war ended so that John and I can heal. If I think the war is going on much longer, I don't think I can bear it. Still, I do need to prove that I wasn't out of my mind to come to Hawke's Cove in the first place. I'm not just hiding; I'm working. So what if the only poetry I make is by planting seeds. I need to feel vital.

Then I mentioned my second plan. "I could raise a cow or a pig. Make some use of the land for the effort."

"Yeah, 'effort' with a capital *E.* Right?" Judy dipped her tongue into the bottom of the jelly glass in pursuit of the last drop of lemonade.

"Right. 'The War Effort,' all caps. Don't you hate it?"

"Yes."

"But you were lucky, weren't you?"

"How so?"

"Ted didn't have to go."

"Teddy did." Judy slowly set the jelly glass down beside the luncheon plate and folded her hands into her lap. "I lost my son to this war."

"Oh, I'm so sorry, Judy. I didn't know."

"How could you? You aren't from here. You really don't have a clue who in Hawke's Cove has been affected by this thing or how. You come from the city and come here thinking it's untouched by the outside world."

The setting sun backlit Judy Frick, and I held a hand up to shade my eyes. I couldn't read her expression and felt like I'd crushed the life out of a good new friendship by my assumptions.

"Judy, I'm sorry. I assume too much."

"Well, you know what my mother said about 'assume'?" Suddenly she chuckled, breaking the tension. "It makes an *ass* out of *you* and *me!*" I reached across the chasm between the chairs and took her plump hand. She squeezed mine, and I knew that she had chosen to keep the nascent friendship alive.

The oil lamp casts uncertain shadows in the kitchen as I write this. I think about Judy and her loss and wonder that I couldn't bring myself to tell her about my loss. Except the two losses are so different. The circumstances vastly different and the comparisons uneven. I wonder if the death of a child one has raised through the joys and sorrows of childhood is as hard as the loss of an infant at birth. I have no memories but grief; Judy can remember her son as a fully developed person. She can see the empty place at the dinner table where he once sat; I see nothing but a tiny coffin. She remembers his childhood; I can only imagine hers.

No, I was a coward and didn't want to debate the issue, or to raise it even remotely. Judy mentioned her loss matter-of-factly, as if to know her, I needed to know this about her. When I offered sympathy,

she rebuffed it. "You go on, Vangie. You
simply go on.

"Teddy was the first from here to die. This
town grieved with me. At first I couldn't
stand the attention, the overwhelming compassion. And then the next boy died, and
Hawke's Cove grieved for his family too. I
realized then that this *place* cared for those
boys. They had been the Cove's boys too.
My grief was Hawke's Cove's grief.

"You see, Vangie, we're only a few hundred here in Hawke's Cove. No one's problems—or joys—go unshared."

I wonder now if that had been an invitation.

May 1, 1944

I'm not being a very faithful journal keeper.
Perhaps it's the wonderful spring air,
keeping me outdoors and at my garden;
what little energy I have left for writing, I
devote to my weekly letter to John. It
seems like rehashing old news to then put
it into this journal. I tell him about the
weather and about meeting Judy Frick. I

try so hard to keep my letters newsy and light. It would do no good to burden him with my anxieties. He is foremost of those anxieties, but how do I tell him that? He'd just write back and say, "It's no use to worry. What will be will be." John is a pragmatist. Neither one of us writes with any depth. It seems to me that we have held each other at arm's length ever since losing the baby. I tell myself it is because it would be unfair to ask John to worry about me that I keep these letters casual.

I find that there are some things that I can't put into a letter, yet I need to put down on paper. Someday all of this will be faded cloth and I will want to remember what it was like when brand-new. I've told myself that this is the time for me to really work on my poetry. It isn't enough to dabble when my hope is to publish. I need to harness my thoughts and observations and whittle them into verse.

I had dinner last night with the Fricks. Ernie Dubee was there, brave extra man to my war wife. The conversation was a blend of gossip and politics of the local variety.

Had we heard the news Everett was running for an unprecedented eleventh term as selectman? Old codfish had been stuck in the office for so long he was ineffectual, yet no one had the heart to vote him out. I knew Everett only as the guy behind the counter at the hardware store who sold my grandmother ten-penny nails and picture hooks. I couldn't picture him without the carpenter's apron he always wore around his waist, odd bits and pieces tucked in there as he sorted through the bins of screws and nails and eye hooks.

At first I thought it was out of some deference to me that there was little talk of the war beyond the usual complaints of shortages and black-market coupons. Then I realized that it was Ernie they were being careful around. At an age when all of his classmates and peers are fighting overseas, Ernest Dubee remains at home. He is a double hostage in that he performs essential war work, policing this small place, and is the sole provider for his elderly and cantankerous mother.

Mrs. Dubee is the sort of woman who becomes granite, a block of a woman with steel gray hair fashioned into a tight little bun and undershot jaw that moves constantly as she plays with her dentures like a horse at a bit.

Ernie was her only, late-in-life child, and I remember when she terrified the bejesus out of all of us who chummed together those summers long ago. Mrs. Dubee's iron grip on young Ernie's ear amazed and embarrassed us as we scattered home late for supper. When Chief Dubee senior collapsed and died at the wheel of his police car, Ernie, at sixteen, was left to manage his mother's moods and finances. His father's life insurance was inadequate, and as soon as he graduated, Ernie took on the responsibility of keeping a roof over his mother's head. Even fifteen years later, the chief's job didn't pay enough for Ernie to keep another one over his own head. The old battle-ax had even kept him from getting married, but that was another story, Judy promised to tell me.

Judy and I gave the men a solid drubbing at cribbage.

I'm not ready for sleep, so I'm back at the journal. Having picked it up again, I find it feels nice to keep going. I keep thinking back to this evening. It's been a long time since I've been out in company. I had almost, out of habit, declined Judy's invitation—except that I realized it appealed to me. A shared meal (I brought a green-bean casserole), a card game. It's been five months since all of it happened—the baby's death and John's abrupt shipping out. Even yesterday, I couldn't have imagined ever laughing out loud again. But I never stopped tonight, what with silly stories and bad jokes.

I don't believe it's in my nature to be sorrowful. I have always been the cheerful one, the one my parents called their joker. Feeling this sorrow has been such an unfamiliar experience that I don't know how to behave. Sometimes I think I'm so weary of it I will just cast it off. And, in the next minute, am so utterly captive to it I feel guilty for having been disloyal. I'm not sure if I'm disloyal to John and the baby, or to the feeling of sorrow itself. I wonder, am I to be permanently changed by this? Will the person I was ever come back?

I stood out on the back porch for a little while after Judy and Ted dropped me off. The air is crisp but not like it is in the fall, spring crisp. Early peepers keep the night from being totally quiet. I had left my bicycle out, and it is overcast enough for me to think it might rain, so I put it in the barn. The strangest thing. I had just the tiniest sense of not being alone in there. Had I heard something, or was it a wafting warm odor that sent a little alarm through me? The moon above the overcast is full, and there was enough light to see shadows, yet nothing moved. I held my breath until I heard the skittering of rodent nails on the rafter above me.

I shake off my suggestibility but do lock my doors tonight. Maybe I will borrow Pal.

My old Glenwood combination range in the kitchen keeps me warm enough to sit and write in this journal. Upstairs I still indulge in the kerosene heater to warm my bedroom before turning in. In deference to John's fears for me, I never leave it on while in bed.

I wonder if I will be able to stay here if this interminable war keeps John away into next winter. It doesn't bear thinking that the war could go on another year. Maybe once fall begins, I will think of going back to

Boston, as if I have simply had an extended summer in Hawke's Cove. Nothing more. Time to stretch out my days into useful activity and endless beach days. Yet it doesn't feel like it used to. Maybe because now I am responsible for it all, the house and garden, the falling-down barn, and the taxes. Funny how it should all have fallen to me. Maybe she knew I was the one who loved it most. My mother, after Dad died, wanted nothing to do with it. Uncle George viewed it as a liability and was frankly relieved when the lawyer said Gran had left it to me. Frances certainly knows she can have the run of the place, but her life on the West Coast doesn't make a visit in the near future likely. Especially now that she's working in an aircraft factory. I haven't heard anything new about Stevie, off somewhere in the Pacific. I include him in my prayers every night, praying that he'll get back safely. It would be nice to share this place with them, Frances and Stevie. Maybe in a few years we will all have children and we'll sit in the Adirondack chairs, drinking scotch, and watch them play tag or hide-and-seek in the barn. I suppose I should see to getting the barn repaired enough to guarantee it will still be standing in ten years.

What did Judy say, stay from planting to harvest and justify my escape from the city?

It is now well past midnight. I look back on what I've written and wonder that my mind can even fathom any sort of future. I tried to sleep but woke up cold and plagued by those vague dreams that are really daylight worries turned into abstract images. Though the room was only a little cold, the cold I feel seems to come from within. I have been so long without another human body to warm me that I am incapable of producing my own heat even with three blankets piled on top. I need the generator of someone else's pulse. When I was pregnant, I was hot all the time, as if my body were a furnace producing manufactured goods. I was so awful to John, home on those weekend passes from his stateside posting, throwing the blankets off on him and, ultimately, leaving the bed for the couch. I wish I could have a little of that warmth right now. I wonder if I will ever sleep beside him again. I miss him the most at night.

He didn't wait to be drafted. He volunteered a few weeks after Pearl Harbor. With his college degree, he was a natural for officer's training school. I was so angry. Not that he'd joined up. It had become unthinkable that one wouldn't join up. I was angry because he did it and *then* told me. It is so like John to make a plan and then bring me in on it at the last possible moment. I would have wanted him to wait until fall, but he said that made no sense. I accused him of going in the spring to avoid having to go to Hawke's Cove for vacation. "There's a war on, Evangeline. We can't be particular. You could take on some war work yourself, not spend the time on the beach."

When John came home that first time, fresh from boot camp and still in his uniform, I thought he looked like a stranger. The wool of his tunic was hard, like a carapace, and I remember a moment's hesitation before I embraced him. Even then I knew that his experiences in the war would separate us from each other. I would be unable to imagine his life, and he would be unable to share it. His letters bear me out. Neutral, reluctant things. But then, here, on last summer's leave, I got pregnant, and suddenly my experience was vastly different from anything he could imagine. It made me less impatient with him.

There is another awful thought, too awful to bear recording, but I will. It has long been stuffed away, buried psychically so deep it is only now that, in the darkest of my private moments, I acknowledge it. I never meant to become pregnant. I did not greet the news joyfully despite John's rapture. It meant putting aside my own plans. I wanted to finish my graduate work; I wanted to keep teaching. Selfish, evil. When John, right here in this room, suggested making a baby, I was speechless. As usual, he made an airtight case for why we should, and we did. Even as we made love, I was calculating my cycle. Hoping it was the wrong time so that we could reconsider this. It wasn't, and I got pregnant immediately. I wasn't thrilled. Once again John's plans had prevailed. Then, magically, I began to want the baby. Everything else receded in my life, and I acknowledged to myself that John was right, though not out loud to him. So now, sometimes, I wonder if John thought I didn't hold onto her well enough.

It is so still, even the peepers have quieted. I can hear the bell buoy on Hawke's Shoals even through the closed and curtained windows. Too erratic to use as a sleep inducement, nonetheless I begin listening for the bell. I count the moments between clangs . . . six . . . three . . . seven beats.

May 3, 1944

I went to visit the Ruths today. Ruth Banks and Ruthie Jones. Two elderly ladies with a passion for gardening. They were great friends of Gran's, and I feel bad about not visiting them sooner. I've been here exactly six weeks today.

When I got to their cottage overlooking French's Hole, they were fussing about a theft. A wool blanket with Ruthie Jones's initials monogrammed on it was stolen from their line, where she'd hung it to air out after a winter's use. The incident was too close to mine, and I told them about the theft of John's clothes. We clucked a little about the state of things, but I'm a little more concerned. If the vagrant Ernie was so certain would be long gone was, indeed, not, then what might happen next?

I stayed to tea, carefully guiding our conversation away from my own peculiar danger zones and getting them to talk about their garden plans for the year. Ruth Banks, dressed like a young girl in her uniform of dungarees rolled at the ankles and a man's oxford shirt, had dirt lodged so deep into her short fingernails I wondered if it was left from the previous year. She kept swatting at Ruthie Jones, who fluttered and hovered about us as we sat in the rose garden on the white-painted wrought-iron benches set there. Finally, satisfied that all our needs were met, Ruthie Jones sat down and promptly dozed off, her little hands cooped in her lap like doves.

Ruth Banks is proud to say she and Ruthie have been together longer than some marriages, and I can see equal amounts of irritation and patience keeping them housemates for so long. Some people say that one of them was married and the other jilted by a lover, but I suspect those stories are made up in that artful way this community protects its own.

When I left, Ruthie Jones handed me a massive bunch of daffodils culled from the thick bed along the southern flank of the path to French's Hole. I placed them in my carry basket, and as I pedaled along the dirt track that runs along the fence line and across the field towards home, the bouquet bounced out. They hadn't been properly tied together, and the jolt strewed the yellow flowers all along the track. I squatted down and duckwalked, gathering the flowers against the crook of my arm and glad no one was around to see me. As I stood up I saw him. Rather, I saw John's plaid shirt as it disappeared into the thick scrub at the perimeter of the field.

"Hey!" I called out. "Stop!" I was too far away to catch up even if I had had the temerity to actually run after the thief. What a sight that would have been: "Angry Woman With Arms Full of Daffodils Gives Chase." I can see the headline now. I'll talk

to Ernie and let him know that this character is alive and well and living in the woods.

I am pleased to write that my garden
seems to be doing well. I got in the lettuce
and squash yesterday, and my starter cups
are showing optimistic little shoots already.
I've been cautioned about having too many
tomato plants and about having a proper
deer-and-rabbit-proof fence. I suppose I'll
have to ask someone to come do that for
me, I don't think I can manage a posthole
digger. I picture my garden like MacGre-
gor's, only Peter Rabbit will be on the outside this time.

Ted has been very diligent about seeing
to my electricity. The electric company will
be out early next week about hooking me
up to the wires Ted has run throughout
the house. Ugly knob-and-wire crawling
along the walls and across the ceiling,
ending in a fuse box now sticking out of
the wall on the cellar stairs. He put in an
extra circuit for when I invest in a Frigi-
daire. Right now the icebox suits me for
the little I keep in it.

May 3—afternoon

I got a letter from John. Roy Tingley in the post office winked as I went to my postbox, so I knew something beyond my mother's weekly plea to abandon my solitude lay in wait for me.

I went into the little park that overlooks the harbor to read it. The onionskin paper is so insubstantial; it moistened quickly from the heat of my hand. I sat on the one park bench, which is backed by a line of small shrubs. It feels a little more private than it really is, and I saw the Sunderland boys looking at me from the path that runs along the waterfront. Howie, or maybe it was Jake, waved a hand in greeting. I waved the hand holding John's letter, and he gave me the high sign.

John's letter tells me very little, and the censor edits so much. He says very little about what he is doing, but mentions mates and pints, so I know he's still in England. Preparing for being somewhere else, I suppose. It's like looking into the ocean—only in the shallowest places is anything revealed—or like seeing that glimpse of red and blue in the woods. There was a man, but he has no face.

John signs his letter, as he always does: *"I love you. I miss you. Your husband, John."*

Not once, not in any of his letters, ever, has he mentioned the baby. I don't know why. Is it because if he doesn't mention her, I won't think of her on my own and become upset? Or is it simply no longer important in his life, because his life is so far away?

May 10, 1944

I met him today. The man in John's blue-and-red shirt. I had gone down to the beach for the first time this year. The water is far too cold to swim in, but the air is warm and I wore my bathing suit. I fell asleep on the sand, the touch of the strengthening sun like a blanket on my back. I wasn't deeply asleep, just in the slight doze warmth and comfort afford. The sound of footsteps coming nearer telegraphed through the sand beneath my left ear. When I sat up, there he was, leaning towards me as if to wake me.

"You're burning."

I knew instantly that he was right, and in the second instant that he was wearing John's clothes. "Where did you get those clothes?" We faced each other across my beach blanket. The May breeze against the burn on my back made me shiver.

"Sears Roebuck." He answered without missing a beat, and I felt my face redden to the color of my back. Of course. There was nothing unique about John's shirt or trousers. Half the men in Hawke's Cove wear them. Except John's plaid shirt has a frayed pocket where time and again he'd caught his pen. This man's shirt had no such pocket, only an unfaded patch where a pocket had been.

"I'm sorry. It's just . . ." I really didn't know what to say.

"It's okay. Your husband's . . . ?" The suggestion of a question was open-ended enough for just about any answer, and it was easy for me to tell him about the theft of John's clothes.

"I don't know why I'm so upset about it.

They were old clothes, and John, well, he won't be wearing them anytime soon."

I'd slipped my beach coat over my sunburn and tightened the belt. Feeling a little less vulnerable I introduced myself. "I'm Vangie Worth."

It was odd, how he said his name. As if after I gave him mine, he couldn't remember that he should tell me his. Almost as an afterthought, he said, "Joe. Joe Green." As if saying it for the first time. I wonder if he's a shell-shock case, although his eyes don't have any of that vacancy to them I've seen in others who come back mentally wounded. No, his blue eyes were lively and met mine as if pleased to know me. Nor did his hand shake. But I was a little surprised at how smooth and warm it was when we shook hands.

"Maybe, Mrs. Worth, you're upset about the clothes because they were a part of your life before the war. Something left over from a happier time."

I know Ernie will be displeased with me, but I don't think Joe Green is our man. I rather like him.

May 13, 1944

I am restless. Despite hours in the garden and long walks, even though I bike to town once a day, I am antsy, as if I am expecting something. Someone. Maybe this is a natural response to the exquisite spring weather. An instinctive time of hope and waiting, planning and growth. Maybe I mistake boredom for anticipation. But, I have enough to do, more than I accomplish. How can I be bored? I fill my days with household tasks, read up on canning and pickling in optimistic preparation for my harvest. I should really give the parlor a new coat of whitewash. I don't believe it's ever been done in my lifetime. The old blueberry-and-milk wash is powdery under my hand.

Sometimes the feeling of waiting forces me out and I walk for hours. Today I left my usual shoreline route and went up through the woods, then over the array of pastures tied together by ancient tracks. Every society—deer, cow, and human—leaves a track specific to its own kind, a thin trail, a trampled path, a two-wheel-cart track. One leads into another, and I follow them all.

If I had the time and stamina to continue west, eventually I would reach the single-lane bridge cast across the salt marsh that attaches us more firmly to Great Harbor. Traditional debate centers on whether Hawke's Cove is a peninsula—the commonly held opinion—or an island. Some traditionalists declare the marsh in flood qualifies as surrounding water. In either case, the bridge is what gives Hawke's Cove its independence.

When we discussed this question at cards the other night, Ted said that there are old-timers who have never crossed the bridge. Never felt the need to. I scoffed at that as legend. "After all, there aren't any trolls beneath the bridge."

Ted settled his cards into a fan, studying them with great concentration. "Really now?" he deadpanned, sending us all into fits.

Still, home from my long walk, forcing myself to eat some semblance of a meal in respect to nutrition and proper human habit, I wait. I stand out on my back porch after dumping most of my meal in the can, and I wait in the dark. Listening. I am not afraid, just waiting. Waiting for John to come home and tell me what we do next. He never said we'd try again for a baby. I cast about in my memory, tracing back every sentence he uttered as I lay there in the hospital bed, the harsh bleached sheets rubbing my elbows raw. Did he ever say, "When I come home, we'll try again"? I don't remember.

It will be better when I have electricity. I'll have the radio then to block out the silence that nurtures my waiting.

May 14, 1944

I saw Joe Green again today. I was prowling along the beach, collecting beach glass for my jar, when I found his footprints ahead of mine. I had the advantage of him. He was leaning against that big rock you can get to only at low tide. For a few minutes he was unaware of me, clearly deep in thought. He smoked a cigarette, inhaling slowly, letting the smoke drift out of his mouth as if reluctant to let

it go. He stubbed the half-smoked cigarette out against the rock and carefully replaced the stub in the packet, and this he
tucked into the back pocket of his trousers. This action brought me into his view,
and he smiled as if he was expecting me.

I smiled in return, waved, and headed
towards him. Joe isn't exceptionally tall,
but is rather thin, though it is hard to say
if it's from nature or illness. Unusual these
days, he wears a beard, and that, too, isn't
clearly deliberate or, like his thinness, from
some circumstance beyond his control. I
have the urge to feed him.

"I'm sorry. I didn't mean to disturb your
solitude."

He pushed himself away from the rock.
"It's a welcome interruption. I'm not always
my own best company."

As naturally as that we fell into step,
continuing along the shoreline just above
where the incoming tide licks at the wet
sand. He saw that I was collecting sea
glass and spotted a few bits for me, placing them into my hand as if we had discussed it. We spoke of neutral things: the
weather, the particular beauty of the sea-

scape today, how May was a slippery month—you just got to enjoy it and it was June. Neither of us asked questions, some instinct keeping us from doing what most new acquaintances automatically do from polite interest. In that twenty minutes or so I learned enough about Joe Green to be content. He is amusing, he can identify certain small birds from a distance, and he can make a flat stone skip seven times before sinking. I don't really need to know where he's from or what he does. He's simply a nice guy. He is not wearing John's clothes. I don't know what he learned about me.

"I must leave you here." Joe and I had come to one of the more prominent deer paths that meander up through the scrub to the woody perimeter of the headland. "Thanks for sharing your walk with me," he said.

I put out my hand, and he held it in his for perhaps a fraction longer than need be, but I felt no need to pull it back.

As I turned towards home, I happened to glance behind and saw that Joe Green was also looking back towards me from the deer path. We waved again, smiling at the coincidence.

I know that I will not share this little moment with anyone. The last thing I want to do is bring down on my head the well-meaning censure of Judy or Ernie. Or John.

May 19, 1944

It seems odd to be writing in my journal in daylight, but the rain keeps me indoors, and I have no taste for housework. My bread is still in first rise. I tease it into rising faster by lighting the heater-side of the stove and setting the bowl of raw dough on the drainboard. The warmth clears some of the dampness out of the kitchen. With my outdoor plans scrapped, I feel like an untethered balloon, allowed to drift whichever way the wind blows.

What news shall I record here? For posterity and for when I look back and remember these days, I'll want to be reminded of little things, the details that make up a life. That the linen towel covering the dough is blue and white, that the bowl the dough rises in is one my grandmother received as a wedding present, that the smell of the oil heating stirs up old memories of the rare cool days in July when Gran lit the stove.

That if I work really hard, I can make older memories overshadow the recent painful ones.

I went to church yesterday for the first time since I've been back. I had gone faithfully to church even after John shipped out. Some nearly superstitious need to house my prayers for his safekeeping in a solid place, as if my homegrown prayers were inadequate to the job. Would God hear them more clearly surrounded by sanctified brownstone?

I went to tiny clapboard-and-shingle Saint Luke's on Sunday. It hasn't shown much decline since I attended there as a girl, flanked on the one side by Gran in her starched cuffs and collar, straw hat with its indomitable silk flower pinned on. Frances and Stevie on my other side. Was it my being the eldest that placed me next to Gran? Or my fidgety behavior? Even on the hottest days, Fran and I wore harsh little Sunday dresses our mothers had sent along with us, little white gloves just touching the place where wrist meets hand, and black Mary Jane shoes with our anklets carefully turned over in measured halves.

Of course I attended Saint Luke's as a teen and even as an adult the rare times I came with John, but it is those childhood Sundays that come to mind whenever I touch the time-darkened wood of the pews and feel the oversoft kneeler beneath my knees. There is a smell endemic to all these seaside wooden buildings, of salt and seaweed and generations of wet woolen coats. I catch myself inhaling deeply when I enter and dip my knee in respectful Episcopalian genuflection.

I was surprised to see Joe Green there. I don't know why I should be, except that I had never seen him in town before. He had knotted an unfashionably narrow tie under the collar of the shirt that looked like John's, but was otherwise dressed as the other times I had seen him. He was one pew ahead of me and on the Gospel side of the aisle. When he raised his head from prayer, I noticed that his maple-syrup-colored hair was just a little too long and crept over the collar of his shirt. He must be High Church, as he crossed himself at the appropriate times. When we stood to sing "A Mighty Fortress Is Our God," his very natural baritone was distinctive in a congregation filled with women and old men. I couldn't help but notice that he seemed deep in private prayer through most of Mr. Cummings's sermon. His eyes were closed, and he intermittently pinched the bridge of his rather aquiline nose.

Joe passed me with a smile and a brief nod on his way out. He didn't stay to coffee hour, and neither did I. I don't know about Joe, but I'm not ready yet to be wholly social. Next week maybe. It felt really good to be in a familiar place, following a familiar ritual. I kept John in mind as I took Communion, hoping that somewhere in England he was doing the same for me.

My dough is ready to be punched down for the second rise. I manage to get three loaves out of it and set these beside the stove on the drainboard. Wednesday is a bake sale for the Saint Luke's Ladies' Society. I suppose I should bake a pie for them. I think they're raising money for an orphanage in England or some such. I really should pay more attention to the announcements.

The rain let up enough for me to dash across the yard and go into the barn. There is something churchlike about a still barn. Dim with the thin gray light of this rainy afternoon, the hushed quality of the open space above my head was disturbed only by the dash of swallows breaking across the width of the small barn and swooping up and out of the open hayloft doors. I'm glad I haven't bothered to shut those doors, although swallows are clever housebreakers and can find their way in anyway. It's been on my mind lately to do something more productive with this place than just gardening. Sylvester Feeney put something in my head the other day when he made his delivery. I came upon him standing in my yard, one hand punched into his side, the other hand gripping the bottle rack with my one quart of milk poking out of it. He was in deep contemplation of the barn. His old dobbin shook her harness at my approach, and he turned to take the empty bottle from my hand. "You oughta do somethin' with it." He handed me my full bottle of milk. "You gotta nuf land for a couple of milkers."

"I don't know how long I'm staying." I handed him money for the milk. "Besides, I don't know anything about cows."

He had no response to this but humphed his throat. It might have been a dismissive sound or one of contemplation or, worse, one of phlegm. He climbed back into the driver's seat and clucked to his horse. "Might be I could rent the space if you go back to the city. Gov'ment needs milk."

And so, when the rain let up, I went into the barn. Two box stalls—filled with the odds and ends of accumulated junk, scrap wood, and rusted tools—are aligned on the left wall coming in. An empty space, probably storage for a cart or feed, is on the right. The loft goes from the midpoint of the barn towards the back and is reached by a wooden ladder nailed to it. I remember the great games of hide-and-seek we played in here, climbing among the boxes and barrels I know to be still up there, being cautioned about stepping on nails as we ran barefoot through the moldy hay.

There are puddles here and there on the barn floor, and I felt drops strike me on the head as I walked around. What counts, though, is how dry it is in the loft. There aren't any puddles directly under it, but it might be too wet up there to keep hay.

However, I didn't get a chance to find out because as soon as I put my hands on the rungs of the old ladder, I heard a car pull up. I was a little embarrassed to greet Ted and Judy Frick with mud on my hands, and it is only as I write this that I wonder how it was I had come to have muddy hands. I had only touched the ladder.

The rain has intensified this evening, and I worry about my ~~infant~~ little plants. The rain makes a sound like applause on my roof. I had intended to cut the grass around the house tomorrow, the mower having just been sharpened and delivered back to me by the Sunderland boys. Even newly sharpened, the reel will never be a match for wet and overgrown grass. I must be more diligent about cutting it.

The rain has also put off the electricity. That's what Ted came out to tell me. I made tea for us, and they stayed nearly to suppertime. Judy suggested that it might be "prudent" to get a telephone hooked up now that the poles will be up my drive anyway. What with my "being out so far." I know she means prudent in light of the vagrant thief being in the area, but somehow I'm less worried about him lately. At the time she mentioned it, I only shrugged, a little like an obstinate child being told something is for her own good. But, now, thinking about it, I know Judy is right. I'm not nervous or particularly given to hearing noises—at least not those that can't be explained away, like raccoons in my trash can—but, maybe there are enough good reasons to be connected to the rest of the world.

May 20 (5:30 A.M.)

I woke up thinking I had heard a cry. Not a baby's cry, as I have dreamt before, but an adult's cry of anguish. Startled upright, the sound only in my head, I suppose I must have made it.

* * *

May 22, 1944

Ernie played host tonight, just for cards, though. No chance the old woman would cotton to dinner guests. Judy and Ted picked me up. Ted's still being apologetic for the delay on electricity, but I assure him, I do not hold him responsible.

Halfway through the game Ernie's mother came home from bingo. She handed Ernie her string bag filled with cans, and our police chief, still dressed in his blue tunic, immediately fell to arranging the cans on the shelf. Gertrude Dubee's undershot jaw nibbled at the air as she debated greeting us, which she finally did with a nod, clearly put off by this invasion of her kitchen. I felt as though I should check to see if my nails were clean.

Ted, bless him, leavened the atmosphere with a joke, and even Mrs. Dubee smiled.

"Hear about the tourist in the market the other day? Asked LaRiviere if he arranged his cans chronologically. 'Nope,' says Riv. 'Alphabetically.' "

I must remember to send that one off to John.

* * *

Ernie took me aside when we stood up to leave. "Met a guy out at the sand pit. Looks like he's been living rough for a few weeks. Told me his name was Joe Green. Might be he's wearing John's clothes."

I shook my head. "No. I thought so too when I met him. But he's not. Besides, John's clothes wouldn't fit him."

"Looks to me like they didn't fit any too good."

"He's all right, Ernie."

Ernie didn't say anything, but fastened the top button of his tunic, keeping his skepticism to himself. "He's looking for work. I told him to go see the Ruths. They've always got odd jobs."

"Thanks."

"What for?"

"I don't know. Being a nice guy instead of a hard-nosed cop."

Ernie's fair skin reddened under the unexpected compliment, and he undid his top button.

"So what was Ernie so intent on?" I know Judy well enough by now to know she'd ask that question the moment Ted shifted into third gear. I have so many things of which I don't speak that this didn't seem worth collecting into that group.

"He's met a fellow he thought might be the thief."

"Is he going to arrest him?"

"No, Judy. He's just a guy down on his luck. Ernie sent him to see the Ruths about work."

"You should hire him, Vangie." Ted put his oar into the conversation. "Face it, you need some muscle on that place. If Ernie thinks he's okay, it would be a good idea to get some help, even if it's just to get the fence built before you lose more of your vegetables to rabbits."

I couldn't naysay that and didn't try. I had them drop me off at the foot of my drive. The night is mild and moonlit. By the reflection of the moon in the puddles, I avoid them and keep my feet dry. I don't know; maybe I should hire Joe Green. Except that I have little money to offer, only my cooking and the hired man's room off the kitchen. Even if he would take it.

As I write this, I balk at complicating my solitude with someone. Facing someone

over a dinner table, making general conversation that allows us both our privacy,
caring whether another person likes my
meat loaf or is just being polite. I'm not
sure I'm up to it yet. Equally, I'm not sure
if John would approve. He was not happy
that I made the move to Hawke's Cove
from Boston. His last two letters have not
chided me, but before that, every one he
wrote somewhere contained his disbelief
that I would continue to stay away from
home, as he put it, and our friends and
families. I haven't the heart to tell him again
that it was for those very reasons I needed
to get away. He has just never understood
my thinking of this place as a refuge.

So, if I invite Joe Green to work here,
will I not be giving up some of the refuge
I have created for myself?

Before I went into the house tonight, I
paused. I could hear the waves, kicked up
by some unseen storm. The normally
placid cove is in motion, frothy rollers
launching themselves against the beach.
Compelled, I left the porch and followed
the path to the beach. It is so warm tonight
that I think perhaps I'll go for a swim tomorrow. Funny, I've put the first swim off

far longer than I would have had this been an ordinary summer visit. Released from the tyranny of finite time, I have all the time in the world. The white sandy path was clearly visible against the dark night and easy to follow. I heard the ducks on the pond by the path protest their disturbance with little mutters of ducky annoyance at my passing.

Where the sand becomes deep, there are rough planks spread end to end. I am like a tightrope walker, balancing along the narrow beams. I took off my shoes to better feel my way along. "Don't touch sand or you're It!" cry my childhood companions, chasing, tumbling into the breast of the dunes. No room in those young lives for sadness or sighing, which is what I hear myself do as I sit on the cold sand.

The moon illuminates the cresting waves so that white lace ribbons come towards me, curl over, and disappear from sight. I think that it is finally time to write poetry again. This thought cheers me as I head back towards the path. Despite my intentions since I arrived here, I haven't written poetry. I haven't written any since last summer. Somehow, being filled with the expectation of a child overshadowed my poetic urges. Procreation subsumed poetry.

As I came back up the path and through the vine-held stone wall, the cockeyed barn holds my attention. Dark bulk against a darker sky, it seems all the more like the crooked man's crooked house. Sylvester Feeney's suggestion keeps coming back to me, and now it occurs to me that Joe Green might fix my barn.

May 25, 1944

In the crazy way of coincidences, Joe showed up at my porch door just as I was wondering how to find him. Since seeing him in church, I've caught sight of him only once or twice in town. Once at the market, where he was buying a loaf of day-old bread. The second time as he was walking along Seaview. I offered him a ride, but he declined, claiming to be walking for pleasure.

He's accepted my meager offer of twenty

a month, room and board. The Ruths sent him my way after hiring him for a once-a-week lawn cutting. "The ladies thought you might need some work done." Does everyone in Hawke's Cove think I need help?

I invited him in for lunch, which he ate like a man forcing himself to slow down. I made him another ham sandwich and gave him the strawberry-rhubarb pie meant for the Saint Luke's Ladies' Interminable Bake Sale. Charity begins at home.

After lunch we carried our cups of tea out to the barn to have a good analytical look around. Joe sipped out of the big mug my grandmother preferred, all the while casting about the barn, poking a nail into the beams, knocking on the walls. He scuffed a bit of the damp hay off the floor, then, handing me his cup, swung himself nimbly up the ladder. Not to be left behind, I set the cups down and clambered up. Joe gave me his hand as I crested the top rung. "The roof is in better shape than you'd think by the general condition of the barn. The few holes I can see can be patched, although I'd recommend a whole new course of shingles. Won't be worth doing unless you make the investment."

"You're a carpenter, then?"

"Not by trade. My father taught me a great deal."

"He was a carpenter?"

"No, just a follower of a carpenter's philosophy." He didn't elaborate but quickly slipped down the ladder. Grateful to be wearing slacks, I followed down more slowly. Joe Green stood open-armed at the bottom of the stairs, as if to catch me should I fall.

I remember as a kid being fascinated by the word "enigma." I loved the sound of it and the sense of mystery it evoked. Well, Joe Green is enigma personified. I asked when he wanted to move into the tiny back room, expecting him to say, "at the end of the week" or some such normal response. Instead he asks if "right now" is okay. I expect him to fetch things from his current situation, and he doesn't. Clearly Joe Green is a man unburdened by possessions. When I bring him his sheets, all I see of personal items are a pocketknife, a thin leather wallet, and a white handkerchief wrapped around something he places in the dresser drawer as I come in.

Joe seems so happy . . . no, that's not it. Comforted. Joe seems so comforted to be here. He took a long time in the bath, then apologized for it. I lent him a robe Stevie left behind years ago. I half expected he'd shave the beard off with John's old straight-edge razor I'd put out for him, but he came out of the bathroom with it neatly trimmed instead. He readily helped dry the dishes and is inordinately pleased to have been given borrowing rights to my small library. As if, having fed his body, I had also fed his mind.

Already I feel my hermit's life getting away from me. I had to plan a meal for tonight, instead of heating some soup or boiling an egg. I write in my journal now in my bedroom, leaning against the nightstand. The lamp is smoky, so I trim it and am left with a little oval of yellow to write this by. John looks at me from the photo on my nightstand. Do I detect disapproval on his face? *Evangeline,* he seems to say, *what have you done?*

Oh, I know that John will have a problem with this.

June 3, 1944

There are rumbles everywhere, even in this small town where the Great Harbor paper is weekly and seldom mentions world events. SOMETHING is about to happen.

Tonight I sit at the kitchen table. The hanging kerosene lamp swings a little and throws too much heat. I feel myself perspire under my hair, and I lift it off my neck and ponder once again cutting it off. I wonder what John would say, coming home to a bobbed wife. Then again, he's never said anything much about my hair. I used to have him brush it, but it never felt as sensuous as I had hoped. He was as matter-of-fact about it as washing the car. John's sensuality is in his work, ever so delicately marking on his sketches where a door or window will go, seeing the finished design in his mind. I've watched him when he wasn't aware, closing his eyes to envision what he will draw, the tiniest of smiles on his lips as he pictures the space. I would not call John a passionate man. Knowing no one else, I assume he is a good lover.

He is always careful of me, careful of my pleasure. But his passion lies in his work.

I lift my hair away from my neck, twisting it into a knot, but the loose pieces tumble back down. Joe has come in, half hidden by the shadows cast by my poor light. He's offered to chip some ice and pour us lemonade. We're going out to the porch.

The lemonade glass felt moist in my hand as we sat out under the stars, letting the cool sea breeze work its magic. We are silent for a time. Then Joe starts pointing out constellations. "Orion's Belt, Casseopeia, the Big Dipper, Andy Hardy."

"Hey," I say, and he laughs.

In leaning to point out the stars, Joe leans close enough for his beard to touch my cheek. I don't move. I don't know if he was unaware of it or not. I was aware of nothing else. But I don't move.

"Just checking to see if you're paying attention," he says, and then stands up.

I heard him early this morning. A crying out like a warning. It was like the cry I thought I had once made.

June 8, 1944

So much has happened. The Allied Forces invaded Normandy two days ago in a most ambitious attempt to end this war. John is out there somewhere. I know that without any word. It is the not knowing *exactly* where that is so hard. If I knew he was in Arles or Paris or Glasgow or Poughkeepsie, it would be so much easier to bear. It suddenly makes sense, all this time in England. I wonder if he went with the first wave to land on Omaha Beach, or has he been one of those dropped by plane? I have spent so much time imposing myself on the Fricks to listen to their radio, memorizing the statistics as they come in, so many dead, wounded, missing. I listen to crackling speeches from Winston Churchill and FDR lauding the thousands who have gone. Forty-eight hours ago I was living in a temperate zone of concern. I worried and prayed. But now. Now I am terrified. Ever since the news broke, I have been sick to my stomach.

Joe came to pull me away from the radio last night, coaxing me along gently.

"They're not going to tell you anything new tonight. You've got to get some rest." He is smart enough not to tell me not to worry, everything will be all right. When I got out of the car, I threw up. He didn't say a word, only handed me his handkerchief and followed me inside the house.

June 10, 1944

Roy Tingley at the post office gently suggested that it might be some time before I got another letter from John, or before mine reach him. Still, I bend to the task of writing him, filling my letters with the bland mundanity of everyday life. *The garden grows well. I've cut the grass. The Ruths are well and send their regards. Judy Frick sprained her ankle last week. Joe Green has begun work on the barn.* I casually mention Joe's presence in my life, as if it doesn't count. But it does. If he weren't there, I would be left standing still.

Joe and I drove to the Sunderlands' today to borrow pump jacks. Joe graciously declined to drive. "Happy to be a passenger, Mrs. W." He calls me that, Mrs. W., in some attempt to keep our relationship businesslike—despite the silly behavior we fall into. Snapping dish towels and one-upsmanship contests as we clear up after dinner. In his mouth, the "Mrs. W." is almost affectionate, not deferential. Still, it is a verbal barrier and allows me to hand him his pay at the end of the month.

The Sunderlands wouldn't hear of payment for the use of their equipment, so I wandered down to the beach while Joe helped them load their ancient dump truck with various bits of scrap destined for the War Effort.

As I came back up the path, a little hidden from their sight, I could hear Jake's cigarette-harshened voice. "You stayin' with Miz Worth?"

"I am."

"Nice lady. I remember her grandmother Florence was a nice lady too. Not a Cover by birth but married a Bailey."

Howie chimed in. "Miz Worth can do with a man about the place. That husband a' hers weren't much in the way of keepin' the place up. Dun't think he much likes it here. City boy, you know."

"Well, I don't know Mr. Worth, except that he's over there, so I'll keep my own counsel."

Sunderland boys liked that response. "Yeah, do no good to speak ill of someone in it." I could tell by the expression on Joe's face that he knew full well the expected response to this was to speak of his own experience. To explain in a word or two why he was here. I could see by the way the brothers raised their bushy eyebrows that they were eager to hear his story.

He gave them—and me—nothing.

I announced my return with a halloo. "Job all done?"

"Could use help other end," Jake said to both of us.

I nodded my okay, but Joe shook his head. "If it's all the same, fellas, I plan to get started on the barn today. I need to get a good start on it before the real hot weather sets in."

"What ya gotta do is lift 'er up with them jacks, butcha gotta be careful ya dun't tip 'er over."

"Naw, Howie, old barn like that'll cave in fore she tips over." Jake demonstrated the collapse with his hands backed together into a V.

As we were getting back into the car, I spotted the raft still lying on the long grass. "So the Navy did leave that with you?"

"Navy ain't been by yet. Guess they don't care. 'Sides, finders keepers. Sea law." Howie walked over to the raft and gave it a proprietary kick.

"Sunderlands found that on their beach," I said to Joe, who was very quiet in the seat next to me, lost in his own thoughts at that moment I suppose.

I pulled the Plymouth out from under Jake's elbow and waved good-bye.

Before going home, we headed into town to pick up a few things at LaRiviere's Market. Joe seemed a little tense going in, and I wondered if the conversation at the Sunderlands' place had made him upset. I know that there is something odd about the way Joe Green came to be here in Hawke's Cove, but we aren't acquainted long enough yet for me to be comfortable asking.

Just as we came out of the market, I saw Ernie charging towards his police car. He saw us on the same side of the street and paused before climbing in. Pal took advantage of the pause and jumped into the front seat.

"Get in back," Ernie ordered the dog, and came towards us.

"Joe Green."

Joe didn't respond, only stood still as I kept moving to meet Ernie.

"Joe," Ernie repeated, and I turned to see why Joe was no longer beside me. "Vangie, can I borrow your hired man for a couple of hours?"

"There must be a premium on help today. You're the second . . ." I was cut short as Ernie motioned to Joe to come over. There was an obvious hesitation before Joe stepped out of his self-imposed suspended animation.

"The Collison twins have gone missing, and I could use a little help locating them. Would you be willing, Joe?"

Joe nodded. "Sure. Can I take Mrs. Worth home first?"

"Just come with me. We'll ride together for a bit."

Joe handed me the grocery bag and followed Ernie back to his car, where Pal drooled over the back of the front seat.

When he got home, Joe told me that the boys had managed to get themselves buried alive in the sand pit. They'd rigged up a breeches buoy over the deep pit using some stolen wire and a couple of turnbuckles nailed to opposing trees. The whole pit is about a hundred feet across and probably thirty or forty feet deep. The town has gotten all of its sand for icy roads and cement mixing from this hole in the ground for decades. It's not the beach sand type of sand, but that nasty yellow dirt that sticks to the seat of your pants and never washes out. When we were kids, we were forbidden to play near the pit, not just because of the inherent danger of landslides, but because no one's mother wanted to wash clothes that had been dragged through it. Joe came home covered, and I despair of getting it out of the knees of his only decent pair of work trousers.

The good news is, Ernie and Joe found them in time. Joe credits Pal's whining in the backseat of Ernie's car.

June 11, 1944

It was my turn to host the card party. It was a little difficult, trying to figure out what to do about Joe. I felt awkward about leaving him out, and equally awkward about including him in a rather fixed group. But, in the way these things sort themselves out, it seemed natural he should join in after dinner.

Judy and I cleared the table, stacking the dishes in the big sink, only running cold water over them to keep the stickiness of my chicken pot pie from hardening. Joe stood up to hand me a plate and excused himself. "It's been a pleasure meeting all of you. I bid you good night."

"Joe." Ernie stood up, knuckles pressed to the tabletop. "Sit for a hand or two, won't you?"

Joe looked at me, and taking permission from my surprised smile, nodded. "I'd like that."

We played hearts for a while, then switched to cribbage when I insisted I wanted to get the dishes done and go ahead and play without me. Joe offered to sit out so that the game would be even, but I really wanted to get the dishes done. I don't mind watching others play.

The conversation this time did come around to the war, what with all the excitement about the invasion. We all believe that this action will help hasten the end of the war. I hear myself speak of it dispassionately, in control of myself. "This will put an end to it. The Germans surely can't resist this massive an attack."

Ted gripped his cards in his hand without looking at them. "An awful thing, all those men lost. But, what else can be done? We have to be ready to do anything to bring about the end. Anything to stop Hitler."

"I suppose it comes down to sacrifice. National sacrifice, personal sacrifice." Once I had said the word *sacrifice,* the room fell silent. The truth is, I thought not of John, but of our child. Judy and Ted certainly thought of their son. Perhaps Ernie was thinking of himself. Standing as I was at the sink, overlooking Joe with his back to me, I could not even imagine what he was thinking.

"Fifteen for two." Joe ended the silence.

Long after I waved the Fricks good night, Joe leaned against Ernie's car. I went to bed, too tired even to go out with them to say good night. Sometime after I had drifted off into that first heavy sleep, I was awakened by their voices.

"Don't get me wrong; I'm happy in my job. I draw a good salary, pension even, if I stick it. I have the respect of this community . . ." Ernie's voice trailed off, and I heard the scrape and snap of a wooden match.

"Did a lot of your friends go?"

"Yeah. All of them. I mean, this is a small place. There were probably only twenty of us of an age to go. There were even a few older guys, Hank Colby and Bert Lamb, who were already in their thirties when we got into it."

"So you stand out."

"Yeah. Something like that."

"And everyone tells you you're doing essential war work, how can the town survive without you, etcetera, etcetera."

Ernie chuckled. "Exactly."

"They're right."

"I know."

"Doesn't make it any easier, though, knowing everyone approves."

"Nope."

I closed my eyes and tried not to eavesdrop any longer. I must have succeeded because I heard nothing until a lead-footed seagull landed on my roof and started a raucous mewing this morning.

June 16, 1944

It's finally gotten really hot. Well into the eighties! I went to the beach right after lunch and ignored the prohibition against going in after eating. In church this morning Mr. Cummings seemed cheerfully oblivious of the June heat, failing to mention either hellfire or brimstone and once again missing an opportunity to bring relevance into his sermons.

Joe continues hard at work, digging a trench, preparing to set up the pump jacks that he will use to support the barn while he builds a new foundation. I felt guilty for skipping off to the beach while he labors on a Sunday. Coming up behind him as he was digging with such rhythmic intensity, I startled him.

"Hey, don't do that to a guy!"

"Come to the beach."

He looked back at his work and made some calculation in his mind, looking at the sky, the trench, and then back at me. "How about in half an hour? That way I'll stay cooled off."

"I left John's bathing trunks on your bed." He didn't argue with me this time, as he has consistently at any suggestion of borrowing John's clothes. He's already spent the pay I advanced him on a Montgomery Ward order, so at least he's got a change of clothes.

It was much more than half an hour later when he finally came to the beach. By that time anyone else around had gone home to wash off the salt and start supper. The seagulls were edging closer and closer in an attempt to shoo me off as well. I tossed them the few crackers left in my beach bag. "Go away, yellow-eyed scavengers!"

I was just about ready to leave when I saw Joe coming along the beach, John's little-used trunks a little loose at the waist, but good enough. He dropped his towel and stripped off his shirt, not hesitating for an instant to plunge into the calm water of the cove. He burst to the surface, shaking the drops from his face, then threw himself backward into the water. The sight of his enjoyment made me go back in. It's been a very long time since I swam with someone. Children and teenagers play in the water, splashing and pretending to be dolphins or mermaids. Adults, unless they are lucky enough to have a float, tend to get the task over with and seek out their books or knitting as soon as possible. Matrons in black swim dresses stand knee deep, entering the sea by degrees, all the while conversing with one another and watching their grandchildren. There is that mystical point where they all duck to their necks, still keeping an eye on the kids and the conversation moving. I've watched them, women like Gran, pale, soft flesh of their arms exposed, white rubber bathing caps protecting their purchased curls, swim skirts floating around them.

Joe and I swam in tandem, not racing exactly, but I think we both enjoyed showing off our form. We climbed out of the water, our suits stuck to us like seaweed, and we pulled at them, laughing at the slightly embarrassing sound of the suction.

There is a strange intimacy in swimming.

The seagulls had reconnoitered our blanket thoroughly and, disappointed, moved on. I toweled off and pulled on my terry-cloth robe. When Joe dropped his towel and bent to pick up his shirt, I couldn't help but notice scarring all along his back, as if he'd been burned or badly abraded. Judging from the pinkish shine of the new skin, it hadn't been long ago. He quickly pulled on his shirt. To thwart my curiosity about his back, he called attention to his hands.

"Oh, Joe. We should have gotten you work gloves." His hands were blistered from the rough handle of the shovel. "I'm sure there are work gloves around somewhere." I blathered on, appalled at myself for not attending to such a simple precaution, then annoyed with him for not looking out for himself.

Back at the house I got down my limited medical supplies of peroxide, the big jar of Vaseline, and my roll of gauze. Cleaned adequately by the saltwater, I spared Joe the Fels Naptha soap portion of the treatment. "Be brave." I poured peroxide over his hands as he held them over the sink. He was stoic for about a minute, then danced around the cracked linoleum, waving his tortured hands and making us both laugh.

We sat down, and I took his left hand in mine and began gently working the Vaseline into the four swellings at the base of his fingers. He had raised, broken, and raised again blisters on his palms and along the crescent between thumb and forefinger, leaving little red ovals burned into the skin. I massaged each finger with a dollop of Vaseline, then carefully wrapped the gauze as best I could to cover the blisters. When I turned his hands over to wrap the gauze, I noticed for the first time that the backs of his hands were mottled, like his back, with evidence of healed burns.

We fell silent as I bent over his right hand. The joking subsided, and I concentrated on my work. Over and over I stroked the jelly, smoothing it, taking off the excess, making sure each bubble was padded in it.

Joe has extraordinarily long, tapering fingers for a man. The kind of fingers we sometimes call piano fingers. He wears no rings. Each knuckle is smooth, but his wrists are delicately etched with fine hairs.

"I think that's enough, Mrs. Worth." Joe's voice was soft, unsettled, and I quickly tied off the bandage.

"Done."

The nausea has subsided, only a lingering knot of tension resides there. It is still hard to eat, but I feel the need to try. Like grief or even great happiness, worry finds its own functioning level. I keep moving.

My garden is doing well. The fence Joe put up the first week he was here is doing its job in keeping out Peter Rabbit and his friends. All the things that are supposed to be growing are healthy, and those things that I am supposed to recognize as weeds are too. I devote mornings to it. I have indulged in a little cutting garden of zinneas and cosmos, and my geraniums and petunias grow with abandon in the window boxes. The whole place looks bright and cheerful if you discount the fact the trim needs paint and the barn now looks more like it's sinking underground. Piles of dirt, stones, and tools lie around it, as if part of some mishandled archeological dig. Joe will set the pump jacks tomorrow, and then, so he says, we will begin to realign the whole building, forcing it out of its seventy-year slump. Joe seems utterly confident that he will be able to carry this off without either dropping the barn or dying in the effort. When I tell him I keep thinking of the Wicked Witch of the East's having Dorothy's house dropped on her, he only shakes his head and cackles, "We'll see, my little pretty."

This afternoon I went to Great Harbor at Judy's invitation. We shopped and ate lunch at the hotel there. Afterwards we treated ourselves to a Bogart movie. It was hopelessly romantic, and I loved it. It was very late by the time Judy dropped me home. I stumbled up the back porch steps and into the dark kitchen. It's an inky night, without moon or stars. I felt for the matches and could find none. "Damn it."

"Damn it." I stubbed my toe on the table. Inching my way through the kitchen towards the parlor, where I had seen some in the dish on the mantel, I was startled by

Joe's voice coming out of the darkness behind me.

"Wouldn't you like some light?"

Suddenly the kitchen was flooded with
electric light.

"Welcome to the twentieth century, Mrs.
W."

I clapped my hands together with the
same enthusiasm I had applauded the end
of the movie with as the houselights came
up. I have electricity. Gran would be so
pleased.

June 23, 1944

Joe has been with me a month. In that
time he has cleaned up my yard, fixed the
other bike, so now there are two . . . ,
serviced the car, dug out the foundation
of the barn to ready it for lifting, built a
better fence around my garden, planned
a fence for the pasture, and kept me company.

He's proven useful in the neighborhood
too. Helping Ted out with a tricky job, cutting up the fallen pine in the Ruths' garden

without so much as deflowering one of their prize roses.

Joe has served as a distraction from my dark thoughts, reminded me what joy there can be in cooking a good dinner for someone who works hard. Given me someone else to think of when I can't bear thinking of John anymore.

Judy says he fills my need.

"What do you mean?" I asked.

"You have a lot of nurturing in you going to seed. He helps you make use of it."

June 25, 1944

The wildest thing. In raising the barn, Joe has found a store of bootleg whiskey. I knew about the rumrunners of Hawke's Cove in the eighteenth century, but this stash is more recent. I suspect it comes from my grandfather's reprobate brother, Ralph. In the way of families, scandal is hinted at, spoken of in hushed tones and only when the children are, presumably, out of earshot. Ralph Bailey had always been a hoodlum and black sheep of the respectable Bailey family. He'd modified a lobster boat to no known fishing specification and taken to long, unaccompanied jaunts, setting out when most boats were coming in. I knew from the gleanings of careless conversation when we were all abed, but not asleep, that Ralph did a bunk, with only a postcard years later to say he was still alive. No one ever heard from him after that card. His name was seldom mentioned, and then only with a roll of the eyes.

Now I guess we know why he disappeared. Clearly he'd bitten off more than he could chew, judging by the quantity of whiskey lying at the bottom of a pit suddenly exposed by the work Joe has done. Maybe he stole it from someone else; maybe the revenuers were hot on his trail. Whatever the case may have been, Uncle Ralph vanished.

"Well, what do I do with it?"

"Only one good suggestion comes to mind with twenty-five-year-old scotch whiskey." Joe had a glint of mischief in his eye as he slid one of the bottles out of its wooden box.

"Drink it?"

In the end it seems best to leave the whiskey where it is for the time being. The pit itself is roughly four by six, maybe three feet deep. The flooring of the barn serves as the pit's ceiling and seems in no danger of collapse, as the walls of the pit are planked. Joe suggested the hole in the ground might actually have once served as a slave hole during the days of the Underground Railroad. That gave me the creeps. Imagine lying in that claustrophic place wondering if the next daylight would be the light of freedom or capture.

July 3, 1944

My little electric lamp lights my journal as I lean against the nightstand to pen these thoughts. John's face in the photograph seems less dark beneath the incandescent bulb, almost cheerful. Maybe I think he seems cheerful because, for the first time in nearly a month, I feel cautiously optimistic. I got a letter from him yesterday. He's all right, if tired and dirty. He's unscathed. My prayers are answered. For the time being.

Roy Tingley fairly beamed as I collected the frail envelope out of my box. A single sheet, so thin it is translucent. He's only written on one side, economy of words more than economy of paper. His upright architect's handwriting is barely marred by the censor.

Dearest Evangeline,

I'm safe and unhurt. I know you'll have been wondering, so I'll say that right off. Since landing here, we've marched for days across this once beautiful land. There are still farms and vineyards that at first sight seem untouched. Then you see the house has only one side left standing and the dogs have been shot. Many of my companions are the same men I started out with, and we count our-selves very lucky. We make slow progress and mostly we complain about our feet. I'm all right otherwise. How are you? There is a Red Cross station here and they will post this for me, so I must end here. We are mov-

ing again. I hold you in my heart. I love you. I miss you.

> *Your husband,*
> *John*

I sat on the green bench that overlooks the harbor. The letter grew moist in my hand, and I folded it and put it away before I smudged the writing.

I was still sitting there, the envelope in my hand, when Joe came up to me, a bag of groceries in his arms.

"Is he all right?"

"He says he is."

"Good. That's good, Mrs. W." Joe set the bag down and sat beside me on the park bench. We were quiet for a moment, each of us staring out towards the harbor, where the fishing boats not out to sea banged up against the pilings, the water rough today with some distant storm.

"He tells me nothing. He never tells me if he's scared or whether he is in danger."

"What do you tell him?"

"Well, I tell him what I'm doing, with the farm, and what my daily life is like. I tell him I miss him."

"Do you tell him you worry about him? Do you tell him you're scared?"

"No. Of course not. I'm careful not to give him something to worry about besides keeping safe. I don't tell him anything which will worry him about me."

Joe had the good grace not to point out the obvious. As soon as I said it, I knew what the point was. "Oh."

"Mrs. W., he's doing the best he can. There are things he's witness to or participant in which he will never tell you. Please don't expect him to."

A moment later Joe stood up, picked up the groceries, and walked off, leaving me to reread John's letter and wonder of whom had Joe spoken—John or himself?

It made all the difference, those words, and now John's face in the photograph looks almost cheerful.

July 4, 1944

We had a big picnic today. All the Fourth of July trappings: potato salad, coleslaw, hot dogs, lobster and littlenecks, too much green salad and not enough hamburger. Most of Hawke's Cove turned out for the Great Harbor parade. Our own auto parade began where the three main roads on the peninsula converge on the road to the bridge.

It was a wonderful parade, all the patriotic good cheer of small-town America as *The Saturday Evening Post* likes to portray it. Hawke's Cove's selectmen piled into the horse-drawn carriage with Great Harbor's selectmen, all of them tossing hard candies to the children waving their little American flags. I am hopelessly attached to such events. The veterans of the previous war filed by. Grim-faced men, many of them wearing scars and empty sleeves.

Then today's soldiers and sailors marched by, on loan to the parade from the local military bases. Next stop Europe. Or the Pacific. I wonder if they will remember this hokey little parade with amusement or derision at our perplexing naïveté. The sustained cheering escalated at their appearance. Our heroes. When will we cheer your return?

Joe insisted he remain behind to help

get the big grills going. The Sunderland boys provided them, oil drums sliced in half the long way and set on cradles. By the time most of the Hawke's Cove population was back from the parade, the grills were hot and the odor of cooking overrode even that of the sea.

I thought about not going to this long-standing traditional event. Many of the people there would be Boston folks who have spent years coming to Hawke's Cove for the summer. The McCormacks and the Hansons know my mother from home. I was certain there might be someone at the picnic who knew I lost the baby last December. It would be unbearable to have some old summer friend come up with well-meaning condolences and lay bare my secret to these new friends who know nothing about it. I don't like the idea of having my grief revealed by accident. Especially to Judy. I should tell her, I know. But the more time goes by, the harder it is to say anything. I should have said something early on, but I didn't.

I told Joe I wanted to stay home and work in the garden. Two days of rain made this new sunny day a perfect excuse. I thought. Joe thought otherwise and talked me into going.

"You have to come, Mrs. W."

"Joe, I don't, but you go. I insist. You'll love it. Lots of food and silly games."

"Exactly the reason you should be there. You don't want to be the only Cover who misses out on the July Fourth everyone else will be talking about all winter, do you?" He handed me the basket with three blueberry pies in it. "I'll bring the car around. You make sure you've got a sweater for when it cools off."

I stood there, big wicker basket clutched in two hands, feeling my reluctance ebb.

We played a long game of baseball. We ate and swam and ate again. The one or two who came up to me, approaching me in that careful way that announces their sympathy for my loss, I either ducked or— Mrs. Hanson—acknowledged gracefully (for me) and no one heard us. There was so much going on I was unable to brood.

It was nearly dark when Joe caught up with me. "Having a good time?" He handed me a whittled stick with a burned marshmallow on its tip.

"I am." I nibbled gingerly at the hot,

sticky glob. "Thank you for making me come. Sometimes I just need to be made."

"I know. We all have to be made sometimes to do things good for ourselves." He touched my shoulder gently. "I wouldn't have come without you, so I'm very glad you changed your mind."

He squeezed my shoulder again and dashed off to join those collecting wood for the bonfire. I think Joe assumes it's my worry over John that keeps me reclusive. I wonder what it is that keeps him so. Maybe if I told him my truth, he'd tell me his.

No fireworks this year. Instead we light a huge bonfire, the volunteer firemen standing ready to douse it in case of air raid. We are all standing in shadows, only our faces are illuminated by the golden red light of the fire that towers above the tallest of us for a little while before collapsing.

No one had called us to circle the fire, but we did, those of us who stayed late, whose obligations on the morrow didn't preclude watching the fire die to the last ember. Judy and Ted had left, and the women with small children. Sylvester

Feeney, up before dawn, was gone before the sun had set. The Sunderland boys, side-by-side as always, poked encouragement at the blaze, thrusting new driftwood into its flame. The eerie light of the fire cast their worn faces into gargoylesque relief. A gust of wind teased sparks from the top of the bonfire, miniature fireworks. A spontaneous ooh and aah went up from the remaining crowd.

I found myself flanked by Ernie and Joe, all of us silent. The rowdy mood of earlier in the day had drained away, leaving us contemplative. Ernie's dog, Pal, cast his exophthalmic eyes towards Ernie in a doggie plea to go home; he'd taken care of all the scraps and wanted his bed.

Ernie snapped his fingers at the dog and bid us good night. He was absorbed into the darkness beyond the bonfire. I heard the Sunderlands' truck start up, and then the fire department pumper. The fire had dwindled to a bed of ash, only an occasional red glow breathed and sighed in the remnants.

Joe was still beside me, seated on the cold, damp sand. "I offered to stay and bury the coals. If you want to take the car home, I'll walk."

"No, I'll help you."

I spread the bits of charcoaled lumber out with an iron rake while Joe fetched seawater in two buckets. He doused the ashes, and I raked. We played like this for a little while, raking and dousing, until there was no longer any steam coming from the hot embers. It only took Joe a couple of minutes to cover the spot with sand. Tomorrow it will look as if nothing had ever taken place. No primeval fire ring revealing where an arcane American ritual had occurred.

I was a little chilled. Joe had sent me back into the house to get my sweater before we left. I was glad of it now and struggled with cold fingers to button it.

Joe set the two empty buckets down and pointed to my cardigan. "You're all wrong there." Gently, he undid the misaligned buttons and rebuttoned them, stopping at the third one up.

He is such a sweet man. The way he has begun to take care of Gran's place, the way he already knows more people in town than I do, the way they all cheered him on during the baseball game—it is obvious he has already come to love Hawke's Cove. I wish John could come to love it. Maybe after the war—*maybe after the war*—how can I write such words and not worry I've thumbed my nose at the devil? Anyway, maybe someday John will come and the scales will fall from his eyes and he, too, will come to love this place.

July 10, 1944

I see that I am getting less and less reliable in journal keeping. I would make excuses, but that's silly. I am, after all, the only one reading this. I *know* why I don't have time to write every night. I'm too bloody exhausted!

Did I mention the whiskey? Yes, I did. Well, we decided to move it from the pit to the cellar under the house. Mainly because it'll be easier to get at. I haven't been down in the cellar in many, many years, and it lived up to my expectations of cobwebs and creepiness. As cluttered with ancient farm paraphernalia as the barn was, it smells vaguely of apples and dampness. In the north corner is a root cellar accessible to the outside by way of a wooden hatch. This is where we've stacked the sixteen wooden boxes of booze. Joe started singing that awful drinking song about ninety-nine bottles of beer, and I threatened to clock him with one. He switched to "Onward, Christian Soldiers." I was supposed to tease him about that too, I know, but his voice is so nice I let him go on. He knows all of the verses.

Sometimes I feel so settled here, as if there is no other life to return to. The city and my mother, my friends . . . they all seem part of another life. The Hindus believe in reincarnation, that we live a bunch of lives one after the other until we get it right. I think it's Hindus. Anyway, I feel as though there is some truth to that theory, except you don't die in between. At least not physically. After living my life with so much good, I am now tested by bad. How I live through this testing period will dictate what my next life will be like. If I can keep myself from thinking about John, if I can keep myself from thinking about the baby, then maybe I can survive this incarnation.

It helps to be here. Just being able to swim or walk or dig in my garden or play cribbage with friends has been healing. Healing. When Joe comes in and stands at the sink washing up, he brings in the scent of useful work, of the sweat of manual labor, the smell of the 3-In-One lubricating oil he squirts on the tools he uses. Generally he trails in dirt across my poor old floor too. I chide him, and he jollies me back, and I know that this is the best place for me to be.

A couple of days ago we went into the town to run errands. Joe wanted to pick up some bags of cement, so we took the car instead of the bicycles. He dropped me off in front of the post office and went on to park nearer the hardware store. When I got done at the post office, I couldn't find the car along Main Street. I walked up and back the length of it, finally coming to a standstill in front of the store. "Oh, ma'am," Everett, the elderly clerk/selectman, called out to me from the doorway, "yer husband's gone 'round back." He walked away before I could correct him.

I didn't tell Joe about that one, thinking he might be embarrassed.

July 16, 1944

I have waited a day before trying to write this. I am so filled with emotion I am numb from the surfeit. I can no longer feel. As soon as I can feel again, I will know how to act. How to behave. Now I am just moving from one minute to the next, from kitchen to parlor to porch. No matter where I am, the letter containing my new reality follows me. It sits on my bureau, the simple declarative sentences announcing my husband's disappearance written by formula, nothing new here for the Army. Just substitute "John Worth" for yesterday's name and send it off. Only they don't send them. That's how you know how serious it is. Two young officers, all tricked out in their dress uniforms come and make you stand in front of them, get you out of the garden where the July sun has warmed the earth into luxurious comfort and you don't mind feeling it on your hands. They have brought Judy Frick, knowing that a woman alone needs a woman at a time like this. Single star. Missing. Accept our regrets, Mrs. Worth.

Everything is being done that can be done. Off they go, relieved to have gotten it over with but mature enough to stay silent until the jeep goes over the rise.

I don't let Judy touch me at first. She knows from experience there's nothing angry about my refusal to be embraced just then. She knows I'll let her hold me in a little while. I think about being thrown off a horse. At first you shake your head, then test each of your limbs to see if anything is broken. Then you take a hand up.

Calling on those reserves of civility we all depend on in ourselves, I thank Judy for being there and assure her I'm all right. Hasn't John been missing since December? Of course, I don't say that aloud. Ted has followed in their car and he comes over to me. They really want me to go in, but I refuse. "I'm okay. I'm fine." Judy takes my hand and squeezes it gently. Ted pats my shoulder. I wave gamely at their departing car.

I look for Joe, but he has slipped away. Then he is there, and I feel him behind me, not touching, only waiting to see if I want to lay my head on his chest and weep. A willing prop in this new drama. I cover my face with my hands, but the tears do not come. I will not let them.

Once I was on some kind of carnival whirligig ride. It was fun; we laughed and screamed our enjoyment. But the ride went on for too long, the teenage operator probably slipping away for a cigarette. Around and around in erratic loops the ride went on, faster and faster, with no one to control the levers. The screaming changed from thrill to real fear. It will never stop. I will die on this ride, my brains exploded from the pressure of spinning. That is exactly how I feel. My world is spinning amok. I had deluded myself that I was in control of things by living here. It was only a mask.

Joe cares for me as if I were a child. He carried me into the parlor and tucked my grandmother's old afghan around my legs just as if I were ill. First he brought me a cup of tea. Then he gave me a shot of the twenty-five-year-old whiskey. That helped to stop the trembling. Then he sat beside me on the davenport and put his arm around my shoulders, snugging me to him, containing the outward me while the inward swirls around. He says neither, "There, there," nor "Everything will be all right." He says nothing, and there is a great comfort in that. Eventually he got up and went into the kitchen to make me a lunch of Campbell's tomato soup and a Pilot cracker spread with a thin layer of margarine.

"Joe, you don't have to do this."

"Yes, I do. Today I take care of your blisters."

"I don't understand."

"You can take a day off being the caregiver. Let me take care of you."

July 27, 1944

For the first few days after John was listed "missing in action," I couldn't make myself leave the yard. What if they needed to find me to tell me it was all a mistake? Or that he's been found alive and well, or that he . . . ?

Joe has thrown himself into the last of the foundation work under the barn. He's jacked it into alignment and built piers out of bricks. Early on in his digging he pointed out that the barn had been built on one granite pier and one hardwood pier in the front; thus its cant to the left was inevitable. Now all he needs to do is fill in the trench. I sat and watched him for hours.

At the end of the week, Ernie, Judy, and Ted showed up to play cards. "It's our turn," was all Joe said, and I saw complicity in Judy's eyes. In view of Judy's own grief, I am reluctant to share mine with her. How can mine compare, how can I go to her for sympathy when her loss is so much greater? So final. If—no, I cannot write those words. Should things get worse, then I can be her emotional equal. Right now I still am allowed to hope. So I turn only to Joe for comfort. I don't weep or even speak, but he tolerates my silences.

This is the second week. I went to church on Sunday. In order to make myself go, I insist Joe go with me. It was a near miss for both of us. I sat for a long time after getting dressed, staring into my cup of chickory coffee until Joe took it away from me and poured it down the sink. He handed me my hat. "I've got the tie on, Mrs. W. We'd better go."

Mr. Cummings wouldn't release my hand until I agreed to let him come and visit me.

"I feel as if I had some terminal illness, the way people are being so kind, so bloody sympathetic." Even as I said the words, I recognized them as cousins to the words I used to defend my decision to come to Hawke's Cove in the first place. Where can I go now?

Joe and I were sitting opposite at a center table in Linda's Restaurant. He'd talked me into buying him breakfast as a reward for going to church.

"No, you're wrong." Joe handed his menu back to the waitress. "People empathize with you. Admire you, even. 'This horrid thing has happened to Evangeline Worth; see how well she's handling it. Maybe we can handle our own bad news as well.' "

"I'm not handling it all that well, Joe. You know that."

"Yes, you are. You're doing fine."

I believed him for a little while because it felt good to.

This morning after breakfast Joe called me out to the barn. He'd finished filling in the trenches around the perimeter of the barn—wheelbarrow after wheelbarrow of stone and dirt dumped and tamped and now seeded. I admired his work and followed him into the barn. In the early morning a soft light comes in from the opened stall windows and the hayloft. In that light I could see that all of the junk is gone. The two box stalls are completely empty and ready for livestock with stall guards and new mangers. The space against the right-hand wall opposite the stalls has been converted into four milking parlors with metal bars separating each space and a cement trench strategically placed where bovine hind ends will project. Electric lights hang at evenly spaced intervals along the center beam above the aisle. The loft is filled with bales of straw for bedding, and the wire mesh silo Joe has added to the outside of the barn stands ready for a delivery of silage. Newly built shelves hold shiny new milk cans and pails, an optimistic vision of a bovine future for my grandmother's barn.

"This is the best part." Joe took my hand and led me to the double doors, one of which has sat open in the same position since I was a child. Joe pulled the door gently, and the two halves joined in a marvelous symmetry. "Even better . . ." He pushed both doors, and they swung open in a wide embrace of the new day.

It occurs to me to wonder what Joe has done with the collection of trunks and boxes stored in the loft. He hasn't mentioned them at all, so I don't think he's done anything with them. He's probably just left them alone. I'm not sure what I expect to find in those trunks. Most likely just Gran's collection of old quilts, too fragile to use, but stored away out of respect for the women of the family who came before her. I still use the one she made me for our wedding. It was her last quilt, a simple patchwork done in blues and greens, reds and yellows. She was getting too doddery even then to do much more than simple patchwork, the fancy wedding ring and stars of her heyday way beyond her strength. After almost ten years of use, the batting is getting lumpy and there are some weak spots in the fabric. I should retire it, but I love the feel of it, a tactile memory of an earlier day.

July 28, 1944

I woke up irritable. It was a nice change from sad. I tried to work out my crankiness on housework, storming along through the downstairs with broom and mop and dustcloth. I got to the kitchen, and Joe had trailed in barnyard mud yet again. "Try using the mat!"

"I'll take my boots off. I'm really sorry . . ." Wisely he decided to go see Sylvester Feeney about our cow-buying expedition next week.

Alone at last, I sat on the back porch steps and let my irritability mount. It peaked at Joe's forgetting to stop at the post office yesterday afternoon, and valleyed when I looked at the securely closed barn doors. Then I thought about the trunks. No better time than the present, I thought, and stood up.

The straw bales are stacked one on the other like yellowed sugar cubes. The air up there is warm and muffled. A paper wasp bumbled along, bumping into rafters until it found the one with its nest. On the wall farthest from the loft doors I saw the two trunks and barrel I remember being there since my youth. The ghostly voices of my childhood companions echoed once again as I see us playing hide-and-seek up here. The huge barrel made a great, if obvious, hiding place, and sometimes two of us would climb in, our hushed whispers melting into mindless giggles as we heard our pursuer bumble, like the paper wasp, among the clutter in the barn below us. The hideout worked only with kids who obeyed the admonition to stay away from the loft.

One of the trunks is a round-topped steamer; the other, a simple black rectangle with travel decals pasted all over it, a record of Gran's European tour. My father used it to go to college. A Bates sticker garnishes the flat top, placed just between the stickers from Lisbon and Paris and just above the one from London.

Hay dust sparkled in the sunlight, turning the light from the loft doors very yellow. I opened the steamer trunk first. As I expected, there are a half-dozen ancient quilts wrapped carefully in sheets. They are patchwork and crazy quilts, rather common, which is a little disappointing. I would have liked to have found one of Gran's specialty quilts. I suppose she divvied them up among relatives long before she died. I refolded the quilts in opposite folds to help preserve them a little longer. This left the grand-tour trunk. In it, my father's clothes. I know that they are his because his varsity sweater lies on top. I took everything out, laying each piece of clothing on the bales of straw to look at them. After my father died when I was a teenager, Gran would tell me stories from his childhood, but not much about his adult years when he was long gone from the farm and making it on his own as a businessman in Boston.

I took out everything. Woolen trousers, white shirts, no collars or cuffs. A narrow tie that I think I remember. I dig deeper and come up with his graduation gown and cap.

I dig still deeper and find the Ruths' missing blanket.

"Mrs. W.!" I hear Joe calling, a tiny note of concern in his voice. I have left him no note, as I would had I gone to the beach.

Besides, my suit waves alone on the clothesline.

"Mrs. Worth?" My bike leans against the house, where I have forgotten to put it away, so he can see I haven't gone for a bike ride.

"Vangie?" He is in the barn now, the worry exposed by this use of my first name. He has never called me Vangie before.

"Up here."

He knows. Even before he sets foot on the ladder, he knows I have discovered one of his secrets. Not the most important, to be sure, but my discovery is a breach of the trust I have shown him. When his head crests the coaming of the loft floor, he sees me standing there with the blanket gripped in my hands.

"You should have told me."

"Yes, but I didn't, and then too much time went by and I couldn't. I stayed here in your barn, I took the blanket to keep warm on those cold April nights. I took your husband's clothes so that I wouldn't be naked."

My Joe, my friend, had been the vagrant thief. "Why?"

"I was desperate."

"Why were you desperate?" It is a question I have wanted to ask.

"I can't tell you."

My anger is volcanic. I spew it in gobs of words that come from some renegade part of my mind. "You take my kindness and throw it back in my face. You must be laughing at me every day, 'Mrs. Worth, ha ha. I stole her husband's clothes and lied blithely about it. I stole her kindness, I stole her trust, I stole her . . .' " I paused for breath. I paused before I said a word I had no control over. I almost said *heart.* He had stolen my heart. With each raging phrase I stepped closer to him. "My husband lies dead in some French forest and you make me worry about you. You make me care what happens to you. It isn't right. There is something very wrong with how you came here. You've lied to me all along."

I struck him. Over and over, cold-eyed and deeply angry at everything that had spoiled my happiness. I pummeled Joe Green's chest because he had lied to me, because my husband was missing and Joe was alive. Because my baby was stillborn and Joe Green had no knowledge of her.

Because I'd known all along he'd been the one who'd stolen the clothes and he'd made me want to be wrong. I pounded until at last he took my wrists in his hands. I could feel our pulses together, mine pumping with almost audible power, his fluttering against my wrist.

"Your husband isn't dead."

He waited until I dropped my resistance, then let go of my wrists, sliding his hands down to take mine. "You must believe me when I tell you I only did what I had to in order to save my own life. I never thought for a moment it wasn't wrong. That surviving itself was wrong. Then I met you and lied from the very first moment. Of necessity." Joe let go of my hands and turned away from me. "Of necessity." He turned back. "Don't think there hasn't been a day yet when I haven't regretted it. Please don't ask me any questions which will force me to lie to you again. Can you understand?"

I stood with my hands at my sides, the hayloft suddenly overwarm and suffocating. I couldn't answer him, and he took this as mistrust.

"Mrs. Worth, the barn is done. Ready for cows. So, when you say why I've left, you could also say I've done one good thing for you."

All of my anger was gone. I watched as he turned towards the ladder, and suddenly the realization washed over me. I cannot bear another loss. Another wrench to my heart. I don't think I could bear to go back to my solitude.

"Joe. Don't go."

He did not look at me, only stood there with his back to me, his shoulders perfectly straight. "Are you certain?"

"Yes."

He turned around then and came back to me to circle me with his arms. I lay my head on his chest as naturally as if he had been my lover. His cheek rested on my head, and he rocked me back and forth. I think we both took comfort from it, that we are both starved for human touch. I clenched the fabric of his shirt, John's shirt, in my hands, determined not to lose him too.

I dream of the baby. I dream of her birth. The pain of the incessant, useless contractions has me doubled up. The black rubber mask over my nose does not put me to sleep; I fight it and remain awake as they cut me. The blood gushes out and the baby stands up, squalling as she never did in life. The blood runs onto the floor, a river in which the doctors and nurses swim. I wake up, wet and lying in my own menstrual blood. "Damn," I say out loud, and climb out of bed, dragging my sheets off. No one told me that after you have had a child, live or stillborn, your periods come on instantly and intensely.

My nightgown and sheets are soaked. I strip everything off. In deference to Joe, I'm fortunate to have my Kotex in the bedroom and strap on the belt and thick pad. I tiptoe down the stairs and into the kitchen to rinse out the mess. Joe wakes up anyway.

"You okay?" He looks like a big, bearded boy standing in his doorway, clutching his blanket around his waist, the other hand rubbing sleep out of his eyes.

"I'm fine. Go back to bed."

"What's the matter?" Being a man, he's a little slow to figure it out. I'm too modest to say.

"Oh." He'd figured it out.

I've boiled enough water for the sheets

and nightgown with some left over for a couple of cups of tea. It's nearly dawn, so I abandon returning to bed. "Make us some tea."

He slipped on a pair of pants; I tightened the belt to my robe. Don't we look a pair? I am gripped with a cramp and grimace. At once the dream comes back to me, and I grimace again.

"Why don't we skip the tea, and I'll fill the hot water bottle."

"What do you know about this?" I asked, suddenly afraid that one of the questions I'm not suppose to ask involves an abandoned wife.

"Sisters."

Oh, there is so much I don't know about Joe Green.

August 2, 1944

Well, we have cows, three to be exact. Not exactly a herd, but Mr. Feeney says they're enough to qualify this place as a farm. We drove to Tylerville on Thursday to attend the weekly auction there. Joe was really reluctant to go, claiming to be superfluous, busy, expected at the Ruths'. It was only when Sylvester Feeney described upstate Tylerville as "the back of beyond" and not exactly a watering hole for anyone besides farmers that Joe acquiesced. That and when Mr. Feeney said he wouldn't go with "just a woman to help bring 'em back."

Joe grew pretty enthusiastic after that.

We drove up in Mr. Feeney's truck with the six-cow trailer rattling along behind us. I sat wedged between the two men and, given I know Joe a little better, leaned right against the centrifugal forces as Mr. Feeney barreled down these impossibly twisting back roads. Miraculously, we arrived at the auction barn alive. The barn is actually a cinder-block single-story building with big double doors at both ends and high rectangular windows all along the side. It looks WPA-built, although Tylerville seems a long way away from any WPA projects. We had passed a camp for conscientious objectors, and I wondered if they had been put to use building it. All along the side of the building, black pickup trucks nosed like Labrador pups on their dam.

Inside was an arena with an auctioneer's podium at one end, and surrounded on three sides by wooden bleachers. Wedged once again beside my two companions, I felt a little seasick every time one or another of the lineup of farmers on either side of us bounced off the bleacher to bid or to catch a friend's eye. I looked around at them. Each man's face stamped with the years of his profession. Deeply lined, roughened by the sun and wind, ubiquitous cigarette dangling from rubbery lips. They all were of an age when they should have been able to let their sons take over. Instead they continue on as they have all of their lives, hoping their sons will survive, hoping their sons will want to come back. The silly First World War tune "How Ya Gonna Keep 'Em Down on the Farm (After They've Seen Paree)" keeps going through my head.

Joe was looking around as well. I wondered if he felt awkward being the only young man present; if the old men wondered about him. He caught me looking at him and smiled.

"Maybe if you limped a little?"

"How do you know what I'm thinking?"

"It's what I'd be thinking. Is this why you were reluctant to come?" Another forbidden question.

"No."

Our whispered conversation was interrupted by the entrance of the first of the sheep to be auctioned. They were so cute I almost abandoned my cow plans in favor of sheep farming. Mr. Feeney shot me a withering look when I suggested getting some.

The air was filled with bleating, and even some of the veterans chuckled at the ram who seemed to be bidding on himself, answering the auctioneer's yodel with loud baas.

"Twenty-one . . . Do I hear twenty-two? . . . Noisy bugger, 'n' he? . . . Who'll give me twenty-three? . . . Not you, stupid sheep. We're at twenty-two . . ."

Just after eleven o'clock, the last of the sheep were herded out the rear doors and the first of the milk cows brought in.

"Keep your hands down." Mr. Feeney shifted his unlit cigarette into the other corner of his mouth. "Let me do the bidding here."

I've made an arrangement with Mr. Feeney. I buy the cows, and he buys my milk. He gives me a good price on silage, and I sell him the cows at what I bought them for if I leave Hawke's Cove in less than a year. He's very careful, then, about selecting my cows. His criteria are mysterious, and cow after cow is brought before the auction block and nary a nod or a wave from Mr. Feeney. I grew a little restless after about seven good milkers came and went, and went off to the little-used ladies' room. The acoustics allow me to hear the bidding even as I wash my hands at the sink. "Lot number thirty-four sold to bidder one-oh-three." That's us. I own a cow! Then I own two more, a cow and her calf.

It's been a long time since I've owned any animals, John being not keen on them in general, and I quickly run outside to examine my new pets. Bessie is a doe-soft black-and-white Guernsey with an inquisitive wet nose. The second cow is a brown-and-white Jersey we dub Mom, and her calf Baby. I can't see the difference in any of them from the sixteen or so that have gone before.

"Pedigree," is all Mr. Feeney says.

Joe and Mr. Feeney loaded the "herd" into the trailer while I watched from a safe distance. Joe got kicked in the knee, but no permanent damage done, he says, although he's still limping a little. Given our earlier conversation, I wisely forgo pointing out the irony.

After dinner Joe and I went out to the barn, where the three cows were happily munching the prescribed amount of feed Mr. Feeney had instructed us to give each one. Joe ran a hand along Bessie's bony spine. "Mrs. W., I think this cow thing is going to be good for you." He scratched the cow behind her swiveling ears. "Not as a distraction from, well, from what's going on, but as a focus. Something positive, productive for you."

"I think that it's going to be hard work. Mostly for you." I watched him stroke the silky skin of the cow. "Joe, I wouldn't have been able to do it without you."

He put his arm around my shoulders and

gave me a little squeeze. "Shucks, ma'am, I'm justa cowpoke doin' my job."

"Hey, cowboy, how 'bout a beer?" We walked back to the house hand in hand.

August 7, 1944

I never knew cows were so regimented. I always tended to think that they simply mooed and chewed their cud and otherwise hung around. Not so. These cows demand to be fed at precisely six A.M., expect to be milked, and moo plaintively if not taken care of immediately. It's worse than a pestering cat begging for dinner.

Joe is so good. He's up and out there taking care of business before I can pull myself out of bed. I stumble downstairs and start the coffee even if sometimes I creep back up the stairs to lie down just till I hear it perking. He never complains, not even joking. Sometimes I think he actually *likes* the work. He bought a soft horse brush at the hardware store yesterday and spent an hour going over the cows as if they were pets. He's even begun telling stories about them. "Mom and Baby wandered down to the very edge of the drystone fence to lie down. Bessie kept herself at a distance." He thinks maybe Mom is the herd leader. Then he saw Mom and Bessie standing head to head, "conversing," he called it.

I shouldn't be surprised. He's treated me like a pet, always taking my emotional temperature and adjusting my climate as best he can. Stopping what he's doing to suggest a walk or a bike ride if he catches me staring off into space. He refuses to take a day off. "And just what would I do with the time?"

"Go into Great Harbor and see a film? Go to the beach for the day?"

"I have no desire to do the first, and I like the beach when everyone else has left for the day."

We do go nearly every nice day. Usually around three o'clock or so. He's done with the sweaty chores, as he calls them, and I've puttered around sufficiently to fool even myself into thinking I'm productive. I pack up a light snack—whatever fruit is available, a box of crackers. A Thermos of lemonade or just cold water. Nothing fancy.

I notice that Joe is careful about the sun on his back. He never works bare-chested, even on these dog days. I expect that one of the reasons he prefers the beach late is to keep the direct sun off those still-healing burns. I haven't yet asked him about those, how he came to have them. His wall goes up almost visibly anytime I come near asking him those kinds of questions. As well as I think I know Joe Green, he is a deeply private person.

August 10, 1944

The Ruths called today to ask if they could "borrow" Joe for a few hours. Besides his weekly lawn-mowing, Joe's been over there once or twice a week more, mostly pruning high branches or lifting heavy things for them. It wasn't long ago Ruth Banks would lift furniture over her head. Well, not really, but she was legendary for never asking for help.

"Vangie, honey, can you spare our boyfriend for a little? Got some clearin' we want done. You come too. We could use the company." Ruthie Jones didn't fool me with her backwards invitation. She meant I could use the company. I still haven't been terribly social. I'm happiest—no, that's not the word. I'm *better* when I don't have to make conversation. I can do it. I've done it in the grocery store, nodding and commenting on the weather before Angela West can ask, "How *are* you?" It's that little inflection that is so hard to defend against. How am I? Fine. Just fine. I have used those words, comforting those who know me a little with a little reply. It is kinder to pretend to be fine. To grab Angela by her round shoulders and shake her and scream, "Just how do you think I am!? My husband is missing and every day I have to read the paper. I have to read every name on the list because he may have been found dead and they neglected to tell me," would be . . . what? Uncivil? Cruel? Not what is expected.

What a beautiful day. A little less humid, the sky brilliant blue over a dead calm sea. In the west, mare's tails swoop, and I know by tonight's mackerel sky that tomorrow it will rain. I did go to the Ruths' with Joe. We bicycled over; my gas ration is dangerously close to depleted. Ruth Banks greeted us with evil-looking hedge clippers, and Ruthie Jones hovered in the background with a yellow apron tied around her plump waist. The four of us marched out to the ancient privet hedge Ruth Banks's father planted to separate the cottage from the roadside. "I'm sick of that hedge. I want a nice white fence with Rosa rugosa fronting it. Sick of being cooped up here behind it. Daddy planted it to keep us in. I think I'm old enough to know not to run across the road without lookin'."

"Besides, it'll be nice for people passing by to see your lovely gardens." I gestured towards the old traditional half cape with its surrounding cottage garden. Every color of blooming flower—blues and reds and yellows, purples and delicate whites—fills six feet in front of the house and all along the flagstone path to the front door. Carefully chosen rocks and bushes stand as anchors to the thick beds, giving a different definition to each.

"That's what Joe said, and I said—didn't I, Ruthie?—I said, why the hell not?" Ruth Banks handed the hedge clippers to Joe and stalked off in search of a saw and shovel.

It felt really good. The physical labor of tearing those seventy-five-year-old bushes out. We chopped and sawed and pulled and dug, and in the end we had a huge pile of vegetative debris piled up in the most unsightly heap. Joe promised to borrow a truck from the Sunderlands and remove the brush.

Afterwards we tracked good old yellow dirt into the pristine kitchen and gratefully refreshed ourselves with peach cobbler and the real coffee Ruthie Jones had produced for us. Ruth Banks dug into her dungaree pocket and pulled out as much money as I pay Joe in a month.

"No, please, that's not necessary." Joe gently grasped her raddled hand with its filthy fingernails. "Real coffee is payment enough."

"Bull. You'll take it 'cause I don't see where you're so rich you don't need it."

"It's too much."

"Call it payment in advance for building the fence."

"Done."

"When can you come back?" Ruth asked.

"Up to Mrs. W. here." Joe looked at me for the answer. For some reason it made me think of John, looking at me to get him out of some commitment.

"Jeepers, people, I'm not exactly a taskmaster. You work it out."

August 15, 1944

It has been a month. A month since this letter was handed to me, and I felt that same helplessness you feel when caught in an undertow. Panicked, you can't remember that simple admonition, relax and you will float to the top. Instead, you fight it and tumble head over heels, so disoriented you try to breathe water.

A month and no word. I lied to myself: It would only be a few days . . . weeks . . . I would hear something. Now, should I tell myself it will be a few months? Years? Ever?

I worry out loud only to Joe. To everyone else I wear my trooper face. "She's such a trooper," I hear them say. The Ruths and the Sunderlands and even, God bless them, the Fricks.

Only Joe hears me pace the floor in the night. Only Joe finds me staring off into space, my hands in the soapy dishwater. Only Joe knows that I never cry.

August 16, 1944

I cut a massive bouquet of zinnias. The tomatoes are still green, but there are dozens of them. Our weather has been nearly perfect, sunny days and misty nights. Enough rain to keep the water table high. I've picked all of the peppers, zucchinis, and beans. Summer squash grows with abandon. My peas were eaten by something early on, so I only managed enough for one meal. I'm disappointed, but determined. Next year I'll try asparagus. I hear our soil is good for it. *Next year.* I write those words and I wonder if I expect another year here. Or want one. John will not live here. His life, rather, our life, is planned around his architectural career, which by his definition is in the city. Therefore I must be demonstrating pessimism. At least I am if I expect to be here long enough to plant next year's asparagus. You plant it very early.

These are the thoughts that plague my nights. Is wanting to be here disloyal to John or hopeless or maybe just selfish? I have a hard time imagining life elsewhere. I don't even miss our Boston flat. I know that I'm truly selfish to continue to pay rent on it and not live in it. Profligate. Still, what if John came home and we had no home? Except I feel as if this *is* home. My home. I realize now that my most recent letters to John, wherever they have been collected to wait for him, are filled with persuasive arguments for living here. Nothing obvious, just a recitation of the more prosaic aspects of living on the farm, of being part of a small community. I tell him how beautiful it is, how kind the people, how at home I feel, how protected. I feel as though I can say anything because . . . No. I won't write that I think he won't get these letters. I won't.

Our days have become very cow-oriented. Joe is up before dawn and into the barn for milking. Mom and Bessie are producing about eight pounds of milk apiece. I suppose this is good, but Sylvester says they'll do better. The calf, Baby, is finally weaned. We had to separate her from her mother even visually. Her bawling was piteous indeed and made even my dry breasts ache. Joe spent a lot of time with her, hand-feeding her, brushing her with his horse brush, and talking baby talk to her. Twice she managed to get out of her pen and into the field with the other two. Interesting, Mom seems to be completely blasé about her calf's absence. Nature's way, I suppose.

I'm being a good farm . . . what? Not wife, *ummm,* boss. I'm being a good boss. I'm better about getting up and giving Joe a real breakfast of oatmeal and bacon, eggs, toast. Whatever he wants. I like cooking for him and am gratified to see less of his ribs when we go swimming. He looks fit.

After breakfast is the mucking out. I don't understand why they wait until they're in the barn to do their business. Beats me. I don't mind the work, though. The barn smells pungent, but not unpleasant. It's the correct odor for a place like that, a scent of purpose.

Sylvester comes by around nine to collect the milk. For the first week he would stand at the high end of the pasture to look at the cows, but now he seems to have decided we aren't going to do them any harm, and he just collects the milk, leaving us with clean cans.

In the afternoon the whole process repeats. Joe has gotten them to come to his call, "Here, Bessie. Here, Mom. Here, Baby. Come home cows . . . !" He's very proud of himself, but I think its really a matter of conditioning.

He was ecstatic the first time they lifted their heads and began the slow sauntering walk up from the lower end of the pasture. "Will you look at that!"

"Don't suppose it has anything to do with associating you with dinner?"

"I think they simply respect me."

While they munch their feed, we milk. We're both getting better at this too, giving each teat its equal share of use, making certain that no milk is left in them. Such carelessness, we've been warned by Sylvester, leads to mastitis.

Sometimes we talk as we milk. Often, though, we speak only to the cows, shushing them with soft voices. The rhythmic pulling and pushing on the full udders, the sound of the milk as it dashes into the bucket, our foreheads pressed against the firm sides of the cows, leaves us a little sleepy with the meditative effect.

I have a radio, a brand new Philco. After dinner we listen to the news and one or two programs. Joe is so tired now he usually falls asleep despite valiant efforts not to. I confess I like watching him sleep. I don't know why. Sometimes I have the urge to lay a blanket over him and let him stay there on the davenport. Tuck him in like a child. I don't. Instead I touch his arm, startling him out of his doze and say, "Cows."

These last days of summer are beautiful. Most nights I go out with Joe when he does his final check on the girls.

Sometimes we sit on the back porch steps afterwards and share a sip of the bootleg scotch or a beer. Once in awhile we go for a night swim, running back to the house chilled from the cool night air. Tonight there was an air-raid drill. We heard the firehouse horn bleat its coded warning. One-two-one-two. Pause. One-two-one-two. The few lights we could see along the arms of the cove blinked out. It is a dark night, and we'd found our way to the beach with a flashlight. We didn't dare return until we heard the all clear, so we stayed in the water, drifting in and away from the shore on the quiet waves. The air was cooler than the water and felt more like silk than in the daylight, as if not being able to see it changed its texture. It was so dark I couldn't see Joe. I felt his wet hair bump against me as he drifted by.

"Did you shut the lights off before we came down?" Joe knows I am less careful about electric lights than I was about the oil lamps.

"I hope so."

"Let it be on your head if the Japs take Hawke's Cove."

I splashed water in the general direction of his voice, but the only response was the sound of his dive. Suddenly he had me by my legs, flipping me into the dark and silky water.

We are given a certain immunity in the darkness. An immunity against being old before our time, against grief, and against solemnity. Just for a tiny little bit. We played. His hands went around my waist and then let go, as if he was suddenly aware of what he was doing.

Tomorrow night he's going fishing with Ernie.

August 17, 1944

Between milking and final check I spent the evening with Judy. Ted had gone with Ernie and Joe, so she and I decided on a man-free evening of a meal out and a movie. "Should we invite Mrs. Dubee along?"

"Judy, you are joking?"

Behind the rims of her glasses, Judy's faded gray eyes gleamed with mischief. "It is a girls' night out, after all . . ."

I waggled a finger in her face. "My grandmother would have said you are a caution, Judy Frick."

"Yes, she certainly would have."

Judy drove her Ford with a certain devil-may-care insouciance that made me cling discretely to the door handle, anticipating around every turn the need for a quick escape. My nervousness didn't escape her notice, and she smirked at me.

It felt good putting on a shirtwaist dress and real shoes with heels, dabbing an appropriate amount of red lipstick on my lips and a touch of nearly dried-up mascara to my spiky eyelashes. I've been too long in frumpy housedresses or old slacks. Rubber boots seem to be my usual footwear, or tennis shoes with a hole in the toe. Joe must think I'm pretty drab. I don't think that should matter to me, but, oddly, it does. Female failing.

Saturday night and Great Harbor was bustling with sailors and soldiers with weekend passes, too much money in their pockets, and a battlefield in their near future. Not since the city had I seen a greater mass of uniforms, all filled with skinny young men with grins on their faces and mischief in their hearts. I know what they all thought. They all thought they should do their utmost to get laid before shipping out. Most of these kids were so young I imagined that the loss of their virginity was of paramount importance. A rite of manhood.

None of these boys looked as if Galahad was their hero. No, more like Lancelot.

As we walked along the main avenue, they came along in groups, eddying around us like the tide against pilings, or in pairs, tipping their caps to us in flirting courtliness. The restaurant was filled to capacity, so we had to wait in the small bar. At least three sailors tried to buy us drinks, but we refused with grace, indicating we were all set with the soft drinks in front of us and pointing to our wedding bands as further proof of our off-limitsness.

Judy shook her head in amazement. "I'm old enough to be their mother, and they want to buy me a drink. Their mothers would be appalled if anyone suggested to them their sons would be trying to pick up an old lady in a bar. I suppose they think I'm ideal to help them slough off the curse of virginity."

"Five years ago these boys were children." I don't know what made me say that, except that with their clipped hair and thin chests, these drunken sailors were painfully young, and I decided that the war had really gone on too long that children should have grown old enough to be in it.

In contrast, John is an old man at thirty. He's had a chance to be a grown-up, to have a wife and almost a child. I threw back the remains of my Coke, choking a little as I did, trying to avoid wondering if he'll ever have a second chance at a child. Will I?

The girls were all right, but seemed to look for Joe when I came in for the night check. "He'll be back. I promise." They just look at me with those amazing eyes and seem skeptical. What makes me think he won't disappear one day like he arrived?

The night air is silky and cloudless. The early crickets are tuning up, prelude to fall. The wind is right, and tonight I can hear the waves as I sit up here in my room. I am filled with a nameless want. No. I'm not honest even on my own page. I know what it is and am familiar with it. This nameless want has been absent from my life for a long time now. I had thought I'd gone beyond it. I have not been touched in so long, I have not wanted to be touched in so long, that I thought I never would again. It seemed best, with no one here to touch me. But I do want it. I find myself thinking the most inappropriate thoughts, thinking about Joe. I tell myself it's proximity. I tell myself it's natural curiosity. I think of his hands, long and elegant and so different from John's square, capable hands. I think of them touching my waist. I think of them . . .

I must stop this nonsense. It is wrong.

It is one of those nights when the water and the air are exactly the same temperature. I ran to the beach barefoot, still in my dress. I planned only to go and put my feet in, but suddenly I am stripping off my clothes and plunging into the sea naked. As warm as the air, the water glides over my body like oil. I swim furiously; maybe if I tire myself out thoroughly, these thoughts will go away. I lie on my back, and my hair, unencumbered by a swim cap, fans out behind me, then lies heavy on my shoulders when I stand. I swim towards the seal rock jutting up out of the water. The rock where Joe once stood, staring out to sea and smoking a cigarette. Phosphoresence glitters all around me as I swim, making me think of liquid fairy dust. The moon tonight is bright enough to cast shadows. I sit in the water and lean my back against the rock, watching as the eddies swirl into and around its crevices. I sit there long enough for the receding tide to expose me.

What is sex, after all, but imagination and touching the right places? Who is to know that it is Joe Green's hands I imagine. For ten minutes I absolve myself of disloyalty and imagine Joe Green's hands touching me.

August 19, 1944

Judy and Ted think Joe has been discharged; the Sunderlands claim they know for sure he's 4-F, although they couldn't say why. The Ruths hazard the opinion that Joe is a conscientious objector, maybe a Mormon or a Quaker. Ernie never says what he thinks. I think maybe Joe's a little of all of those things.

I watch him when he doesn't know it. Sometimes his naturally mild expression hardens against some interior pain, and I know that whatever the genesis of his being here in Hawke's Cove, here on my farm, it has a bitter taste. When he first came, he was consistently cheerful. As we've grown accustomed to one another, and he's seen some of my drearier moments, he's allowed himself the luxury of being quiet. Of having reflective moments unassailed by my interfering. I don't ask, "What's the matter?" I let him be. These pensive moods never last very long. I'm not sure if it isn't simply against his nature to be morose for long. If I go to call him to lunch, he breaks into a smile and throws off whatever it is that has kept him unsmiling and broody.

This morning I went out to the barn to find him sitting on the milking stool, his hands still, his cheek pressed against Bessie's side. He didn't hear me come in, though Bessie swung her head around to see. Joe patted her nose and began milking.

"Hi." I came up behind him. Some impulse made me lay my hands on his shoulders. I could feel the muscles work as he milked.

If he had shrugged a little or spoken of neutral things, I would have dropped my hands with a little playful slap. He did neither, only leaned a little against my touch, so that I knew, in that moment, we have inadvertently become important to each other, and so I left my hands there.

He still calls me Mrs. W. As long as he does, the borderline is safe. We acknowledge the barrier.

August 21, 1944

If I hadn't needed the preserve jars, it would never have happened. If I hadn't decided to go with Joe instead of sending him alone to town. If I hadn't been greedy for his company, he wouldn't know this about me, and I wouldn't now have to suffer his feeling more sorry for me than he already does.

Mrs. Sutton had only heard of my being pregnant, not of my loss. She sometimes plays bridge with my mother but left for Florida before I was due. She is one of the few people we know from Boston who spend time in Hawke's Cove. She is not a close friend. I can barely write this.

I hear Joe in the kitchen; he should be

outside mending the fence, not worrying about me.

It was the way it happened that keeps exploding in my mind over and over the way an accident will. I have this impression of this tottering female, perched on impossibly high heels, hands waving in the air, but I'm sure this is a grotesquerie grown out of my distress.

"Vangie, sweetie. How's the baby!" She came clattering towards us as we left the hardware store. "Was it a boy or a girl? How wonderful for you, did I hear girl? And this must be John. Still not overseas? Where's the baby, let me get a good look at her!" Words fell from her red lips like rain, no, like hail. The assault was blindly vicious and unstoppable.

A wall of numbness shut out her voice. I went deaf, although I could see her lips moving and knew that she was exposing my secret to the world. To Joe. I must have dropped the bag because I see myself looking down at the scattered lids and seals.

I don't remember Joe getting me into the car, although he says he fairly strong-armed me away from Mrs. Sutton, pulling

me out of her reach. I only remember seeing her lips still moving as we backed away
from the curb. Joe said nothing as he took
me home. Instead, he took my left hand in
his, holding on to it even as he passed the
car through its gears. It was only mid afternoon, but Joe poured me a glass of the
bootleg scotch. Then another. Until the
numbness was replaced by sleep.

When I woke, he was sitting there, in my
room, on the edge of the bed. I don't know
if he'd been sitting there the whole time—
by now the sun was quite low—or if it was
the feeling of his weight on the bed that
awakened me. All I know is that I was glad
to see him, glad of his touch as he brushed
the hair away from my eyes. "You know,
Joe, scotch isn't a cure."

"No. But it can make things go away for
a little while." His voice was a raspy whis-
per.

"You speak as one who's had to make
things go away."

He only smiled a little. I crawled out from
under the afghan with which he'd covered
me and sat beside him. I might have joked
about compromising positions, but my
heart was too sick. Joe took my hand in

his and stroked my knuckles with his thumb. Soothed a little by his touch, I began to talk.

It was the first time I have spoken of Molly as someone who had actually been part of my life. Not just the lost baby, the stillborn who beat herself to death trying to be born. The child I had named. *Molly Anne* or *Charles,* those were our names for our unborn child. The child we never considered ever losing. It was only when John showed surprise at my wanting to put her name on the grave of an unbaptized fetus that I realized he didn't understand the depth of my loss.

"By the time they realized I would never dilate enough, it was too late. They cut me, but she was already dead, strangled. It was likely, they told me, that she wouldn't have survived anyway. She was too early. So that was that. Tough luck, try again. Except that John ran away. No. I don't mean that. He was shipped out before I got out of the hospital. He wouldn't have been there at all except she was so early."

Joe snugged the afghan around my shoulders to warm my shivering. "He came to see me, as he did every day just after breakfast. You see, they gave him compassionate leave, and he had a few days home with me before going back to base. But then he'd gotten his orders. Joe, the grief was washed off his face by the excitement of finally going overseas. He couldn't even wait until I was discharged. They hadn't canceled his leave, but he was anxious to get back to base, to be with his buddies. He was excited.

"I was still being sedated. They do that so you can't face your grief head-on. I was still groggy when he came in and told me. I don't recall the time between his telling me he had to go and his leaving. It seemed like minutes, although I know it was a couple of days. Even now, when I think of it, it seems like it was the same day as we lost Molly, but it couldn't have been. Joe, I don't even remember if we said we loved each other. It has been as if I lost them both."

Joe shifted the afghan back over my shoulders.

"It was the expectations of other people which finally drove me here, where no one knew of my loss. At home they expected me to weep, then they expected me to get over it. I've done neither."

"Not wept?"

"No."

"Why?"

"I wish I knew. I wish I could. It's as if some spigot is turned off too tight."

"Or maybe if you cry, you'll feel as though you *have* gotten over it."

I nodded. "Sometimes I feel as though I need to remember every detail, no matter how painful, in order to make her real. You see, otherwise I might convince myself it never happened, that she had never been. I don't want to do that. I want to mourn her completely."

"You'll never lose her entirely." He pressed a soft, comforting kiss on my forehead and stood up to leave, pausing a moment in the doorway, one hand pressing against the jamb as if to hold himself in. "And you haven't lost your husband. He will come home to you. There is no doubt in my mind."

Now I hear Joe banging around in the kitchen making a dinner I won't want to eat.

When I write to John, I won't mention

this incident to him. I know that he hopes I have gotten over it. I don't mention Joe much to him either; it wouldn't do to have him know how important Joe is to me. He might get the wrong idea.

August 22, 1944

I really don't blame Joe for telling Judy about the baby. About Molly. At least he had the sense not to call her on the telephone. The party line is a notorious well for gossip around here. I didn't know he had spoken to her until she showed up this afternoon. Judy is not a flutterer. She walked into my house and put the kettle on. I was shelling peas at the kitchen table.

"Joe did the right thing telling me. You're not to get angry at him." She stood with her feet apart and her hands on her hips, daring me to disagree.

"He was concerned for you. I think you scared him a little, closing down like that. Of course, he would fall on that man's remedy of scotch to cure you. Lucky he didn't kill you."

"Well, it got me past the worst." I got up and took down two teacups from the shelf. "The truth is, I'm glad he told you. I'm sorry I haven't been more honest with you. That I do regret."

"Look, Vangie. We all have things bottled up inside of us which aren't always for other people's consumption. Don't waste time regretting not telling me. This is how you need to deal with your grief. I know. When Teddy died, it took me a year before I could bear to speak his name out loud. I closed the door to his room and wouldn't let even Ted in there. I thought that if I could just keep it exactly as he had left it, he would somehow still be in there. We all do inexplicable things to help ourselves get through. Then with John going missing, well, you don't have to say anything about that either. Unless"— and here she squeezed my elbow to better hold my eyes—"unless you need to. Then you mustn't hesitate."

Her lecture concluded, Judy finished her tea in two quick swallows and went on her way. I waved to the departing car, then hunted down Joe Green.

"Mrs. Frick made me promise not to get mad at you."

Joe was on a ladder, replacing the top hinge on the right-hand barn door. "Can you keep that promise?" He didn't look down as he asked his question, just kept turning the screwdriver.

"I really don't have a choice." The ladder wobbled a little as he bore down against the long screw. I stood at the bottom, one hand on either side, and lent my weight to hold him steady.

Done, he came down the ladder and took me by the shoulders. "Mrs. Worth, we always have choices." He let go of me and bent to pick up the toolbox. "It's really a matter of regretting or accepting our choice and then sticking by it." With his free hand he pulled a renegade piece of hair from the corner of my mouth. "Are you angry with me or not?"

"No." I sighed and tucked my hair behind my ears. "No, I'm not angry with you Joe."

Tonight we were able to pick up the classical station out of Boston very clearly. They had a broadcast of Verdi's *Aida*. It was so pretty we picked up our coffee and brought it into the parlor. Joe turned up the volume and sat beside me on the davenport. We didn't try to converse; we listened, the music creating private imagery for us both.

"I've always loved that opera." I didn't stand up right away, even though it was getting late. It was too comfortable sitting there in the soft afterglow of the music.

"Yeah. I've always been a big fan of my namesake's work."

When I gave him one of those perplexed looks he knows how to get out of me, he laughed. "Guiseppe Verdi. The Italian Joe Green." I responded with a playful poke in his ribs, and he got off the davenport.

Joe took my cup into the kitchen, then went to check the girls. I was still sitting there when he came back in. "Good night, Mrs. W.," he called from the kitchen. I didn't hear him move from the kitchen to his room, and I knew that he was waiting. I went to the Philco and shut it off, watching as the little star of light from the tubes faded slowly away. Then I went into the dark kitchen, knowing he was still there.

It was as if we stood in a shimmering,

beautiful bubble. We could only step to its center; if we backed away, the bubble would burst. So gently, honorably, we kissed good night.

I sit here now and write those words and tell myself it was a chaste kiss. A kiss between friends. Nothing more. That's what I tell myself. I start a letter to John that I think will never reach him.

August 25, 1944

I fill my days with gardening. Weeding, harvesting, pulling, I clean up the garden and make room for the latecomers, the winter squashes and the endless trail of pumpkin vine. I boil and steam, cut and mash, and fill my preserve jars against starvation or want. I put up. That's what they call it. Putting up.

I've put up pickles and relishes, stewed tomatoes, puree, and sauce. I've canned a cellarful and have no hope of ever consuming it all. I'll give some to my friends at home, who still think I'm quite mad to be here playing at farming. I'll give them jars of homemade goods to prove them wrong; I am not playing.

I'll give some to the Ladies' Society of Saint Luke's for sales. Although, everyone always ends up buying their own stuff back because there is so much of it.

I put up strawberry jam this spring and blueberry preserves this July; sweet pickles, sour, and some variation of both. We've learned how to make butter from Mrs. Feeney, so I've plenty of that. I am industrious and patriotic, and I would trade it all for real coffee.

Joe thinks I should enter some of my better stuff in the fair. Maybe I just will.

He's frantically getting the rest of the barn roof shingled. The hurricane season is upon us, although the sky continues lovely blue and the air remains gentle. I can see him from my kitchen window, nailing course upon course of dark gray asphalt shingles the Sunderlands sold to me.

In between shifts of preserves, I went out this morning and handed him shingles. I could tell even from the kitchen window that this was one of those days when that inner devil was plaguing him. Yesterday he had whistled in time with the hammering of the nails, sometimes forgetting himself and singing a line or two from some song or other. Today his shoulders were rounded and he moved more slowly, the rhythm more erratic than the pattern of shingles would have dictated.

"Want some help?" I called from the ground.

He peeked over the edge of the roof at me and nodded. "What about your canning?"

"It can wait. You look like you could use a little company."

"Can't argue with that."

With Joe on his knees and me just to his left, we sidled along the roofline in a bizarre line dance. One-take-a-shingle-two-hammer-three-hammer-four-hammer, one-take-a-shingle and slide.

The barn roof is gently pitched, so it isn't particularly tricky to stand on once you get yourself up the ladder. However, taken with the rhythm of the work, I got a little careless and almost lost my balance. Joe caught my leg, and I grabbed his shirt collar, hauling myself back into balance.

"You saved my life." Even though I said

it to be funny, it came out sounding sincere.

"And you saved mine."

We haven't repeated our good-night kiss. We carefully part company now.

Joe's gone off to check on the Ruths. Ruth Banks fell yesterday. Although the doctor doesn't think anything is broken, she's confined to the couch for a little while. Ruthie Jones is such a helpless little thing that it seems prudent to check in on them once a day. They call Joe their boyfriend. "Here comes our boyfriend!" they chortle whenever he drives up. They play at flirting with him. He must have been a good son, the way he treats them as if they are his maiden aunts. I send them some sweet pickles, but Joe picks them an armload of field daisies. "A little like bringing coals to Newcastle, don't you think?" I say, but Joe only shrugs and gives me that little-boy smile and tells me that even gardeners appreciate getting flowers. Practicality versus romance. That's us.

We claim to have found Ruthie's blanket in the woods and suggest that a mischievous dog has been the culprit. Mentioning, without actually blaming, Roy Tingley's new puppy. Isn't it fortunate that there are no holes? I claim to have washed it for her before bringing it back, saying that it was "pretty filthy." No harm done. Their gratitude is embarrassing, and they mention it every time I see them. I have never lied well. I wonder why I feel like the guilty party. I'm just the accessory.

I've decided to enter my "New York Style" dills in the Great Harbor fair.

Labor Day, September 4, 1944

This is my traditional departure day. Gran would bundle us all off on the train that runs from Great Harbor's run-down little depot. Fran and Stevie and I would press against the window, waving madly at Gran as if we couldn't bear to leave her. And then, in the next instant, we'd long for the first sight of our parents waiting for us at the station in Boston. Then there would be the tearing apart of the three cousins as Fran and Stevie continued their journey to Worcester by car with Aunt Audrey and

Uncle George. Even though we had spent upwards of six weeks together, locked in some dispute at least half the time, we grew despondent at the annual fall separation. We always promised to write; we hardly ever did. Reunions with school chums and busy lives filled the void quickly. Besides, we always got together for Christmas. And Gran would venture down from Hawke's Cove to complete the group.

On the train we passed the time with card games, which slowed down as we began to tell what it was we liked best about the summer just past and then to set goals for ourselves for the winter. "By next summer I want to have kissed my first boy." This when Fran was thirteen and I, a lofty fifteen, claimed I had already passed that landmark. "It was really quite disappointing." I liked being blasé that year, affecting a somewhat jaded attitude towards everything poor Fran wanted to do.

The looking back done, we looked forward. Things will be different next year; I will be older, wiser, more beautiful, mature. Resolutions and goals for the year were launched in New Year's fashion on those Labor Days of our youth.

"Well, I'm going to play shortstop." Stevie was twelve and kissing completely immaterial to him. I wonder how he is now, assuming he's still in the Pacific. He was all right last I heard, a month or so ago. I must remember to include him in my prayers and to stop being so single-minded about John's safety.

Now here I sit, on my own doorstep, on a hot September Labor Day. Glass of lemonade at my hand, journal on my lap. I'm watching the last, hallelujah, course of shingles go up on the barn. I stay put. I linger in Hawke's Cove to imagine goals kept out of reach by the war. We live in the present; the future depends on too many variables. For the present I will keep cows and finish the garden off for the year. I'll bring barrowloads of seaweed up and cover my plot with it to nurture this sandy soil for next year. That's as far ahead as I dare plan. If I am here, the soil will be ready. For the present I will wait patiently for word of John. Oddly enough, I am content. I've put out a feeder and chickadees are coming to it.

It seems to me that Stevie never did play shortstop. I think he broke his arm that year sledding.

I won an Honorable Mention for my pickles. Joe encouraged me to try, but then wouldn't come with me.

"You've got to come, Joe. It won't be any fun without you."

"You are too kind, but no. I don't like fairs."

"That's the oddest thing I've ever heard. What don't you like about them?"

"Crowds."

"Oh." I got it then. It was the Fourth of July all over again. Joe's weak excuses to stay in Hawke's Cove. Only this time there was no community picnic to set up. It was the same reluctance he showed in going to Tylerville, until I assured him it was a back-water. Crowds. Crowds of soldiers and sailors. I keep steering clear of the obvious truth about Joe Green. I came to Hawke's Cove to be reclusive and lick my wounds. Joe Green has too. I know my reasons. I suspect his.

While I digested all this, he watched me, his blue eyes with the thick black lashes, watching me like a cat at a mouse hole. He must have seen the doubts in my mind because he touched my face. "I can't go."

"How long to do you think you can get away with never leaving this peninsula?"

"For the rest of my life." There was no joking lilt in those words. Only a calm resignation. Not unhappy, not a complaint. Simply fact.

September 9, 1944

When I peek through the windows of the post office, I can see little brown cardboard squares like a tic-tac-toe board, the closed boxes of those who have gone home. The whole place seems to have sighed a breath of relief, as we do when beloved company leaves. I have never experienced this phenomena before. As a girl, I always assumed that the natives pined after us, the summer people. When I was very little, I imagined that Hawke's Cove closed up like school at the end of term. This was well before Stevie brought

Ernie home and we pumped him for information about life after Labor Day.

Ernie was patient; yes, we go to Great Harbor for school; the market does cut back a little on its hours, the gas station too. It gets quieter; you know everyone on the street. So Ernie said then and—now I've seen it for myself—so it remains.

What he didn't tell us was that, far from slowing down, Hawke's Cove seems to abound in activity after the summer folk leave. Potluck suppers for social and charitable reasons; the bridge club starts up again after a summer's respite. I can't talk Joe into joining the choir when I do. The Hawke's Cove Civil Defense is looking for members and this he joins. Now twice a month he gets to make sure blackout curtains are pulled and headlights masked. I've taken up with the Red Cross chapter in Great Harbor. I help put together ditty bags for servicemen and hand out juice and cookies at the blood drives.

The war goes on and on. I thought— hoped—that the invasion in June would put an end to things. It lingers instead, pulsing with intensity one moment, hopes rising with troop movements. Then things settle back into an acceptance of the war as a permanent fixture in our lives.

And there is no word on John. I tell myself that no news is good news.

Maybe I joined the Red Cross because they are part of the effort to locate missing men. Maybe subconsciously I thought if I give of my time, they'll try harder. I said this to Joe, and he didn't laugh at me. "Tell you what. If you'll organize a blood drive here in Hawke's Cove, I'll give."

We both have our ways of helping the effort.

September 12, 1944

I woke up this morning having dreamed something that left me with the oddest feeling of being held. Touched. I suppose that it was an erotic dream, but I have no recollection of its content. When I woke up, I wanted to believe that I had dreamed of John. But when Joe came into the kitchen, I knew that it had not been John I had dreamed of.

September 15, 1944

Sylvester borrowed Joe to help cut the last hay of this year. The deal is, Joe will get paid and I will get a discount on the hay. I packed Joe a good lunch, two ham sandwiches, sliced tomatoes from my garden, a slice of apple pie made from freshly picked apples I bought at the farmstand near the bridge. A Thermos of coffee. Haying is hard work. I go for a long walk instead of eating. I no longer enjoy eating alone.

September 17, 1944 (4:30 A.M.)

I heard him again in the night. I've heard him several times, crying out a warning, then making a sound that might be weeping. Tonight I went down when the sound didn't stop. I stood in the middle of the kitchen, listening. The moon is brilliant, and I didn't turn on any lights. I was torn—should I wake him, or should I just put my hands over my ears against that pitiable sound and let him fight whatever devil plagues him in his sleep? I have never told him I hear his nightmares.

Then I heard him say my name. "Vangie." It was distinct, and I thought he must have woken and heard me even though I was still.

"I'm here, Joe." The moon lay across his sleeping form, and I could see that I was mistaken. He opened his eyes to the sound of my voice. I looked at his confusion.

"What's the matter?" He moved to sit up.

"You were crying." I touched his cheek where I could see moisture reflected in the moonlight. "I came to wake you."

Joe touched his face where my fingers had been and looked at me in surprise. "I was dreaming."

"I know. Then I heard you say my name, and I thought you were awake." I sat beside him on the low, squeaky cot. "Do you want to tell me about it? About your dream?"

He had rubbed away the telltale moisture with an embarrassed swipe at his eyes. "No. I don't think I can remember it. But it must have been a doozy."

"It helps sometimes, Joe. It helps to say

them out loud. Sometimes telling banishes them."

"You've heard me before?"

I nodded. I felt a little like being caught out as a voyeur.

"I really don't remember it."

"Is it the same one every time?"

"If I can't remember them, how can I know?" He sounded plaintive.

"I frequently know I've had a dream made up of the same images as others. Certain elements repeat themselves. I don't always remember the context, just that when I wake, I am left with a feeling of loss or anger or grief."

"I'm falling. I'm always falling into an abyss, and I'm reaching for someone I have no hope of grabbing. I pull my hand away empty. Then I scream."

It was chilly in his room. Irrelevantly I thought, he should light the kitchen stove to keep warm. I must have shivered, because Joe put his arm around me.

It would have been so easy to lie down next to him, to pull the quilt over our shoulders and spoon together for comfort, for warmth.

I shivered again facing my own abyss and stood up. "Good night, Joe."

"Good night, Mrs. W."

I feel as though I am on the borderline of good and evil, loyalty and disloyalty, fidelity and . . . I have never stepped over any border before. Never driven too fast or sworn in public or drunk to excess. I have always been a good girl. I was a virgin on my wedding day. What I want now is over the line; what I need is placing me at that invisible border where faith hesitates. I can almost justify it. I keep putting myself in temptation's way. I keep putting Joe there. The fact is, I love being there. This thing, this unspoken, unacknowledged thing between us keeps me alive.

September 23, 1944

The Ruths stopped by today with Ruth Banks's niece, Jean. She's a nurse cadet, training in Boston. Ruth Banks is so proud of her, of all the hard work she is doing at the hospital and in her studies. She seems so young at nineteen. Doing things most of us would be too squeamish to do. She told me that her patients are almost all men sent home from overseas to receive medical care. Her bravado weakened a little when I asked her whether all her men recovered.

"No. Some die despite our best efforts. Many others go to a rehab hospital to learn to function with their injuries. You know, amputees and paraplegics."

"So the men you see receive honorable discharges and go home when they leave the hospital?"

"Not always. You see, the whole ones, those whose injuries aren't maiming, generally those fellows go back if they are listed as fit for duty. Although not many of those come through our hospital. If they need to be shipped stateside, usually they are pretty seriously damaged. I mean, I have had plenty who got well. But most others are discharged."

"But some go back?"

"Some. In fact, I hitched a ride here with a former patient on his way to the air station in Great Harbor." Jean put her hand over her mouth. "He kissed me when I got out of the car. Said, even though I was beautiful, he hoped never to see me again."

"So even if John was found, if he was sound, then he'd just go back?" Even as I asked the question, I could see her adult manner slipping.

"*Umm.* I don't know, Mrs. Worth. I don't know what they do with POWs."

"POW?" I hadn't thought that John might be held prisoner. Knowing what we now do about Nazi camps, I felt a physical tightening around my heart. I have always pictured John simply separated from his men, making his way across France or wherever. When I allow myself to imagine it, I see him going farm to farm, hiding in haylofts and accepting the kindness of French farmwives with black skirts and bottles of red wine on their tables. I never thought he might be a captive. "I don't know that he's a POW. No one has said that."

Clearly uncomfortable with my response, Jean tried to change the subject. Ruthie Jones pointed out the last of the September tomatoes sitting on my kitchen windowsill. "What nice big fellows those are. Are you still getting new ones?"

"Jean, if he's a POW, wouldn't I be notified? Aren't POW names released to the Red Cross?"

"I don't know."

Joe came in just then, the screech of the screen door cutting off the conversation. I felt like a bully, and Joe's appearance helped dispel the tension I had somehow brought to the room.

Ruth Banks accepted Joe's kiss on her wrinkled cheek. "Jean, let me introduce Joe Green."

Joe turned to shake Jean's hand. "Pleased to meet you. Your aunt's spoken of you often and with pride."

Jean blushed a little with pleasure and looked up at Joe with an obvious coquettishness, which was quickly replaced by a look of recognition. "Don't I know you?"

Her slightly rude examination of his face washed the smile off Joe's face. "No. I don't think so. I probably look like someone you know."

"I do, though. In the hospital. Have you ever been in . . ."

Joe cut her off. "No. Never."

"I'm sure I've seen you." Jean was persistent, and I could see that this was a trait that probably served her well in her field but was quickly wearing thin in my kitchen. Both Ruths looked a little embarrassed.

Joe had turned his back on her and was washing his hands at the sink. "I can assure you, we've never met before." He stuffed the hand towel over the drying bar and darted out of the kitchen.

With a stubborn tilt to her head, Jean kept at it. "I never forget a patient. I think I had him on the burn ward last year when I was a first-year student."

I remembered the shiny patches of pink on Joe's back and hands.

"I think he would remember being in the hospital if he had been, Jean. You don't forget something like that." I took down the large tomatoes from my windowsill overlooking the barnyard, where Joe stood absolutely still, as if gathering himself. "Besides, I'm certain he would remember you."

It came out more catty than I meant it, and they left shortly thereafter, warm tea still in the bottom of their cups. Joe was gone from the yard when I saw them out.

I gave them my last tomatoes as a conciliatory gift.

It was a beautiful fall evening. We walked to French's Hill to look out over the western side of the peninsula and enjoy the sunset. "Red sky at night, sailor's delight." We stayed until the first star peeped out, and we spontaneously recited the star poem "Star light, star bright, First star I see tonight, I wish I may, I wish I might, Have the wish I wish tonight."

"Isn't it funny how some things are just part of everyone's history?" Joe made this observation as we folded the wool picnic blanket. "Like putting a tooth under your pillow or saying 'bless you' when someone sneezes."

"And the rule against telling a wish aloud."

"I think I can guess your wish."

"It isn't what you might think. Some things are prayers, not wishes."

"I'll tell you mine."

Our hands had come together, the blanket edges between them. "Don't tell me, Joe, or you won't have a hope of it coming true."

"Some things are wishes, not prayers."

"And some wishes come true." We still held the blanket between us.

An owl swooped past, its sudden and unexpected appearance breaking the spell.

I wonder now what Joe thinks my wish is. Probably to find John safe. It isn't. That's the prayer. I wished instead to know who Joe Green is.

Maybe that's his wish too.

October 1, 1944

Joe and Ernie brought home sixteen flounder. I took their picture with my Brownie. If the picture comes out, what I will have is a shot of the pair of them, looking like pleased peacocks, each holding an end of the string from which hang these ugly flat fish with both eyes on the same side of their head.

I've been snapping pictures with abandon lately. I had forgotten that I brought the camera with me and only discovered it tucked on the shelf in my hall closet. It was one of our first major purchases after we got married, and, oh, what a thrill it was to have the money to buy it! Tangible evidence of a properly launched career. Mostly John used it, taking far too many pictures of me. The novelty wore off after a bit, but he hauled it out again when I was pregnant. I'd forgotten about those until I picked the heavy black camera up and discovered film in it, which I knew was an undeveloped record of my pregnancy. I opened the back of the camera and pulled out the roll, exposing the film to the sun.

Now I take pictures of my farm and the cows, and hope to record a different kind of waiting. I caught Joe out by the barn yesterday, surprising him into a self-conscious smile. I'll have to buy a scrapbook.

It's nice that Ernie and Joe have become chums. All of Ernie's pals are overseas or dead, and Joe has only me to keep him company otherwise. John always enjoyed having a couple of friends who weren't part of our "couples." I realize that his letters always mention some buddy of his. Their names come and go. Now I know that it's because these men disappear from his life. Transferred, wounded, or dead. I wish I knew who was with him now, now that he's disappeared from my life.

Anyway, we had a fish fry tonight, just the three of us. The Fricks are off doing something in the city. There was so much fish left over that I sent Ernie home set for at least one more meal, for him and his mother, and he promised to deliver another plateful to the Ruths. My house still smells of fish, and I boil apple peelings and cinnamon.

Our breath clouded tonight as we walked across the yard to check the girls. A few trees have already turned color. The scrub oaks rust into brown, but the few maples in the distance have brightened to orange and red. The evergreen conifers stand out. I have been scrupulous with my ration cards and know that I could take a "leaf-peeking" trip north, but I know that Joe won't go. Judy would go with me, and I realize that it isn't the thought of traveling alone that puts me off. I am filled with a sense of limited time. I don't want to spend any of it away from Joe. Even a day.

October 3, 1944

I've begun writing poetry again. I feel as though there is enough distance between what happened in December and now that I can bear to put words down that might hurt. That doesn't make that much sense, but I seem so impacted with emotion that putting down meaningful words may help to ease the pain. I haven't been able to understand that until now. The lines I wrote this morning had nothing to do with Molly, and yet that had been my intent. I wrote long lines, as I have always done, then began to rearrange them into stanza form. The lines had nothing to do with children or maternity. Nor did they want to say anything about the war and John. Instead they seemed to have everything to do with Hawke's Cove and Joe. God. I hope no one ever sees this schoolgirlish writing. I gave up finally and let the words run on. I won't use this journal to record them, particularly as unfinished as they are. Two poems, one theme. Home.

The pasture is gold and red. A cow path is worn into the slope toward the pond.

Bessie, Mom, and Baby, now as tall as her mom and still called Baby, are reclining on the grass and goldenrod, chewing their cud with dignity. Their ears twitch against the insects. Looking at them, I see my third poem.

October 5, 1944

After lunch today we took a walk to the beach. The cows followed us as far as the pasture goes, then lowed gently as we moved out of sight and down the wooded path. The beach was quiet beside a calm sea. The lower fall sun struck sparkles in the deep blue water, and in the distance, the horizon looked ruffled in that peculiar mirage that occurs when the sea and sky meet.

As Joe and I stood on the dune over-looking Bailey's Beach, a squadron of Hellcats, F6F fighter planes, flew overhead in a noisy display. There are so many planes flying in our airspace that the population of Hawke's Cove has grown quite inured to them. Anyone having a street corner chat might pause with a quick glance skyward, barely missing a syllable in the conversation. No one pays much attention these days except war-happy boys who play at soldiers and keep track of the planes that keep our peaceful refuge mindful of the war.

Joe studied the squadron, one hand shading his eyes against the southeastern glare. He stared with such intensity that I touched his arm. He didn't seem aware of me, or that I had touched him. He continued looking at the squadron until they flew out of sight. For the first time since I've known him, he allowed the unhappiness to show, which before I had only seen when he thought himself alone.

"Joe?"

"I'm sorry." Casting off the gloom with an observable effort, he smiled at me and walked towards the path. "I was lost in thought."

"About the planes?"

He didn't answer but kept moving towards the house. I followed, noticing that his shoulders still drooped with the weight of his thoughts. I decided that it was time for him to tell me his story.

"Joe." I trotted a little to catch up with him. "Joe, wait."

He slowed down, but didn't pause.

"Joe, it helps to talk. It helped me to tell you my story. About Molly."

"I have no story."

"We all have stories, Joe. Don't you trust me?"

"I asked you once not to ask me questions I could not answer. I will not put you in an indefensible position of knowing too much."

He abruptly stopped in the middle of the path, turning on me and grabbing my shoulders as if he would shake me. "Please do not ask me again."

I struggled against his grip, hurt by his tone. "I just want you to know that when you're ready, I'll listen. And there is nothing you can say which will make me think of you differently. Or feel differently."

"Mrs. Worth, there you are wrong."

"Joe. You've called me Vangie before."

"I called you from a dream." Joe let go of my shoulders and took my left hand in his. He rubbed his thumb over the thin gold band on my ring finger. "It was a dream."

We have skirted around each other all day. I went to a Red Cross meeting, and when I got home tonight, he had gone fishing. I ate alone, mustering only enough interest in the process to make oatmeal. He must have eaten dinner with Ernie because there were no dishes in the sink. He still isn't back and it's past eight.

I went out to check on the girls for the night and found Joe there. He sat on the milking stool, his back against the barn wall, hands clasped together in what might have been prayer. We didn't speak at first. I didn't know what to say, and clearly neither did he.

Finally I used the most neutral of comments to ease the tension. "No luck fishing tonight?"

"I never went fishing. I went for a walk."

"Oh. Just as well, I don't think I could face eating another fish."

"I knew that. That's why I didn't go. I'm such a good fisherman."

We laughed that little, overdone laugh of people who believe themselves over a hurt. "Cows okay?"

"Yep. Chickens too." Gesturing to our

new chickens roosting happily in the boxes he'd built for them.

"Are you okay?" I meant it gently, not wanting to open the subject again.

"Yeah. A little tired, that's all. You?" Standing now, he faced me as he asked this, and I met his eye. There was a puzzling moisture in them. Not tears exactly, but liquid emotion of some sort. Its genesis I can't hope to know.

"I'm pretty tired too."

Tired of wondering.

October 7, 1944

I got a letter today from my mother-in-law. Arnold Scheerbaum was killed. A tiny part of me is glad that I can't reach John. Arnold has been such a good friend since high school. He was an usher in our wedding. There have been others, and even when I could get a letter to John, I've not told him about their deaths. Some superstitious fear that he'd lose hope for his own survival. Maybe I should have told him. Maybe then he'd have been more careful.

There is so much I should have told him, and in my darkest moments I think that I will never have the opportunity to tell him the simplest and most complicated facts of my life. I will never have the chance to say, "Do you want peas or carrots for dinner?" I'll never again have the chance to say how sorry I am I lost Molly. How sorry I am that I screamed at him that night, blaming him somehow for not being there when I needed him, even though he was only two rooms away. I blamed him for making me want to have the child he gave me and for my then not being able in the end to have her. I hadn't wanted her. I hadn't wanted her. Not at first.

I never told John how sorry I was.

Sometimes I feel almost healed. I pick at the scab until I bleed so that I will never allow myself to heal without a scar.

Today I wrote the poetry of anger and release that I have needed to write. I worked for two hours, my back pressed up against the sheltering dune. The October air is closer to winter's than summer's, but the sun warms the sand and I luxuriate in it. Solid blue sky, cloudless and birdless this afternoon. My hand scrawls along the lined page of my notebook, and when I am done, I am amazed at the anger lodged there. Anger at myself and at John. Anger at the world for its war. Even anger at Joe. So much richer and more interesting than the poetry of happiness. Nonetheless, I tear it all up, scattering the scraps in the rising breeze.

I think that maybe I've given up hope for John. The knot of tension in my stomach in recent days has lessened, replaced by a hollowness.

October 7—late afternoon

I biked to the post office this afternoon after lunch. Roy Tingley admitted to breaking the rules and peeking into my poetry magazine, shyly confessing through the service window that he "scribbled" a little. I offered to read his stuff, and he was inordinately pleased at the offer.

I saw two naval officers leaving Ernie's office, just readjusting their caps to the specified angle. That reminded me that I wanted to invite Ernie and the Fricks to dinner on Saturday, so I headed across the street. The door to the police department office was wide open, and I walked in. Ernie's back was to the door, and he was leaning over to scratch Pal's spine. In the moment it took me to step fully into the small office, Ernie covered his face in his hands.

"What's the matter, Ernie?"

"Oh, Vangie, I didn't hear you come in."

"Now, what if I'd been Al Capone?"

"I'd be sorry."

Ernie walked to his desk and fussed a little with some papers on it, dropping a file folder on top of a glossy photo. "So, what brings you here, another unexplained theft?"

"No, a dinner invitation."

"Cards?"

"Probably. Can you bring your board? Mine's harder to use for five."

"Joe'll be there?"

"I expect so. Why?"

Ernie leaned his knuckles against the desktop, then thumped them against the file folders. "You saw the Navy in here?"

I nodded.

"They're looking for a deserter."

"Not Joe."

"Ruth Banks's niece claims to have seen the pilot of that missing Hellcat in your kitchen."

"She's mistaken."

"I told them I had no reason to believe that was true."

"Oh, Ernie."

"Vangie, you might mention to Joe that they were here."

Some instinct made me take Ernie's hand off the file folder, and I picked up the glossy studio photo of a naval officer that lay beneath it. Ernie and I looked at each other. The weight of our complicity bent us over the picture of a beardless Joe Green.

I had to ask. "Ernie, would you have said anything to me if I hadn't walked in here? Would you have warned Joe yourself?"

"I don't know." He didn't look at me.

I lay the photo back down on the desk.

Ernie lay the folder back on top of it. "No. I do know. I would have told him."

I cursed myself for not taking the car into town. The two-mile ride never seemed so long. I pushed the pedals and felt as if

I weren't covering any ground at all. I felt as though I could have run faster. It was past five when I got home, no sign of Navy jeeps in the drive. None had passed me. Either they believed Ernie, or they were taking their time.

Joe was still mucking, and the practical side of me left him to finish the job while I threw Spam into a frying pan with leftover potatoes and began to slice tomatoes. If he had to go, he would go fed.

I called him in to eat before he began milking. I could feel the panic rising as every minute brought us closer to hearing a jeep pull into my yard. I said nothing while he ate, only watched him until he realized I wasn't eating and he looked into my face and read there the obvious worry.

"Vangie, what is it?"

"The Navy is looking for you."

Joe carefully laid his knife and fork across his plate and then went to rinse them off. That done, he wiped his hands on the hand towel as he has done for months and hung it across the rack in the same careless lump he always has. "Mrs. Worth, I'll be in the barn. The girls need milking."

"No!" The kitchen chair fell over in my haste to get to him. "Okay, you'll be in the barn. But, Joe, you'll be in the whiskey pit."

"Please, no more hiding. I'm tired."

"Please, Joe. Please. For me. I can't lose you too."

We had to move Bessie to get Joe into the pit. I scooped an armful of straw for him to lie on. As Joe eased himself into the pit, I heard a car come into the yard. Joe reached up and touched my face. "You don't have to lie for me."

I took hold of the hand that touched my face and kissed his fingers. "Shut up and let me do this the way I want to. I'll be back in a few minutes."

I braced the plank cover as he lowered it, making me think of a dead man closing his own coffin lid. I led Bessie back into her stall, scattering a little straw over the bare planking. Then I went out to meet the MPs.

They were cordial enough for military police. Calling me ma'am and saying lots of please's and thank you's. My lies were believable. "My handyman left a few days ago. Said he wanted to move on. Didn't say where. Have a look around if you want." All kinds of lies. Except when they asked me to look at the photo. "Oh, no. That isn't my handyman. Joe's much older than that." I supposed that the picture had been taken when he first joined up because the youthful face in it, with its crisp short hair and beardless jaw, seemed, to me, to be a boy's.

Mercifully, they seemed satisfied. I walked them out of the house, where I had taken them in an effort to look unconcerned, ergo innocent. One of them spotted my clothesline. "If your handyman quit a while ago, whose clothes are those?"

"My husband's."

"And where is he?"

"I wish I knew. He's missing in action."

"I'm sorry, Mrs. Worth. I had no idea." To his credit, the young MP seemed genuinely sorry for his brash questioning.

The second, somewhat older, MP had no such compunction. "If your husband's overseas, why did you wash his clothes?"

"That, sir, is none of your business." Leaving them to think I had some war-wife fetish about my husband's clothing, I shook their hands and walked back into the house. I hadn't lied; the clothes hanging there were John's.

October 10, 1944

I have spent the last forty-eight hours leaving Hawke's Cove. I am now hurtling back to Boston on the evening train from Great Harbor. The whole of my possessions are packed into the trunk my father took to college. I will not be back anytime soon.

I have not allowed myself to think, to feel. Wisdom would dictate that I not write down any of what has happened. But my heart demands that I do. I crave to record it. I write partly to sort out my jagged emotions and partly to be sure that I never forget any detail of what has happened. For the second time in my life I feel the need to not let something get away from me.

As soon as the MPs left, I went into the barn and released Joe from the pit.

Defiantly, he settled down to milk Bessie. I grabbed a pail and stool and went to work on Mom. For a long time the only sound was the hiss and dash of warm milk into our pails. I couldn't see Joe on the other side of the wall separating the stalls, but I could hear every time he stopped milking. Each time there was a pause in the sound of milking, I waited, pausing myself, listening for his sigh.

Finally, "My name is Spencer Buchanan."

I held still.

"I am a deserter."

I pressed my forehead against Mom's side and waited.

"When I crashed into Hawke's Cove, I thought that it was an act of divine retribution, that I was going to die. When I didn't, I realized that true divine retribution was in living."

"Retribution for what, Joe?"

He stood up and brought his full pail over to the worktable. "Murder."

I lifted my pail and brought it over to him. He said nothing as he poured out the milk from both our buckets into the milk can, careful not to spill a drop. He continued to be silent while he washed out the pails.

"Joe, war isn't murder."

"I shot down my own man."

"Joe, surely it was an accident."

"Yes. That's exactly what everyone said. An unfortunate accident of war."

"But you're not satisfied with that?" I pulled myself up on the worktable and sat there watching Joe pace back and forth in the aisle, as if, the milking done, he was at loose ends.

"No. You see, the sin is that it meant nothing to me. I had become so used to war and death. I barely knew the kid, and I couldn't even remember his name. He was so new to the squadron that he didn't have any buddies to keep me mindful of his loss. Then I was shot down and sent stateside to heal. Jean Banks did nurse me. She does remember me. I'm one of those deemed fit to return to active duty. After I had healed up they sent me to Great Harbor's naval air station to await new orders. I had been reassigned back to my old squadron in the Pacific. I hadn't flown for a long time, so I took the Hellcat out to get some practice in.

"It was only as I was back in the air again, in a peaceful sky, that the significance of my sin came to me. It wasn't in killing him; it was in forgetting him. When the Hellcat's engine seized, I thought, 'Aha! God has found me out for the sinner I am.' The things which flash in your mind in those situations . . . Well, at first I thought, 'Good. How can I live with myself, knowing how hard I've become, how little life means to me? I deserve to die.' Except that, in the end, I survived despite my guilt because I wanted to. So, Vangie, you tell me, how can I go on with this evil living in me?

"When I crawled up onto the beach at the foot of your property, the only thing I was certain about was that I wasn't going back. I'd had enough of it. I'd done my bit, and it had utterly corrupted me."

"Joe. You're one of the gentlest men I know. You were in a horrible situation—"

"Vangie, don't. You can't explain it away. Any more than you can explain wanting to put a headstone on your nameless child's grave. You just . . ." He took my hands and gripped them until they hurt. "You just feel it."

"Joe." I lifted my hands to his face,

smoothing his hair away from his brow, needing to touch him as reassurance to us both that he was all right.

He held my face in his work-hardened hands and smiled. "Vangie, you're crying."

I wiped my cheeks in utter surprise. "So I am."

We both wept then. I wept for Molly and for John. I wept for this man, for who he had been as Spencer Buchanan, and for the Joe Green of now. We wept for each other, and then we kissed as naturally as breathing, and it was like drinking passion. We clung together there in the soft warm light of the barn, and our clinging became love.

It has grown quite dark outside, and the train window gives me back my own face as I stare out. I can see the reflected face of the woman in the seat in front of mine. She is about fifty, tight gray curls peek out from beneath her hat. The fur collar of her coat is a little worn where it folds over. She dozes, her lips pursing now and then to some dream. What would she think of me as I sit here, writing all this down?

* * *

Not one word passed between us. The hay in the loft served as our couch, and afterward Joe covered us with one of the quilts from the trunk. I felt as though if we left the barn, we would break the spell. That as long as we were in there, we would be safe. What we did would remain safe.

We dozed, then woke, and made love again. This time lingering over it like an expensive meal. Not thirst, but hunger satiated. We still kept silent, afraid of what needed to be said. Unprepared for putting words to this thing that had happened.

Sometime around dawn I heard the chickens scratching around their pen for grain, clucking and muttering in general complaint. The cows, left in as if to authorize our being there, shifted restlessly in their stalls, waiting for Joe. I felt him leave our nest, stooping over me, carefully pulling the quilt up over my bare shoulders, whispering for me to stay put. I must have dozed again because suddenly he was back and beside me in the hay.

The third time we made love, the sun coming through the cracks in the loft doors brightened the hay into a yellow glow. I took in the deep blue color of his eyes, the pink scarring on his back, and breathed in the pungent scent of his sweat. And I knew it wouldn't happen again.

We're getting close now. The train just pulled out of the last stop before home. I feel as if I have to hurry and finish this.

We spooned together in the warm, itchy hay, nuzzling each other for scent. Then he asked me, "Will you regret this?"

And I answered, "Never."

Joe went to move the cows from the little paddock next to the barn to the big pasture for the day. Dressed, I slipped down the ladder and stopped to collect the fresh eggs from under the chickens. I was pleased to have three eggs, two for Joe, one for me.

I heard Sylvester Feeney's truck outside. I thought to myself, he must be in a hurry today. He's driving his truck. I bumped the barn door open with my shoulder to greet him. I hoped the flush of inappropriate happiness wasn't too obvious.

It wasn't Sylvester's truck, but a jeep. It wasn't Sylvester, but two Army officers who were getting out of it. I stopped somewhere between the open barn door and them. I thought: *Army. Not Navy. Would the Army be looking for Joe too?* They stepped towards me, hats under arms, and I knew that it wasn't about Joe they had come. "Mrs. Worth?"

I felt the eggs drop from my hands as they came towards me with the news that my husband had been found.

My silent traveling companion got off the train at the last stop. I'm near home now. My mother will be there at the station, expecting me to be beaming and overjoyed with the news that John is coming home. I am. I am the happy wife, my husband restored to me. I am happy. I have been so long waiting for this moment that I am at a loss how to behave. I am so afraid of what I will find. How changed we both are.

There is an old, old lady, Mrs. Grace, at church. Every Sunday she works her way towards the Communion rail. She leans on each pew end as she makes her way from the seat where she and her family have worshipped for generations. She always insists on kneeling, a long and painful-to-witness operation. The usher steadies her as she rises from receiving the Sacraments.

I looked at her a few weeks ago and wondered if she regretted anything in her long life. I thought then that I would rather regret the committed than the uncommitted. What we have done rather than what we have left undone. I write these words and wonder that I feel no guilt. Like Joe not feeling guilt over the dead pilot. But, like Joe, will I later feel the magnitude of our sin? I probe my soul and feel as though what we have done will only live with me as a gift.

It is hardest of all to write this. Joe vanished. He must have seen the soldiers. I ran into the barn to see if he'd slipped back into the whiskey hole, but it was empty. I called his name, and when he did not answer, I knew. I knew that the choice was taken from me. The decision to stay with Joe or to go to John. Joe had made my decision for me. An act of love. Throughout the last two days I have struggled to accept his gift. Alternately, I am grateful and hurt. And angry. Angry that he assumed there was a decision to make.

* * *

I filled the last hours of my life in Hawke's Cove preparing to leave. I called Sylvester Feeney to tell him I was going home, to arrange for the sale of the girls. I asked if he'd seen Joe. He hadn't.

I let myself be held by Judy, who wisely said nothing but made herself useful in getting the details of my departure worked out. She never asked about Joe, only said she'd make sure he was all right when he got back.

She simply knew he'd come back once I was gone.

I didn't, of course, tell her about us.

I slept only a little, listening for Joe to come back. Hearing only the bell buoy on Hawke's Shoals.

I had a last dinner with Ernie and Judy and Ted. Our card playing was uninspired, and we all felt Joe's absence and my departure. We promised ourselves we'd keep in touch; the Fricks have even promised to come visit. Ernie just argued that he expected me back next summer. I made that typically New England "we'll see" response. I think I'll never see Hawke's Cove again.

Sylvester says he'll hire Joe when he gets back. He'll need the extra hand now that the herd's expanded. I went to the post office to collect the last of my mail and close my box. I watched Roy insert a brown square of cardboard into the back of it, adding to the winter's tic-tac-toe design.

Ted will come and undo all the work he did to get me into the house. He'll drain the pipes and shutter the windows. He'll have the electricity, water, and the phone turned off. Ted will take care of the details; I'm not to worry, says Judy. I'm only to be happy and think of getting my husband back on his feet.

Ernie drove me to the station. We filled the twenty minutes with inconsequential chat, careful of ourselves. As we got out of the car at the station, I thought of the question I had meant to ask him long ago.

"Ernie. Did you ever date my cousin Fran?"

Ernie lifted my heavy black trunk out of the cruiser and set it on a railroad baggage cart. He smiled and raised his eyebrows in mockery of his adolescent self. "I was head over heels about Frances. But she deserved better than a small-town cop, and I hope she found it."

"Ernie, she would have had to go a great way to do better than you. But, she's happy." I looked him in the eye. "Are you?"

It was an odd question, spoken likely only because of my own contorted feelings, but Ernie didn't seem nonplussed. "Yeah. Happy enough. You take what life gives you."

I hugged him hard, and he handed me onto the train.

My landmarks are beginning to appear as we speed along the track. I am almost home. My mother will meet me at the station and take me home to my empty flat. I'll make up the bed and buy some groceries to fill shelves bare since April. I'll wait for the phone call that will tell me my husband has arrived and where he is. I'll go to him then. I'll bring him home. We have another chance.

When I went to Hawke's Cove, I was desperately unhappy. My baby was dead, my husband gone, my future unimaginable. I went there to heal and to wait. Joe Green eased my waiting, affected my healing. He was my constant, my anchor.

What I have had in Hawke's Cove will always be with me. As Molly will always be with me. As Joe Green will always be with me too.

Four

Vangie—1993

Evangeline Worth closed the black-and-white composition book and held it for a long time in her lap, her hands placed gently on its cover, as if waiting for the heat of the words to cool.

She fished around in her cardigan pocket for a hanky and touched at the corners of her eyes. She remembered so distinctly the pull of that train as it left Great Harbor, the pull on her heart as she left Joe Green behind. Reading these long ago entries had stirred in her the emotions of a young woman.

The midnight chiming of the mantel clock lifted her eyes from the book. Too late even to bother with tuning into *Letter-*

man, she simply removed her glasses and lay on top of the bed with only an afghan to cover her. She rested, letting the old feelings riffle through her. After a few minutes she got up.

The reflected light of the Victorian lamp on her bureau wobbled as she pulled open her underwear drawer. Beneath the neatly folded stock of undergarments, white cotton and practical, was a brown kraft envelope, addressed to her and postmarked "Hawke's Cove, October 13, 1944." Inside of the envelope was a handkerchief. On one edge was monogrammed the initials SJB. Cached between the neat folds were two metal rectangles embossed with his name: Buchanan, Spencer J., and his numbers. His first letter and these dogtags had come in this envelope, and into it she had carefully hidden every one of his subsequent letters in their nearly fifty years' correspondence. In this way they had stayed alive to one another.

"If you had been my wife, you would have gotten these at my death. You saved my life, but it is as Joe Green, not Spencer Buchanan I live . . ."

* * *

The one consolation of age was wakefulness. A little sleep before dawn would be enough, so Vangie went into the kitchen at midnight and heated water for tea. She hadn't read the early letters in a long time. She'd never read them boldly, like this, spread out on the kitchen table. These letters had been read slyly, sometimes one staying tucked in the pocket of her skirt for hours before an opportunity to savor it arrived. It was a dangerous game they played. A plain white envelope dropping through the mail slot onto the floor along with bills and magazines.

That one passionate night would simply have faded into a sweet memory had he not sent that first letter. Their correspondence had kept love alive even as the passion of the early letters, like the passion of early love, evolved into loving devotion.

She let the tea bag steep as she lifted the first letter from the pile on the table.

Vangie heard the mantel clock strike six. Outside a jaybird squawked, reminding her that she hadn't filled the bird feeders. Well, she'd do that after a little nap. Her eyes felt the strain of the night's long reading, not strained by the physical effort, rather the exercise of so much memory. All of her emotions pressed against her eyes, and she covered them with the tips of her fingers as she lay on her bed. Vangie had read far enough that the rest she could rehearse from memory. Time speeded up even as the pace of his letters had slowed.

One hand left her eyes and stroked the blanket beside her, fingers gently plucking at the place where John had been. She could only picture Joe as she had known him; she couldn't remember John as he had been. The inexorable progression from youth to age had erased each preceding stage as completely as an eraser blurs a chalk line. Powdered memory of a vital young man; when she thought of her husband now, she only saw the old man he'd become.

It was the last good reason to never see Joe again. Without the blindness of daily contact, their individual changes would be a shock. She still imagined dark hair the color of maple syrup; perhaps he still envisioned auburn curls loosened from her old-fashioned braid.

Vangie got up and gathered the letters together and stuffed them back into the kraft envelope. Once John had picked up the mail, handing her the envelope without so much as a glance or smirk of curiosity. She thought about the cartoon characters her children had watched, tossing lighted bombs back and forth in a deadly game of hot potato. The bombs always exploded, and the blackened creatures with frizzled edges regrouped and went on with the chase. How would they go on if her bomb exploded in John's unsuspecting hand?

Now Charlie, her youngest, her fourth child, had potentially pulled the pin on the grenade.

Five

Charlie

"Mom, do you think I could talk with your friend Judy?"

"Charlie, Judy's been in a retirement home for two years. You remember, I told you she moved in after Ted passed away. I'm not sure how she is." Vangie tapped her temple.

Charlie shrugged. There was so much he didn't pay attention to as his mother nattered on about people he didn't know. He was glad, on the one hand, that she still was active and interested and sometimes had a better social life than he did. But, on the other, he didn't feel compelled to remember details about all her elderly friends.

"Well, I need to speak with folks who'd have been there." Charlie noticed that his father's head jerked a little, as if John was waking from a nap. He patted his father's arm. "How about that guy, the policeman."

"Ernie spends every winter in Florida. Doesn't come back till May."

John Worth rolled his head a little to the left. Vangie daintily wiped his chin with a tissue and spooned another mouthful of mashed peas towards him. Sometimes she had to take his chin as you would a reluctant baby's. This time he opened up easily.

"Well, who else? How about that farmer—what was his name? Joe?"

Vangie was beginning to regret ever telling Charlie about her friends in Hawke's Cove. "Charlie, drop it for now. We'll talk about it later."

John closed his mouth over the spoon, but kept his right eye on Vangie, studying her face as she looked, not at him, but at the mess on his lunch plate.

"Mom, why don't you come with me?"

Vangie held the spoon in midflight towards John's closed mouth. She let the thought ripple through her like a chill. Then, "I can't leave your father."

She lowered the spoon again and reconfigured the brown mash against the edge of the plate. "Can I, John?"

Charlie was always amazed at his mother's tenacity. She insisted that there was nothing wrong with his father's mind, that it was only his treacherous body that had failed. If you wanted to get Vangie Worth's dander up, talk in front of John as if he weren't there.

Charlie loved his father, but had a hard time keeping up both ends of a conversation and rarely visited unless his mother was there. "Tell your dad about your trip, your story, your friends . . ." Charlie would start a monologue, looking at John Worth, at his father's unsteady head and dangling hands, but telling his anecdotes to his mother. Sometimes he would sit in his car in the parking lot of St. Elizabeth's Home and force recollections of his father to mind so that he would remember how his father had been before and, thus, open up a little with him as he was now.

A late-in-life son, he had still been taught the important boy things by his dad. How to pitch a knuckleball, how to be a good Red Sox fan, how to drive. How to be a decent man. John Worth may have been strict, and not given to playfulness, but he was quick to praise and slow to anger. Sometimes Charlie reviewed this litany as he climbed the cement steps of the building, making himself be a good son.

"Mom, it'll only be a couple of days. That's why he's here. To give you a break."

"Charlie. You know better than to talk like that. I don't need a break, and I don't need to go to Hawke's Cove."

John's good left hand suddenly flew up, striking the edge of the tray where it stuck out over the table attached to his chair. The remnants of lunch splattered Vangie where she leaned towards him.

He had meant to touch her.

Six

John—1993

It was Hawke's Cove that came between us.

My fault really. I couldn't hide my disdain at the sight of the little, ugly farmhouse. For all of Evangeline's rapture about the beauty of the place, what she showed me was a huge disappointment. If I thought we were going to a traditional summerhouse, airy ceilings and wraparound porches, I was greatly mistaken. Grandmother Bailey's place was a tumbledown, four-square, and primitive wreck. Evangeline loved it. Cedar shingles so old they looked like loose teeth clinging to the sides. The trim paint had long ago faded, leaving streaks of dark gray beneath. No gutters, no amenities. Beyond it the decrepit barn, sagging on a misaligned rock foundation, a putative carport tagged on, giving the whole structure the look of an old man leaning on a chair.

The yard was another whole horror. Spikes of stringy yellow grass mixed with patches of unidentifiable growth that looked vaguely cultivated. The place had been, in some incarnation, a working farm, and only the acres beyond the barn looked appropriately bucolic. A long, broken stone wall meandered down towards the tree line, beyond which, Evangeline assured me, lay the water.

Evangeline looked at me with expectant eyes. I pulled on a smile, but those perceptive green eyes had seen my distaste. "It's a bit different than I had imagined." Wrong words. Fighting words. My wife said nothing, it being in her nature to swallow her anger until she formed the right words to vent it. I swallowed too. I'd reserve judgment until we got inside. Who knew, maybe it had a charming interior. I muscled the two suitcases up the clumsy steps through the screened porch with its torn screen and welter of gardening equipment and leftover clothing from God knew how many generations of Baileys.

It was neat and clean, but this house had never qualified as charming in its life. Wallpaper of an insignificant yellow in the kitchen, a peculiar blue on the walls in the room Evangeline quaintly referred to as the parlor. The stairs to the second floor were narrow and steep, with a weird twist that caught the suitcase in my left hand, making me bang my knee. "Damn!"

Evangeline stood at the top of the stairs, with a mixed look of disapproval at my epithet and disappointment at my initial reaction to her beloved Bailey's Farm. I was still newly wed enough to want to please her, so I grinned. "It's great, Ev. Simplicity itself."

She turned on her heel, and I followed her down a short hallway to the bedroom. At last, a perfectly lovely room. Again with yellow wallpaper, but the sun hadn't faded it and the pattern of light pink-and-white dogwood blooms was still fresh. Calico curtains, and a ball-fringe bedspread, worked in a traditional early American motif, covered the antique spool bed. Although I prefer contemporary furniture, I could appreciate the quality of the antiques.

"It's lovely, Ev. Really." I put the suitcases down gently and took her hand. She had wanted so badly for me to love this place, this Hawke's Cove.

"John. Sweetheart. You don't have to love it right away." She kissed me. "Just eventually." I could see that she was choosing the seductive way out of the argument, and I went along willingly. Even as we made love on top of the antique spread, I thought to myself, *please don't let us have to come here every vacation.* There was a world out there I hadn't yet seen. I was just at the start of my career. I had plans—a successful architectural career, a designed home, European vacations, and, eventually, children. Hawke's Cove never figured in my life's blueprint.

Later, sitting in the inefficient kitchen as Evangeline fried some chicken in a deep cast-iron pan, I sketched. Take out the wall here, replace the huge combination range with a modern electric stove and the soapstone sink with a real countertop and a double-sink unit, maybe bump out an ell as a breakfast nook. My doodling caught Evangeline's eye, and she didn't smile.

"I like it the way it is."

"Just some thoughts on paper, darling. It's what I do."

"It's mine. You can't change it."

I'll admit that that particular choice of words made me angry, but I was still mellow from our lovemaking and I simply folded the paper and put it aside. When I took out the trash, I saw it crumpled up and lying on top.

Evangeline Bailey had caught my eye for the first time on the arm of another boy. I'll never forget it. She was dressed for the Fall Cotillion in a stunning pale green dress that flowed around her like cream. She reminded me of Vivien Leigh, all auburn hair rolled under, one tiny little renegade lock trying to break free from the rest. Her pure green eyes glittered and kept stroking her date's face with beams of excitement and pleasure. I was certain they were in love. No woman looks at a man with that kind of adoration who isn't in the throws of a reciprocal love.

She was a senior at Smith, majoring in

English literature. I, a graduate student at Harvard, in my last year of architectural school. The Fall Cotillion was held at the Tremont, and in those days anyone who could rustle up a tux attended this first major intercollegiate social event of the year—what my daughters, many years later, would call the meat market. Then, perhaps more than now, we were encouraged to select from our own gene pool.

My own date was a girl from my hometown of Providence whose parents and mine were bridge chums. Celeste and I had known each other since crib days, and she held absolutely no attraction for me. We liked each other well enough, but anything more would have been slightly incestuous. Still, Celeste looked good on my arm, and we both intended to find many other dance partners.

As soon as I could, I tapped Evangeline's partner's shoulder. He was gracious, affecting a faux European bow as I took his girl's hand. "John Worth." I felt myself bow slightly and was immediately embarrassed at the imitation.

"Evangeline Bailey." She curtsied in

neatly playful response, and my embar-
rassment faded.

I liked the feel of her in my hands. Even
through the white gloves, I felt her warmth.
She was a good dancer. I was not, but we
looked nice circling the ballroom floor to a
waltz, the "Emperor Waltz," if recollection
serves. Her flowing green gown wound itself between my legs, and she watched my
face as we danced, not like most girls, who
look to see who is watching. I greedily
asked for the next dance. She said yes. I
asked if I might write to her. She said yes.
I let go of her at the end of the evening
and asked if I might kiss her. And she said
yes.

Her date, it turned out, was her cousin
Steve Bailey, and her adoring look, not
passion but amusement. "Stevie's the fun-
niest!" She exclaimed as she introduced
him to me at the punchbowl. Frankly, he
never seemed all that funny to me, and
even as a middle-aged man, I always felt
slightly outside of their jokes.

It was our poor luck to have been young
adults in the midst of the Depression. A
generation before us had enjoyed easy
privilege, riding on a false and treacherous

wave. We were more circumspect, building up a lifelong habit of denial and economy. At school we worked hard to receive scholarships. Many of us worked hard at after-hours jobs to keep our places at college. When I asked Evangeline if I could call her, I was already toting up how much pocket money I would need to ˙earn beyond my weekly salary, as gofer in a local architectural firm, to afford a long distance call. After the first call, I eked out enough to take the train to Northampton, forgoing the "T" and walking from one side of Cambridge to the other to get to work.

The brilliant fall foliage had backed off to old brown, the early November days already crisp harbingers of winter. Heading west, I noticed that nearly all the leaves had dropped, even the recalcitrant oaks, leaving bare silver-gray limbs. My train made its halting way toward Springfield. I changed there, taking a local up to Northampton. I watched from my window at each stop as ladies clung to their hats against the mischievous wind, and men buttoned their threadbare overcoats. My own coat was a little too small for me. I had grown an extra inch or two since beginning college, and maturing had added breadth if not weight. I would have been more self-conscious, but at least my coat was clean and free of mending. I wrapped a crimson-and-white muffler around my neck, leaving the coat unbuttoned, attempting the look of rakish student instead of overgrown boy. I had left my gloves in my room, and I plunged my hands into my pockets as I beat my way towards our agreed upon meeting place at the station clock.

She was there, bundled in a loden green boiled wool coat that somehow made her look like a child, tiny. Her eyes peered out over the top of a thick scarf wrapped around her lower face. She didn't have a hat on, and her auburn hair was charmingly windblown. She saw me coming through the crowd and waved. "I didn't think you'd know me all dressed up like this. I wanted to wear my ball gown."

"I couldn't not recognize you."

Since meeting, Evangeline and I had corresponded. Her letters were full of snippets of the poetry she was writing, just the stanzas she was pleased enough with to share. I complained she had never sent me a whole poem, but she replied in her next letter than she hadn't yet finished one worth reading.

We shook hands as we met on the train platform; then I ducked self-consciously to kiss her cheek. She smiled in reply, and we stood in awkward hesitation before she pointed to the exit sign. "Let's go some-where else."

I had saved enough to take Evangeline to lunch, although I was grateful she de-clined dessert and I drank only water. It seemed as though we could fill every mo-ment we had together that first visit with chat. I told her about my family, skirting the universal story of lean times, keeping to the general description of family mem-bers—mother, father, two sisters. I talked about my chums at school, those class-mates who were interesting fodder for sto-ries.

I even, eventually, told her about my poor brother, Charles. I suppose it must have been the genuine interest in her bril-liant eyes or her clever probing that made me tell her about him. I rarely spoke of him.

Something I said gave her an opening, and she asked, "You only have sisters?"

"I had a brother, Charles." Somehow she knew from my voice, or from the way it was always hard for me to say his name, that this was an important story to me. Usually if asked about him, I would mumble something neutral and move the subject away from my brother. Instead, when she asked, I told Evangeline Bailey about losing Charles in the Spanish flu epidemic of 1918.

"He was ten. I was four. The flu had already taken so many of the very old and the very young we actually thought it was moving off, going away like epidemics do. Charles was perfectly healthy, perfectly strong, and this insidious villain came up behind him and took him down like an executioner. Simple symptoms at first, runny nose. Grumpiness. I remember that he tripped over my soldiers and yelled at me. I was pretty little and I started to cry. Immediately he felt bad about scolding me, and he helped me to set up my little troop again. But when I asked him if he wanted to play, he just shook his head no. 'We'll play tomorrow.' It was the last thing he said to me."

Somehow our hands had joined over the tabletop. I had been looking down at them, not seeing our hands but my brother's as he set up my soldiers on the bare wood floor. When I looked up, there was a compassion in Evangeline's eyes that startled me into finishing the story.

"I had been in the way while Charles was sick, so they sent me to my aunt's house. No one told me anything. I suppose they deemed me too little to understand. When Aunt Juliana came and told me that Charles had gone to sleep with the angels, I understood completely what had happened."

With her soft look of compassion and the gentle squeeze of sympathy for a long ago loss, I fell in love with Evangeline Bailey.

She walked me back to the station, although I protested and wanted to see her safely back to her dorm. Evangeline would have none of it. "I don't need an escort." The time between arriving at the station and the actual departure of the train is a mean time. Unless you are hardened to simply saying goodbye and leaving someone standing alone on the platform, conversation generally peters out. The time is too short for saying anything important, so we are forced into mundane inanities or silence. We stood on the platform under the departures/arrivals sign, our fingertips touching in speechless bond, reluctant to separate until the conductor called and it was really time to go. Again I bent to kiss her, and this time she gave her lips to me. I snugged the scarf back around her neck and chin. "Keep warm."

She pulled the ends of my scarf and smiled. "Keep warm yourself, John Worth."

I was glad to see another girl, also putting a boy on the train, wave to her. She and Evangeline didn't wait for the train to pull out before turning away, arm in arm, heading for the exit. I had a momentary sense they might be laughing at us.

The next time I was able to see her was just after the semester break. The dawning of 1935 seemed to be a heralding of a new hope in a hopeless world. Although the

European tribulations distracted us, I paid them little mind beyond their use as a political or philosophical topic during late-night conversations with my fellows. We all sounded as if we were remote from it, as we were. None of us were dust bowl farmers, none of us yet soldiers. I paid more attention to the WPA, wondering if my untried talents would fit in there. Otherwise, the dreams would be postponed and I would join the rest of the new graduates in the search for work in a workless world. Still, Roosevelt was our hero in these Democratic halls; socialism was intriguing. We stymied our parents.

In Northampton, Evangeline worked hard on writing the one perfect poem. We wrote to each other almost daily, and at least on paper, our nascent passion was flourishing. I went up again late in February. I had saved enough to spend the night in a cheap rooming house my parents would have been appalled to think me in. But now we had the whole weekend to see if this correspondence of ours was translatable into conversation and more.

* * *

The air was cold but dry, the day wind-
less, so we walked out of doors for hours,
her arm linked through mine. The air was
so still I could smell the fragrance of her
hair, pulled off her face in a Bohemian
braid. She wore a little beret, and I kidded
her that she looked like a little French girl.

"Nonsense. I've never even been to
France. I just happen to like this hat." She
skipped ahead of me on the sidewalk and
pulled the green hat off her head, twirling
it around her forefinger before planting it
back on, a little cockeyed and jaunty. All
day long each new expression charmed
me, and I fought not to reach for her. Finally she slipped her arm from mine and
took my hand in new intimacy. "Show me
your room."

"I don't think that would be a good
idea."

"The sitting room in my dorm isn't at all
private. And I'm cold!"

She wanted privacy. Against my better
judgment and with a conspicuously beating heart, I led the way.

I felt like a thief, letting us into the
musty hallway. I had been cautioned
about guests, but it was midday and no

one was home. I gestured to the sitting room with its overstuffed Victorian furniture and heavy, claw-footed tables. Evangeline shook her head no. She did not touch my hand again as we crept up the stairs.

"It smells like Hawke's Cove." Evangeline sniffed the air as she unbuttoned her overlarge green coat.

I looked around the room, noticing for the first time its whitewashed tongue-and-groove boards, the simple dresser and single bed, the brown painted floor. "It smells like what?"

"Damp old wood. Mildew."

I pressed the door shut until I heard the latch click, then pulled the single straight-back chair into the middle of the room. I offered it to her, but Evangeline sat on the bed. I sat on the chair and threshed my imagination for a safe conversational topic. Somehow, after a few minutes, I moved to sit beside her on the bed.

We were young. We were full of ourselves. We leaned into each other and kissed. Then kissed some more until the whole world existed only in our mouths and in that part of me that I knew I had to keep to myself or else ruin a wonderful thing. I told myself she couldn't possibly know what such kissing was doing to me. Finally, with great reluctance, I pulled away. "We should go before the landlady gets home."

I know my voice was husky, but I was surprised when she echoed me in a similarly thickened voice. "Yes, we should go."

It would have been the moment to abandon all ethics, to cave in to a mutual passion that seemed less and less sinful as the moments went on. We were a bright young couple of college students with all the skills to debate the rationality of giving in as opposed to obeying some societal prohibition against what was natural. Nowadays, kids don't seem to debate that. But we didn't give in. I didn't press her because I knew right then that I wanted her as my wife. She needed to want me as a husband. Being lovers was a different, sullied, version of the pure love I had for Evangeline.

We tiptoed as cautiously down the stairway as we had gone up it. To the caution add guilty pleasure mixed with a certain misplaced virtuousness. After all, we had done nothing irrevocable.

Once the idea of marrying Evangeline got into my head, there was little else I could think of, although I managed to keep my mind on my studies well enough. Every other thought centered on seeing her, being with her, and asking her to marry me. I had ambition. I had a reasonably certain future as an architect, and in the meantime, I could support us comfortably enough on what I could make as a junior draftsman. Providing I got a job soon. After graduation I planned to use family connections, which almost certainly guaranteed a position of some sort in one of the surviving firms in Providence or Boston. We would live in romantic poverty as I rose in the ranks and Evangeline wrote poems. In five years we'd have a home, children, the good life. Oh, I had it all mapped out. An affliction of my profession, drawing out plans.

I knew that she had feelings for me. Evangeline was affectionate with me, even passionate. She never mentioned other boys and always answered my declarations with "I love you too." She kept her green eyes on my face and smiled with equal brilliance whether I had just arrived from Boston or had just been out of the room.

We sneaked into my room in the boardinghouse each of the four or five times I scraped together enough money to make the trip. We never did more than lie on the bed, keeping still, keeping the noisy bedsprings from drawing attention to us. We spent hours kissing and talking and kissing some more. Once she inadvertently put her hand on my penis. Feeling the hard desire there, she didn't pull it away as though burned, but removed it slowly, as if trying not to startle an animal.

Evangeline was different from the other girls I knew. She had a sense of the absurd, offset by a compassion that I attributed to her poetic soul. If she was sometimes a little too Bohemian, it only charmed me deeper into wanting her.

All the way to Northampton I kept one hand on the letter tucked into my breast pocket. It felt like a live thing, something that needed to be stroked in order to keep the words on the page in place. I must have looked like someone making a perpetual Pledge of Allegiance, but I cared less how I looked and more how Evangeline would react to my news.

It was mid-May, close to the end of term. Evangeline would graduate the next Sunday, and I would receive my master's at Harvard's commencement on the same day.

This trip to see her was unexpected. We had planned to see each other in Boston in the week after our respective ceremonies. Until yesterday, we had both expected that I would be heading back to Providence. Now I didn't have to, and the whole world seemed to open to me like the pages of a book I knew the ending to. I had called and told Evangeline to meet me at the station and be wearing her best dress.

I saw her from the train window as it pulled into the station. Just as the first time I had seen her, she was wearing green. A pale blue-green dress with a belted waist showing off her figure. The watery color set off her red-brown hair, and I thought she looked like a Monet. She saw me through the gritty window and waved.

"I was so surprised to hear from you. Is everything all right?" I kissed her a long time in greeting, holding her against me, against the letter. She pulled away and repeated, "Is everything all right?"

"Couldn't be better." I fought not to blurt out my good news. "I'm taking you to dinner. Not luncheonette food, real dinner."

I waited until the fresh strawberries and cream had been set before us. Before she could touch the mounded whipped cream with her spoon, I took her hand, pulling the silver out of it. "Give me both your hands."

I gathered her two little hands together and leaned a little forward. "I've been offered an entry-level position at Darling and Geer."

She smiled broadly, but I could see she didn't understand what this meant for her.

"It's entry level, as I say, but I'm guaranteed to rise quickly." My words were coming out more quickly than I had rehearsed, so I pulled the formal letter out of my breast pocket and handed it to her. I wanted her to read for herself that this was a man's job. Not a boy's. That Darling and Geer were located in Boston. That I was no longer going back to Providence.

She smiled again and handed it back to me. "I am so happy for you. It sounds exactly like what you wanted. Good for you!"

"Good for us."

When she'd handed me back the letter, Evangeline had picked up her spoon. It paused now halfway between the cream and her lips. "Us?"

I still held her left hand. "Marry me, Evangeline."

There are so many imperfect moments in our lives. Moments that we edit to convince ourselves that they were perfect; by choice recollection, we improve upon them. This memory has never needed any polishing. It was perfect. Evangeline set her spoon down and gave me both hands. And said yes.

"Yes." She was looking at our gripped hands, clenched together as if I were pulling her into a boat. "Are you certain, John?"

"You are the only woman I have ever loved. I can't imagine life without you." The words flew out of my mouth like those of a dime-novel character's. But I would never take them back. They were then, and now, the truest words I have ever spoken.

* * *

The first time Hawke's Cove came between us was almost immediately after my
proposal. It seemed that she planned to
spend the summer there, with her doddery
Gran and younger cousins, as she had always done. It took a fair amount of persua-
sion to convince her we needed to plan a
wedding and find a place to live. I didn't
want to wait until fall. I wanted to elope. I
wanted to be a newlywed right away.

"John, I told you weeks ago I always
spend the summer at Hawke's Cove."

"Well, now I'm going to be staying in
Boston. Starting a new job. I need you with
me." I played the pathetic lover card. "I'll
miss you, too much to do a good job.
Don't you want to be with me?"

"Of course I do. Why don't you come
weekends?"

"I can't afford to do that. Not yet." In my
mind Hawke's Cove seemed like a likely
summer resort for an established architect,
not a dogsbody like me.

In the end we compromised. She went
for two weeks in July. I avoided going at
all.

We married in January of 1936, a beautiful winter wedding, where I met her grandmother for the first time. Florence Bailey was still pretty straight and energetic at that time. When she shook my hand, she pulled me down into a headlock of an embrace. "You treat my granddaughter well, young man. She deserves it."

I assured her that it was my only goal. Florence released me, patting my cheek with one gloved hand. "Good. See that you always do."

Evangeline sneaked away for a week's visit that following summer, but did not go again. Her grandmother suffered a stroke just before Easter 1937. The family moved her home to Boston to live out her days irascibly, but more conveniently, with them. Then, in 1939, Evangeline's grandmother passed away.

When she left the farm to my wife, I was mystified, but a little excited. I expected something different. When I finally saw the place, I understood completely why Evangeline's cousins hadn't protested. Who in their right mind would want to take possession of a charmless, antique wreck of a sentimental farmhouse?

* * *

It sometimes seems as though the progression towards war shadowed my progression towards those objectives I held so dear. Black and white, thesis and antithesis. War and Success. I got my first big promotion, and Hitler invaded Czechoslovakia. Evangeline published her first poem, and the Nazi war machine moved inexorably forward. Paris was invaded, and I received an important design assignment. I was making good money. Evangeline was happy taking graduate courses at Wellesley and being a teaching assistant in modern poetry. The Japanese bombed Pearl Harbor, and I signed up.

Despite the horror of the world situation, Evangeline and I managed to have five very happy years. We felt selfish and blessed at the same time. Two or three times in those years I acquiesed and went with her to Hawke's Cove. I tried hard to like it. But, I don't swim and hate sitting on a hot beach. There was no social life to speak of. None of Evangeline's summer friends came any more, all grown now and with lives of their own. But it was the house I most despised. Evangeline was stubborn about it. Belligerent almost in her refusal to have me do something with it. Maybe if she had let me . . . Well, she didn't, so no sense going back over that ground. Soon enough we were distracted by the war.

By some twist of military planning, I spent the first two years of the war at home. Well, not exactly at home, but close enough to make good use of weekend passes and even get home for dinner on a weeknight or two. With the draining away of young men into the war, new opportunities opened up for Evangeline, and she took a college-level teaching position even before achieving her professorship. She stepped in as interim assistant professor of romance poetry at Northeastern University. "It's not my favorite, but I can make it work." Evangeline, who frequently had to suffer the Longfellow allusions to her name, did make the best of it and filled my ears with her happy chat about students; complaints, mostly pro forma, about the administration; and lament that just as a young man seemed to "click," he'd vanish into the war machine. I could say nothing about my own life apart from her, and so it was easy for me to let her ramble on. I bought her a new briefcase for Christmas.

In June of 1943 I got an unexpected bit of leave. I say unexpected because, although I had put in for it, leave was so dicey in those days, getting it amounted to pure luck. I called Evangeline, but there was no one home. I knew that the term was over and she was probably at school cleaning up her room, rolling the posters from her classroom walls and tucking them gently into the cardboard containers, finding a box to carry her houseplants back home, lingering over a cleaned-out desk and imagining the next term's young faces.

I had other ideas for her. Over the past few months I'd been thinking about starting a family. We'd touched on the subject once or twice before. Evangeline wasn't ready the first time I mentioned it; she was just finishing up her graduate work. The second time, just not interested. "Not yet, John. Not yet." That was eighteen months before, and now, despite her career and her success at placing poetry in literary journals, I thought the time was right for my wife to look at motherhood with enthusiasm.

It was Bill Carmichael's fault, proffering snaps of his newest baby—round-faced and of an indeterminate sex, but clearly doted on by its parents. I held the photos much longer than decency would have required, and Bill chafed me. "Say, Worth, when are you and that beautiful wife going to get busy?"

"After the war."

"Don't wait that long, Worth. You'll be too old or dead." I saw the straight line of his mouth and knew that he wasn't truly joking.

It was inevitable that I'd be shipped overseas. It was possible, perhaps probable, that I'd be killed. I could leave Evangeline a widow. Or a widowed mother. When I asked myself which was better, I came up with mother. At least she would have some part of me to hold. Besides, what woman doesn't want to be a mother?

In the end I simply surprised Evangeline by coming home. And was surprised in turn to find her packing for Hawke's Cove.

"Sweetheart, I told you two months ago

I was going to the farm to meet Fran. We've been planning it for a year."

"Of course. I shouldn't have bothered with getting leave."

"Oh, John. Don't be a child. You'll come of course." Evangeline pulled my dresser drawers open and began taking out my casual civilian clothes—dungarees I wore to putter around the yard, a couple of flannel shirts, and my rarely wet bathing suit.

"John, this will be great. You remember Fran. You liked her very much when you met her at the wedding. She's only east for a week before heading back to California. Poor thing, she lives under threat of bombing all the time. She needs a little Hawke's Cove to relax."

I swallowed my annoyance and smiled at her. It would do no good to spoil our reunion by quibbling about its location. Besides, giving in graciously on this would earn me consideration when I offered her my own wish.

The farmhouse was no more charming to me this time than it had been in the past. It had been a rainy spring, and the feeling of damp was pervasive. I was hesitant to put the Plymouth under the wobbly carport, but my wife claimed it was just fine. Frances would join us the next day. Evangeline would meet her in Great Harbor at the little depot that abutted the naval yard. I wasn't keen on her going there with all those sailors, but she was adamant she wanted to have a few minutes by herself with Fran.

"But, for now, I have you to myself!" I reached across the bed to snag her and pull her down. We wrestled until we broke apart in laughter. "Let's make a baby," I said before I could govern my mouth. I had thought to broach the subject to her in the car on the long drive, but lost my nerve. Somehow, I believed that the whole subject was a woman's province. It should be the wife who says, "Let's have a baby."

"What?" Evangeline sat up, tossing her unfashionably long hair over her shoulder. "A baby? Why now?"

"It's time. I mean, don't you think? That we should at least be thinking about it?"

"No." I could tell she regretted her bluntness by the way she dropped her eyes and then squeezed my hand.

"Ev, we've been married seven years;

we're not getting any younger. I don't want to be too old to play baseball with my son." I began to list the reasons to go ahead. Even as I did, I could see the debate in her eyes. I knew her thoughts, knew that the undeniable centerpiece was the implication she would have to abandon her own plans if we went ahead with this most natural of plans.

She got off the bed and walked around the tiny yellow-and-pink room, coming to light at her grandmother's vanity table. "I have thought about it, you know. But, John, I've mostly thought of children as far in the future. I mean, my mother—and yours—have certainly badgered me about it, in their own subtle ways, of course. But you? Why now?" What she meant was, why now during this war when anything could happen?

So I told her. "If anything happens to me, I want to know you've got something of our marriage, our happiness, to have besides memories and a few photographs." I took the brush out of her hand and stroked her hair the way she liked me to. "Is it so wrong to want to leave you with my child?"

She didn't answer with words, only a lit-

tle sound that might have been acquies-
cence. Or defeat. I lifted her from the bou-
doir chair and carried her to the bed.

As I had hoped, once she was pregnant,
Evangeline embraced the idea. We were
lucky in that, for once, Hawke's Cove
proved to be the right place. "All that fresh
sea air," she said when I commented on it.
She was happy, happy that the administration agreed to let her teach until she
was ready to stop. I was less happy about
that, and we argued about it. "Why can't
you just relax and enjoy being home? You
can still write poetry, you can spend the
time getting ready."
"Sweetheart, I can't just sit still for nine
months. Besides, if I stop now, who knows
when I'll get back to it. It's only an interim
position; it won't always be there for me.
Besides, teaching isn't like factory work. I
won't let myself get tired."
"It's not right."
"Don't be so old-fashioned, John."
"I'm not being old-fashioned."
"I'll give it up if I think I'm embarrassing
my adult students."
"Evangeline . . ." I don't know what else

I could have said to dissuade her from hanging on to her job.

I never loved her so much as when she was pregnant. Other men's wives looked like whales; mine was graceful and blooming. She kept at the teaching long after I wanted her to, but did cut back to two sections. She was healthy and surrounded by family and friends who jealously guarded her from doing too much or eating improperly. I came home as often as possible, always amazed at the ensuing changes week to week.

Our baby was due in early March. We lost her in December. Evangeline blamed herself, but of course I didn't. I'm not sure I convinced her of that, that in no way did I think her responsible.

It is all a blur to me. The doctor coming to me in the waiting room. I hadn't been blooded yet in war, but my wife had been in childbirth. She was so doped up I'm not sure she understood that I had received my orders to go. She lay there, pale against the white pillow, her green eyes brilliant as if with fever.

"Evangeline, I got my orders. I have to go before you're released. I wish I could go home with you, but I can't. I'm just lucky I was here when . . ." I couldn't finish the thought. She looked at me with unfocused eyes, and I prayed then and there that I be returned to her soon. It would be unthinkable that she be left alone after all of this. I leaned over to kiss her forehead, but I'm not sure she knew I was there.

I know I angered her when I questioned the placement of a headstone with a child's name on it. I think she thought I was hard, but it wasn't that. It just didn't seem right. That I'd had to have that conversation in a censored letter made it seem all the more harsh, I know. Our letters to each other in those first few weeks were terse, as if we'd never written to each other before. I suppose it was understandable; we hadn't had time to grieve together. How do you grieve on paper? I thought it best we simply get on with getting over it. No sense in bringing it up every letter. It was like running in a race; you put so much energy into going forward that it's hard to stop even at the finish line. I kept moving. Like when Charles died, I worked hard at not letting it stop me. I wanted Evangeline to do the same. I didn't expect her to flee to Hawke's

Cove. I would have rathered she stay close to her parents. Even though I hated the idea of her living alone, in so remote a place, I said very little about it. I guess I hoped she'd tire of it and when I got home, if I got home, be happy to return to our life in Boston.

It was a very long time before I allowed myself to hope that might happen. I was one of the survivors of the ill-fated glider drop. Assigned to a battalion making its way across France, I was sent with ten others to reconnoiter a village a few miles to the east of the command center. I was the lieutenant, the one responsible for carrying out the mission. We should have been able to do it, to get to the village, to rout any Germans dug in, and get back in half a day.

I have not looked back on what happened in almost half a century. But it doesn't fade, the memory. The ambush, the sight of my men shattered in front of me. The sound of their grunts as bullets tore through their bellies. There was no screaming. It was that fast. Instinct or luck saved me as I found cover enough to return fire. It was the first time I had fired my weapon at a human being. But they weren't human beings at that moment. They were the enemy.

I fired again and again. A kind of tunnel vision afflicted me, and the only thing I was aware of was the crowns of their helmets barely visible over the burrow I had some-how not seen as we walked upright through the fields towards the village, as if we had been tourists not soldiers. There were two of us left of the ten, me and a boy who hunkered down behind me, shar-ing the cover of rock and brush. He fired his rifle over my shoulder, so close to my ear that it has had ringing in it ever since. Then he stopped firing and slowly sank away from my side to pull himself into the fetal position against his mortal wound. I stopped firing long enough to hear German voices all around me. I put my hands in the air and gave up. I gave up because i wanted to survive to go home to Evan-geline.

The memories all blur into one image, one overriding memory. That of walking. For days, weeks, we walked, my captors and I. Through fields and burnt-out farms, fording rivers and beating our way through old-growth forest. We were heading due east, but they would not tell me where. Periodically I would be left with one guard while the others, about fifteen or so, went off. Sometimes one or two would be missing after these skirmishes. The others would rest, and then we'd move on. As we went, three other prisoners were added to our group. It felt so good to be able to hear English, to catch up on the progress of the invasion. I thought maybe that this small platoon of Germans was heading home to Germany.

Every day I survived by keeping my thoughts on Evangeline. I prayed she would not give up on me.

There was one German who spoke some English and liked to practice it on us, telling us that once they won the war, he would like to go to New York. Claus shared cigarettes with us to get us to talk with him. One day one of the Americans, Hank Ramirez, walked a little too far away from the group. Claus was close by, and we all knew that Hank was just taking a leak in the bush. The platoon leader gave Claus a nod. Without a backward glance, Claus shot Hank dead. After that we refused to speak with Claus, even though the craving for a cigarette was oppressive.

Eventually we joined a battalion, and the remaining other two prisoners and I were added to another, larger, group of Americans headed for a POW camp. We were loaded into a canvas-enclosed truck—tightly packed, stinking, nervous, and homesick. Mostly silent. The youngest among us weren't necessarily the most afraid. They were the first to talk, the ones who wanted to make it all seem normal by asking normal questions. "Where're you from, Sarge?" "When'd you get captured, Lieutenant?" "Anybody got a cigarette?" We stopped only once while the Germans refueled the truck with jerry cans of gasoline. We weren't allowed to get out, even to urinate, and the odor in the truck worsened. One, a PFC old enough to have been in the war for some time, began to cry. He self-consciously rubbed his eyes with the clean end of an otherwise filthy handkerchief, then sighed and went back to sitting quietly crammed between his mates.

I looked around in vain for a familiar

face, anyone who might have been with me before. I realized I should be glad there was no one I knew. I could imagine they were still alive.

I entertained myself throughout the interminable ride with thoughts of Evangeline, whom I knew to be alive and well. I did not picture her where she was, at Hawke's Cove, but where I wanted her to be. I pictured her, over and over, standing in our little garden behind the triple-decker house we lived in. I dressed her in my favorite green dress and seated her on the wrought-iron bench I would put there someday. I was too superstitious to place children at her feet, but saw myself bringing her a rose. I slept with my dreams bending and twisting my imaginings into something grotesque. The rose become a rifle.

For the thousandth time I wished I had not left all her letters in my pack, which the Germans made me abandon at my capture, but had kept them in my shirt, where I would still have them.

I consoled myself with the thought that once I was in a POW camp, Evangeline would come to know what had happened to me. Perhaps we could even get letters to each other. If the Germans would give me a piece of paper, I would write to her and tell her how much I love her, how thoughts of her had kept me alive. How we would try again for a baby. That, if she really wanted to, we could spend time in Hawke's Cove. I kept my sanity by formulating plans for our future.

We determined that we were in one of three trucks, a small convoy of prisoners. Every now and then the trucks would pull off the road and over the motors we could hear the drone of airplanes and even the thud of bombs not too distant. Closer, the sound of shelling, percussive and rhythmic like distant drums. In the last hours of night, just before the pearling of dawn, the truck in front of ours was hit by a shell. The remaining two trucks skirted the smoking remains of the first one and sped down the road. Through the slits in the canvas we could see the burning wreckage and hear the cries of the dying Americans.

A big redheaded private sitting next to me began to rock. Holding his head in his hands, he repeated over and over, "I want to go home. I want to go home." The man on his other side quietly put an arm around the big soldier's shoulders. "I want to go home too, sonny. We will. You just bet we will."

I wanted to believe him too.

At about noon the next day we were finally allowed out of the trucks. A temporary POW camp had been arranged at the site of a bombed-out factory. There might have been a hundred of us. We outnumbered our captors by four to one, but they held the guns and the sure knowledge of where we were. Food was sparse and unpalatable. I ate because I would die otherwise, and I was determined not to do that. I spoke of Evangeline to anyone who would give me an opportunity. I needed words to hold on to, anchors to keep my lifeline secure.

One English-speaking Kraut loved to badger me. He'd heard me speak of Evangeline. "Hey, butty," he'd say in that thick German accent. "Bet some guy fucking your vife. Bet she fucking right now." He tried so hard to provoke me into anger so that he could shoot me, but his words were so ludicrous he failed.

* * *

The rumor went through the makeshift barracks, unstoppable. American forces were nearby. They just had to find us. Someone who spoke a little high school German had heard. Indeed, the Nazis seemed anxious. More guards were on than normal. In our restricted world, every detail had significance. Even the most pessimistic among us shouldered his way to look out of the window to watch for rescue. We had been in the factory-prison for more than two months, and even the big red-headed private looked fragile. Not one of us had the strength to walk the length of the building without sitting down to rest halfway.

"What if it is true?" Al Biondi asked me, his breath foul with bad digestion. "Can it be true?"

"I don't know, Al. They might just end up bombing what they think is a German holdout. They might not know we're here."

Al only shrugged, too weak to care much either way.

After a whole day of listening to the shells exploding in the near distance, we began to expect our guards would begin to execute us in preparation for abandoning the makeshift prison. Instead, at about nightfall, the Nazi guards herded us into an interior room. We barely fit. Then they sealed the metal door and left us. I don't know how long we stood there, too many of us to do more than take turns sitting down. No light at all. We stood trapped in the small blind room, listening to the sound of bombing around us and the soft whimpering of grown men beside us. We stood for days. Some died and, packed as we were, did not fall.

Asleep and awake, I thought of Evangeline, promising her I would not die.

That I would come home.

I did come home. Spiritually numbed, emotionally wounded, but grateful. The Allies did not bomb the already bombed-out factory. They came and they opened the door. I had survived, and the only thing I wanted was to go home and begin again with Evangeline.

Except that she was different. Somehow, in some subtle way, my wife had grown

away from me. Not cold or distant or un-
loving. Simply slightly different.

Those postwar years flew by. Even now,
when I think back, as old men are wont to
do, I see a flow of years punctuated by
incidents, arguments, slipshod little memories that stick to me. I remember things. It
is all I can do now. Remember.

Like two people who have been separated by a fierce argument, we tried hard
to put our war years behind us. I could not
speak of what I had seen, and Evangeline
did not speak often of what she had, except in the most anecdotal and mild way.
I knew she had bought three cows; I knew
that she had won a ribbon for her preserves. She spoke of playing cards with
the Fricks, people who remained in our
lives via Christmas cards and occasional
visits to Boston. I asked for little else from
her. I suppose, in some ways, I discour-
aged her. From this distance, I can see that
I resented the apparent happiness she had
found in Hawke's Cove. I think she was
cognizant of the dichotomy of our war experiences and, being a sensitive person,
kept her adventures to herself. Truly,

though, she didn't seem to mind, and it was of the future we spoke most intimately.

I was plagued for a long time with bouts of depression. Not the clinical kind so popular now, but a deep sadness that stalled my ability to keep moving. So unlike myself. Before the war and, especially, after it I was driven to achieve my goals. So when I felt the walls close in on me and I turned snappish at my wife, and suddenly nothing seemed as though it was going the way I planned, Evangeline would ask me to tell her what was bothering me.

"It helps, to speak about it, John. I know. When I could finally speak of the baby to"—she took a swallow's-worth of hesitation—"to Judy, I felt better. Not less sad, just better for having said her name out loud."

She was so patient with me. Evangeline could always tell the difference between a bad mood and despair.

"Darling, there is nothing I can tell you. There is nothing to discuss. You know that I would prefer it if we never spoke of any of it." I think I meant both our experiences. We shoved the war into a box and went on with our lives.

We were fully engaged in pulling our lives back together in those first couple of years. I was doing well at the firm, but longed to strike out on my own. Evangeline was working hard on her dissertation. We wanted to try for another child.

We had Julie in 1947, followed closely by Amanda in 1949. In 1954 I decided to take the plunge into my own firm. In all that time Evangeline hadn't spoken of going to Hawke's Cove. I diligently paid the taxes on the property and the few maintenance bills that came along, but not once did she suggest we spend any time there. I certainly didn't broach the subject and was more than glad the whole Hawke's Cove obsession seemed to have run its course. Spending a long time there must have worked it out of her system. So it seemed a brilliant idea to sell the farm and use the proceeds as seed money.

"Sell it? My grandmother's farm?" Evangeline was still in her regular clothes even though she was four months pregnant with the surprise of our midlife, Charlie. "I don't know, John. Why not just mortgage the property?"

"Ev, we haven't been there since the

war. It would be a far better use of the value to convert it into cash rather than take on debt. I have this perfect opportunity to enter into a business debt free. We never use the place; it's probably tumbled to the ground by now. Besides, it isn't worth hanging on to this tax burden just for a two-week vacation someday. If I'm as fortunate as I think I can be in business, our vacations can be worldwide. How would you like to go to Paris? We'll be able to do that within a few years. But not if we hang on to this white elephant. Put sentimentality aside, Evangeline."

If I expected her to argue, she didn't. Neither did she smile. I had won my point, but I never knew at what cost. Or why she gave in so readily.

If perfect happiness eluded us, we had enough of imperfect happiness. It all went by so fast. The business was everything I expected, hoped for, except that it was all-consuming. Every day was a balancing act between clients, subordinates, and family. Too often family lost out. If Evangeline and I never recaptured the soul-deep closeness of our days before the war, I could only blame myself for being a harder, less fun-loving man, one always preoccupied with his career. Sometimes I wonder if the war changed me, or was I always destined to be so dour?

My ruling passions were to provide for and protect my family. To do this I had to work hard. I wasn't alone in this. My peers, the men who had been there, they, too, picked up the rhythm of their abandoned lives with a few missteps and then marched on. We had years to make up for, which seemed to disallow frivolity.

I would listen to the sound of laughter coming from the television room or watch my children playing hopscotch in the drive-way. How often did I hear Evangeline's laughter mixed with theirs or watch her jump from block to block with her arms straight out from her sides and the girls teasing her about stepping on a line. I watched them. It never occurred to me to join them.

"It's in the top desk drawer, left side." Evangeline was in the kitchen, phone to her ear, shouting at me to pull a manu-script out of her private desk. Her editor was on the phone. I remember everything about that moment. How the October sunlight was golden through the last of the maple leaves in the yard in Cambridge. How I missed Julie, off on her school trip to Washington. I could hear Amanda's music on the record player, a young Elvis Presley. Charlie was upstairs too.

"Honey, can you get it for me or talk to Meagan while I find it?"

"I'm looking . . ." I rooted around in the desk drawer. She had said left drawer. I was certain she had said left. I closed my hand on a photograph. Impulse made me pull it out from under the notebook pages with their tattered edges. I looked at it for a long time, trying to place the face. A young, handsome, and bearded man dressed in clothes I remember owning. I recognized the barn as the one at Hawke's Cove. The man was looking at the camera with a mixed look of surprise and pleasure at being photographed. I flipped the photograph over. "Joe Green October '44." I closed the left-hand desk drawer and opened the middle one, where the manuscript lay.

I handed Evangeline the manuscript

pages, and she bent over the counter, phone under her chin and finger aimed at the lines written on the pages. She'd already published one volume of poems and this was to be her second.

Rootless, I walked upstairs. I peeked into my children's rooms. Amanda was lying on Julie's bed, taking advantage of her big sister's absence to use the record player. She smiled and waved at me. Charlie lay on his bed sound asleep. I bent and covered him with his security blanket. At seven, he was theoretically too old for a blanket, but we had learned through the girls that a child will let go when it's time and not before. Besides, I didn't want Charlie to grow up as fast as his sisters had. One minute they were babies, the next teenagers. What would Molly have been? Almost twenty years old. I closed Charlie's door and went back downstairs.

I could hear Evangeline's good-natured laughter as she worked with her editor.

What good would it have done to hand the old snapshot to her and say, "And who is this and why do you have this in your most private drawer? Who is Joe Green and why does he look at the photographer with such love?" What good would it have done? It explained a little the thin wall between us that had been there since she put her arms around me in the VA hospital. It explained a little her acquiesing so easily to selling the farm. I knew that I should be happy about that, as if there had been some competition I had won.

I put the photograph back in Evangeline's drawer.

My dear wife of fifty-seven years has just left me sitting here, fed and wiped and remembering. When she mentioned that place, Hawke's Cove, I saw the look on her face. One instant of sweet temptation.

It was Hawke's Cove that came between us.

Seven
Charlie

As it turned out, the Clintons had decided on Martha's Vineyard, and the advance teams quickly deserted Great Harbor and dashed all hopes of booming tourism for the little towns in the area. Thus, it was with no trouble at all that Charlie booked himself a room at the Seaview Bed and Breakfast in Hawke's Cove.

Charlie followed the concierge up the narrow and steep stairs to the front bedroom. "We've owned this place since eighty. Nothing done to it for years, maybe since it was built. It was a rooming house, but, of course, we call it a B and B. Rooming houses were real popular back in the twenties and thirties. Whole families would

come and spend the summer here, sometimes got to feel like family to the owners."

Charlie hoped fervently that the New
England reticence would kick in soon.

"The best part of this room is this."
Mrs. Smith threw open the French doors,
which led out onto a tiny balcony. "We
were gonna put in sliders, but the con-
tractor said these were classier, and even
though they were way more expensive, I
think he was right and do class up the
place, dontcha think?"

Charlie nodded in polite agreement, but
when he actually went out on the balcony
after his garrulous hostess left the room,
he was swept away by the view.

The Seaview was well named, and the
whole of the cove was laid out in front of
him, shimmering in the late spring afternoon. A single sail was etched against the
horizon, then disappeared over it as if Co-
lumbus had been wrong. Beneath Charlie,
the beach road followed the curve of the
bay, defended by the seawall that held
back the threat of erosion most of the time.
Charlie thought how spectacular a storm
would be, beating the water over the top
of that wall, and he could imagine how im-

pressive the sound of the surf. His mother had told him about the storms of her youth, including the 1938 hurricane that became the storm against which all others were judged. Even though she hadn't been in Hawke's Cove at the time, she had a way of telling the story, gleaned from others, that had made it seem part fairy tale, part cautionary tale, and for a year or so he feared the sound of the wind.

Charlie shook himself out of his reverie and went back inside to change into jeans and polo shirt. Afterwards he fished out his notebook and smiled in satisfaction. It had taken only three phone calls to get the information he'd needed about the missing pilot. Spencer Buchanan had been a twenty-nine-year-old Navy pilot who had seen action in the Pacific but been sent home after being wounded. He'd been one day away from returning to active duty. Born in a small town near Chicago, unmarried. Thirty-nine kills to his credit. Looking at war through the eyes of someone who had been too young for Vietnam, but old enough to watch television news, Charlie could imagine that this Buchanan guy might have gone AWOL with good reason.

Thirty-nine kills. Enough was enough. Maybe he figured he'd done his share. Except that World War II was not an unpopular, politically-charged conflict between Americans and their leaders. Story after story told of men anxious to get back to the front. The enemy was clear and truly evil.

Charlie did the math on the back of the notebook. If the guy actually bailed out and came ashore, today he'd be almost eighty. Supposing this fantasy tale was real, he might on the other hand, be dead from old age. Or, like his own father, debilitated by a stroke. Or, maybe lost in the mists of Alzheimer's. Charlie flipped the cover back over his notes and dropped the notebook onto the double bed. Enough story. There must be someplace close by to get a decent cup of coffee.

Charlie hooked a left coming off the porch of the Seaview and headed towards the harbor. Thrust into the cove like stone arms, the jetty defined the protected channel into the harbor. The harbor was still fairly empty, only two or three early arrivers having tied up to their moorings this soon in the spring. The two remaining commercial fishing boats were tied up to the Mobil pier, and Charlie could see the salvaged Hellcat floating on a barge next to them. The finders had lost no time in claiming their prize, and the scuttlebutt was already circulating that they hadn't contacted the Navy before they pulled her out of her resting place. Well, that was someone else's story. Charlie just needed a little proof that the pilot, Spencer Buchanan, had indeed died. Or had not. In the first instance, he'd write an oh-what-a-pity-prime-of-life kind of story, enjoy his weekend in Hawke's Cove, maybe even catch up on some sleep. If it went the other way, well, he'd figure out how to address that unlikely scenario should it arise.

The old travel writer in him reared up to claim his attention as he wandered along the seafront. His mother's stories had centered so often around the farm that he'd never imagined the beauty of Hawke's Cove's waterfront. Here were buildings not only unchanged since the nineteenth century, but, even better, ungentrified. No antique stores taking their names from previous uses, such as "The Loft" or "The Chandlery"; no coffee bars and overpriced clothing stores. Charlie smiled; no, he'd keep this place to himself. He liked the slightly run-down look of the waterfront's working marina. Cracked pavement not cobblestones meandered between the lanes coming up from the harbor and onto the main street.

He stopped at Linda's Restaurant to get a coffee to go. Too late for lunch and too early for dinner, only a few patrons sat at the counter. Grizzled old men in green-and-black flannel or khaki-colored work clothes; greasy baseball caps pushed back away from their foreheads in a nod to civility. The day's paper was broken into segments and spread down the length of the counter; wordlessly they swapped sections. Charlie leaned against the counter casually while waiting for his unflavored black coffee.

"How're the Red Sox doing?" Charlie asked conversationally to the man holding the Sports section.

"Good enough for spring training."

That seemed to close the traditional masculine conversational gambit, so Charlie opened his other one. "Interesting about that Hellcat, isn't it?"

The man nodded, sipped his black coffee, and went back to his reading. Charlie
had just about written off getting any more
response when the man shook the paper
back into its folds and said, "I remember
when it went down. I was a boy, but I went
out lookin' fer it with my uncle on his lobster boat."

Charlie sat on the stool beside his new
friend. "What became of the pilot? Did they
ever find him?"

"Dunt know. Dead acourse. Sunderland
boys found his life raft floating empty."

"Can I ask you a question?"

"Don't mind."

"About the time the pilot crashed, did
anyone show up here? I mean, did any
stranger show up and stay?"

"We always had a lot of strangers show
up. Some left, some stayed." He looked at
Charlie. "Still do."

"Well, I'm doing a story on the Hellcat.
Kind of a human-interest angle, that being,
what if the guy came ashore and stayed
here? Made a life."

Charlie's new friend began to chuckle,
then gurgle in a near choke. All down the
counter the men laughed, nudging each

other. Charlie looked at them all and judged that they were either of an age to have been away during the war, or too young to have made note of any strangers in town.

Sitting on the end stool, though, one man wasn't laughing. A pair of very blue eyes studied Charlie as if trying to place him, a slight smile creased into his neat white beard. "What's your name?"

"Charlie Worth."

"Well, Charlie Worth, it makes an interesting story." The blue-eyed man got up and walked towards the men's room. As he passed by Charlie, he clapped him on the shoulder. "Good luck with it."

Charlie walked across the street from the restaurant and sat on a park bench to drink his coffee and think out his next move. Clearly he needed to interview people who not only had lived here then, but had been adults and not away in the war itself. Women, then. Maybe he should visit Judy Frick in the retirement home. His mother was skeptical about her faculties, but it was worth a shot. Who else then?

As Charlie contemplated his story, he

kept being distracted by the quiet charm of the town. Standing on the roof of the movie house, a gull complained loudly, its mewing the quintessential seashore sound. At five o'clock the taped chimes in the Methodist steeple began to play hymns. Charlie thought he recognized *A Mighty Fortress Is Our God,* but he wasn't sure.

A little blue Mazda, a couple of years old, pulled up in front of Linda's Restaurant, parking a little over the line into the next space. A tall, slim woman got out, and Charlie admired her over the rim of his cup. Dressed in city chic, she wore her dark hair in a French braid that trailed to the middle of her shoulders. As she shut the door of the car, she glanced at him and acknowledged his admiration with a little smile. He couldn't tell how old she was from that distance, thirty or forty. A woman, not a girl. She went into the restaurant, and Charlie was tempted to go back in. Before he could talk himself into it, the glass door opened and she came out with the blue-eyed man who'd asked his name. They looked at Charlie as they stood beside the car, their equal movements defining them as father and daughter. Then, in an identical manner, they both waved a little greeting towards him. Taken by surprise, Charlie raised his hand in self-conscious response.

Eight

Charlie

The rising sun caught Charlie unawares, waking him with a soft touch that made him dream of heat before opening his eyes to recognize the small, eastward-facing room of the bed and breakfast. He hadn't planned to rise with the sun, but the faint smell of toast and the overlying scent of coffee made sleep less attractive than eating, so Charlie got up earlier on a Saturday morning than he had for years.

"Din't expect you till eight-thirty," Mrs. Smith remarked as she handed him a cup of coffee. "Breakfast will be another few minutes, so whyn't you sit out on the porch. Paper's out there."

Charlie settled into a porch rocker and

squinted against the rising sun breaking into shards against the slightly choppy cove. At this hour the only traffic along the roadway that separated the B and B from the seawall was the occasional pickup truck. Most had some combination of fishing rods sticking out of the bed or stuck in PVC pipe fastened to the front bumper. Without exception, each also had a dog sticking out, tongue lolling against the force of the breeze, floppy ears waving madly, and that peculiar doggy expression of suffering delight universal to each.

Distracted away from the paper, Charlie gave up and simply enjoyed the view. It puzzled him, why hadn't his family ever come here? He knew that his parents had sold Bailey's Farm before he was born. Still, they could have come and stayed in one of those "rooming houses" Mrs. Smith remembered. Charlie shook his head against the thought; he could not picture his father in a rooming house under any circumstance. Smiling to himself, Charlie tried again to read the paper.

A dark spot in the sky caught his eye, and Charlie put the paper down again. An osprey working the shoreline rose straight up, beating his wings against the sky like a swimmer treading water.

Charlie knew that although his mother had never come back to Hawke's Cove, the place lived on in her psyche. As his father's time in the war had been for him, living here was her defining experience. It was only after his father had had the second stroke and ended up in St. Elizabeth's that his mother had told him his father had been a POW. So deeply held was that secret that John Worth's own children knew nothing about it. Was it due to shame or an understandable desire to put such an experience so far behind him it could be forgotten? They always spoke about how horrific the Vietnam war had been, all the syndromes and traumas that accounted for antisocial behavior. It occurred to Charlie, the veterans of the Second World War hadn't been allowed that excuse. They were welcomed home as heroes and then asked to move on. How do you do that?

Once again the osprey took aim, and this time he committed himself to the drop, then rose like a phoenix from the sun-splintered dawn sea, the bright silver curve of a fish in its talons.

The smell of bacon set Charlie's stomach juices to flowing, and he stood up to go back in. The sight of a jogger running at a decent clip along the seawall made him pause. The jogger, a woman dressed in the unaffected clothes of a serious runner—shorts, T-shirt, and dirty white running shoes—began to slow as she saw him standing on the porch. He smiled as he recognized the woman with the blue Mazda. "Morning!" he called out as she passed.

"Nice one," she responded in the liturgy of limited acquaintance. Then, to his surprise, she paused on top of the seawall, still running in place. "You're the columnist Charlie Worth, aren't you?"

It didn't completely surprise him to be recognized. He'd had his picture beside his column now for a couple of years. "Yeah, that's right. You've read my stuff?"

"Nope." Her braid swished from side to side as she kept up the in-place running. "I've read your mother's." Then she was back in forward motion, leaving only the impression of an encounter behind her.

After breakfast Charlie went down to the dock where the barge loaded with the hulk of the F6F Hellcat was tied up. The two fishing boats were gone, and the harbormaster sat enjoying the undisturbed scene. Too soon the summer people and their floating palaces would be there, demanding attention from those who served and making his life difficult with their often preposterous demands for all the comforts of home while roughing it. Coming from a long line of fishermen and scallopers, Steve West did not look at boats as pleasure. Nonetheless, the harbormaster's job was decent—good pay and benefits and a nice little office stuck out on the end of the pier. Charlie's sudden appearance at that office's door was not unexpected. Since the Hellcat had been raised, there had been a lot of faces peeking in, curious about this artifact from a time long gone.

"Can I ask you a few questions?" Charlie introduced himself to Steve and then jumped into his prepared list of questions. "When they raised the plane, did they find any remains of the pilot?"

"Nope. No sign of anybody."

"Sharks get him?"

Steve chuckled. "Maybe. Though there aren't too many man-eaters in these waters. If he'd been further out, then maybe. No. I think he just went the way of so many lost seamen. Sea doesn't always give up the bodies. Just happens."

"So you think he just got tired and floated away?"

"Be my guess."

"The reports say that he radioed his position and that he was okay."

"Then you know more than I do."

Charlie leaned against the doorjamb of the tiny ten-by-ten office. "Can I show you a picture?"

Steve muscled his wheeled chair back and reached for the coffeepot, holding it up in silent offer to Charlie. When Charlie shook his head to decline, Steve poured some of the already thick liquid into a grimy cup and then reached for the glossy military photo. "So, what was the guy's name?"

"Spencer Buchanan."

"And you think maybe he's still alive? Living here?"

"That's the line I'm taking." Charlie let Steve hang on to the picture for another minute before asking, "Any ideas?"

Steve shrugged. "Well, not really."

"Are you sure?" Charlie had detected a little hesitation.

"Okay, he doesn't look like any old guy I know, but he kinda resembles a guy I grew up with who was killed in Vietnam. Scott Green."

Charlie wrote the name on his pad. "One more question."

"Shoot." Steve got up and moved towards the door. A powerboat had come into the harbor as they spoke, and he pushed past Charlie in the doorway to stand outside and signal it.

"Has anyone been by to see the Hellcat who's been particularly interested in looking at it?"

Steve laughed outright. "Yeah, every man who ever dreamed about flying, every member of the VFW, and every small boy who makes model airplanes."

"Okay. So, tell me"—Charlie stood back as Steve caught the painter tossed to him by the powerboat's owner—"has there been anyone clearly not interested?"

"Well, probably the only old-timer who hasn't shown up is Joe Green." Steve wrapped the line around a cleat, knotting a proper hitch. "Scott's dad."

Nine

Maggie

Maggie Green finished signing checks, still unused to stopping at the *N* and not continuing on with the hyphen, then "Shofsky" as she had done for six years. When she had finally convinced Ethan that their's was not a successful marriage, he had come back with the accusation that she had been the uncommitted one, not even taking his name completely, but adding him and his name as an appendage, not a husband. Maggie shook that memory out of her thoughts and stacked the bills neatly in a pile to go to the post office this afternoon.

She could hear her father in the kitchen, on the phone with Ernest Dubee in Florida. Every year Ernie went down to Key West with his lady friend for the cold weather, and every year he invited Dad to go. It had become a superstitious exercise, in that he always asked and Dad always said no and then they went on with their lives. Dad would have been hurt not to be asked, and Ernie would have collapsed from the shock if Joe Green had ever said yes.

Thank God he hadn't gone. It had been so wonderful to come home when things had gotten ugly with Ethan. Her parents had separated several years after Scott had died. Her mother had begged Joe to leave Hawke's Cove. She couldn't stand being in such a small place for life where everyone knew her pain. Her emotional pain had eventually become physical pain, and she slid into a hypochondriacal maelstrom out of which she now tormented her second husband. Maggie could take her mother only in small doses, and although Denise lived much nearer Boston, Maggie fled to Hawke's Cove and Joe. There they were, the pair of them, both marriage failures, or as she sometimes kidded, matrimonially challenged.

"Great, we'll see you when you get home. Love to Marilyn." Joe hung up the kitchen phone and began to make a pot of coffee.

"So Uncle Ernie is on his way home?"

"Yup. Doesn't seem possible another winter's gone. Maybe I'll go with him next year."

"Yeah. Right. And I'll win the lottery." She slapped her father on the shoulder in comradely fashion. Everyone knew Joe Green couldn't leave Hawke's Cove. Limited agoraphobia. It never got any worse; he roamed around these sixteen square miles easily enough. But he couldn't cross the bridge.

"I've been thinking about inviting that Charlie Worth guy to dinner. You being an old friend of his mother's and all."

"Leave me out of it. You want to have a date, you don't need an old man around."

"Dad. Stop it. Not a date." The only complaint Maggie had about living with her father was his infernal suggestion she find another mate. *Don't let yourself be alone at this age.*

"Don't you want to meet him? I mean formally."

"No."

If Maggie was mystified by her father's

reluctance to meet with the son of his old friend, she kept it to herself. Like a five-year-old, Joe Green could be inexplicably contrary at times. If she pushed, he'd get his back up.

What didn't surprise her was her own interest in meeting Charlie Worth, admitting to herself without compunction that it was his mother she was most interested in. One of Maggie's most treasured possessions was the framed poem Evangeline Worth had sent to her parents celebrating her birth. There had been one for Scott too, but it had disappeared sometime after his death.

From the time she had discovered a volume of Evangeline Worth's poems squirreled away between paperbacks on the living room bookshelf, Maggie had adored her poetry. She especially loved the volume *Hawke's Cove Remembered.* "Mystical night of sand and sky . . . speak to my heart of the passion of place."

As an adult, Maggie recognized now that the "passion of place" was not Hawke's Cove but that passionate plane where physical and emotional love exist and the place Maggie seemed to be just one side of or the other.

Maggie drove past the Seaview on her way to the post office. She wasn't surprised not to see Charlie on the porch. Of course he wouldn't be sitting there, still leisurely taking in the view four hours later. Only people with three weeks of vacation ever sat still. Still, she didn't chide herself for driving past, even though going to the post office by way of the shore road was a little out of the way. Maggie didn't even claim to herself to be doing it because she enjoyed the view. Besides, it felt sort of nice, being curious about someone. Since Ethan, she'd seemed unable to work up the energy to care.

Maggie waved to friends standing in front of the hardware store as she made the turn to park in front of the post office. It's what she liked best about being here, even if it was only a couple of days a week. Someone to wave to. As a cardiac care nurse, Maggie pulled three twelve-hour shifts a week at Mass General. That left four days to be home. By sharing a condo with another divorcée, Maggie was able to keep expenses down enough to justify living in two places.

Maggie dropped her handful of envelopes as she got out of her car. When she bent over to retrieve the fallen bills, her purse tipped, spilling out all of the change she'd tossed into it over the past week. Quarters, nickels, and dimes rolled under her car and the one beside it. "Damn." Maggie squatted down to pick up the money. A pair of running shoes appeared in front of her, and she lifted her head to see whose they were.

Their owner squatted beside her, gathering up the loose change and handing it to her. "I think that's all of it. No, wait." He reached under the other car, snagging a quarter. "Reminds me of a joke my mother used to tell."

"Which was?"

"Guy's in an outhouse. When he stands up, fifty cents falls into the hole. So, he takes out his wallet and tosses in a five-dollar bill."

"And the punch line is?"

"Well, I ain't goin' down there for four bits."

"My father told me that joke back when it was a quarter and a fifty-cent piece."

"Inflation," Charlie deadpanned. "I'm Charlie Worth. But then, you know that."

Maggie laughed and extended her hand. "Maggie Green." She noticed his eyes widening at her name. "Yes, Joe's daughter."

"Hey, I'm doing a piece about Hawke's Cove, and I wonder if you'd be willing to talk with me?"

The fire horn blasted its noontime alarm, startling Maggie. "Shit, I'm going to miss the window! It closes at noon on Saturday!"

Ten

Charlie

Maggie's sudden flight left Charlie on the sidewalk wondering exactly what it was he was going to ask her, but certain that the first question was if she'd join him for lunch.

Charlie discovered that Linda's Restaurant was the only restaurant on the peninsula except for the hot dog stand near the public beach, which was, in April, still shut up tight. Returning triumphant from the post office, Maggie had readily accepted his invitation and then led him across the street to the coffee shop.

"This is the first time you've been here, isn't it?"

"Yes. Though I've been sitting on that porch wondering why that's true. It seems as though we should have been here as children. This place was very important to my mother." Charlie held the glass of water the waitress had placed in front of him, turning it around and around so that the fine lines of crazing left by hundreds of washings glittered in the sunlight filtering in between the cafe curtains. "She just left and never came back."

"Did she ever say why? I mean, clearly the place loomed large in her imagination. Her poetry, especially in her third volume, is filled with it."

Charlie felt himself grow a little warm. "You know her stuff pretty well."

"Oh, yes. I love it. It's so full of emotion. Longing, fear, loneliness, and waiting. And it can be so sexy too. Especially her most recent volume."

Now Charlie felt a full bore blush rise above the collar of his polo shirt. "I hate to say that I've read so little of it. I suppose I'm a little embarrassed. A mother isn't supposed to write sexy poetry at seventy-something."

Maggie laughed. "Hey, and how old do you have to be to willingly, underscored, willingly give it up?"

"Sometimes we're just forced to." Charlie smiled to cover the extent of his blush. "You know what I mean."

Maggie held up a ringless hand. "I do."

The conversation seemed to have slipped into something a little too intimate for such new acquaintance, and Charlie pulled it back to living in Hawke's Cove. "So, you live here full-time?"

Maggie shook her head and told him about her living arrangements. "But, I could be happy staying put here. It was a great place to grow up. Of course, when my parents split, I ended up living in Quincy. I went to high school there. But, in my heart, I was always a Cover."

The waitress brought them their lunches. Maggie poured oil and vinegar over her garden salad and raised a professional eyebrow at Charlie's hamburger and fries.

"Hey, the twilight years are overrated." Charlie sprinkled salt on his fries. "Your parents divorced after your brother died?"

"A year or so after."

"I'm sorry." Charlie knew that sounded as if he were sorry for her long ago losses, but, in fact, he was sorry that he was revving up to be a reporter. He liked Maggie

Green. He took advantage of a large bite of hamburger before asking his next question. As he chewed, he watched Maggie's hands daintily folding overlarge pieces of lettuce into mouth-sized packages. Before he could swallow, Maggie caught him with a question of her own.

"So, tell me about your story. What have you found out?" Maggie pulled aside the curtain to get a look at the Hellcat. "I hear you're trying to find the pilot." She looked back at him with innocent curiosity, mildly amused at the idea of someone surviving the crash and living here all these years, not threatened by it.

"Nothing much. My leads are all fifty years old."

"You should talk to my dad. He was here then."

"I'd love to talk with him." Charlie felt that evil blush grow again. This time the blush of duplicity. He would never have made a good investigative reporter.

After lunch, which Maggie insisted was dutch, they walked over to the pier and the Hellcat. With tacit permission from Steve West, they climbed onto the barge and walked around the hulk, which stank with accumulated seaweed and dying sea life, smelling, as Maggie put it, like maximum low tide.

"Can you tell anything from looking at it?"

"No. No skeleton sitting in the cockpit, leather jacket and rakish scarf around his neck."

"So what if this guy did make it to shore? Why would he stay in Hawke's Cove? It's pretty limited."

"That's probably why he did. If he did. And we have no proof anyone did." Charlie reached out a hand to Maggie, helping her off the barge. "It's a dumb story, but it's gotten me here."

"I'm glad it did." Maggie didn't let go of his hand until both feet were firmly on the pier.

"Maggie, I have a photo I'd like to show your dad."

"Show it to him at dinner tonight." Maggie fished for her car keys. "That's an invitation."

"Great." Charlie felt himself grin. "Thanks."

Eleven

Joe

Sometimes he took memories out to savor, especially as some piece of music evoked an emotion-steeped recollection. Sometimes the urge was so strong in him to call her. "Hey, do you remember that night we stood under the stars and I taught you the names for constellations? Our bodies so close, yet so innocent. Do you ever think about the time in the barn when I held you in my arms and you leaned on me? Angry at me. Needing me. And, Vangie, do you recall how our fingers intertwined long after our bodies had separated?" But he never called.

Joe waited for the last long chord of the music coloring these memories and then snapped off the CD player. Trouble was, he had too much time on his hands. The job at the movie house only filled his nights, and, too often, reminded him of romantic notions he should have conquered after all these years. His days he filled with what was at hand, tinkering in the house and potting about the yard, doing a little care-taking for the big new summer homes that took up valuable pasture space. With Maggie's return, the empty house seemed all the more oppressive as she dashed off to this meeting or that group or yet another class in some fad du jour. When she was in Boston, it was easier because he had nothing to compare his idleness against. He could sit with his music and his thoughts and not feel somehow guilty for wasting the time he seemed to have in abundant measure.

Joe heard the Mazda crunch up the clamshell driveway and quickly removed the disk from the player. Maggie always got after him for leaving the CDs in the player long after he'd listened to them. Peeking out of the parlor window, Joe watched his daughter bound up the front steps, and knew that Maggie was bursting with some news.

"Hi, Dad!" Maggie breezed by him, throwing her bag on the chair and following it with a dramatic flourish that recalled the adolescent Maggie. Guess who I had lunch with?"

Joe smiled and pretended to ponder a list. "Well, I ate tuna in the kitchen, so I know it wasn't me." He stroked his trimmed beard. "I give up. Who?"

"Charlie Worth."

Joe felt a frisson of anxiety. He studied Maggie's face for suspicion and saw none, only a brightness unclouded by any disturbing revelations, a high color to her cheeks that he hadn't seen for a long time. Joe lay a hand on the top of his daughter's head. His foreboding seemed inappropriate to her pleasure.

"I invited him to dinner."

The dread shivered through him.

Joe Green sat on the single park bench that overlooked Hawke's Cove's waterfront. Fishermen lined the twin jetties casting into the channel, hoping to catch something. Joe could see the harbor water boil, baitfish being chased by blues. Watching the fishermen, Joe thought wistfully of Ernie. Fishing was only fun for him when Ernie was around. On countless dark nights they stood side by side in their waders, casting silently into the invisible ocean, waiting for that telltale tug on their lines. Mostly just releasing what they pulled in. At some point, never guided by a clock but by some internal timing, they reeled in their last cast and sat in Joe's truck, swigging lukewarm coffee from a Thermos and eating the sandwiches they'd bought at the market.

Joe wished Ernie was at home so that they could go out tonight. He felt his belly quicken with apprehension at the thought of Charlie Worth coming to dinner. He wished he had the comfort of a fishing date to think about. Some target to project his thoughts towards, some proof of a future.

Sometimes he and Ernie said very little to one another those nights. But when they needed to talk, they could, and Joe just wanted someone there he could talk to if he wanted. Vangie. He should talk to her. He didn't even know her number. What would he say, "Hey, call your kid off"? No.

This was his legacy. His secret. Not theirs. They had another one.

The F6F bobbed from side to side on the barge. The salvagers had forced the landing gear down, so she sat on her own supports, bolstered by props beneath her wings and nose. The single engine was black with corrosion, so that none of her identifying marks were clear. She had been a stranger plane to him, and he couldn't remember the numbers, only the feel of her in his hands. The smell of burning oil as her engine caught fire.

Sitting in the warm April sunlight, sheltered from the prevailing southwest breeze by the windbreak of pines behind him, Joe forced himself to conjure the spine-jarring belly landing on the hard water. From above, the gray-green ocean swells had seemed maternal, soft and round. He remembered pulling up slightly so that the tail would slice through the water first, the nose slapping down a moment later. He closed his eyes and saw himself hauling out the life raft and inflating the Mae West. It was dusk, nearly dark with a new bank of clouds shrouding the sun. Soon it would begin to rain, and the longest night of his life would commence. Joe folded his arms across his chest at the memory.

"Dad?"

"Mags. Hi. Just enjoying the sun." Joe patted the bench in invitation to join him. He was glad of the interruption, afraid of where his thoughts had been going. This was his here and now. Maggie. "Sit down for a minute."

"Can't. I've got a lasagna to put together, and I want to make homemade bread for tonight."

"Getting a little fancy, are we?"

"Dad." Maggie's voice was a throwback to earlier years when his observations were challenges to her adolescent autonomy.

Joe glanced sideways at his daughter, amazed as always to see what a lovely woman she had become. Tall, self-assured, stylish without being a slave to it, Maggie Green-without-the-Shofsky was his finest achievement. Surviving achievement.

"What's this Charlie guy like?"

"Very articulate, good sense of humor."

"Sounds like his mother."

"I don't know, Dad. You can be the judge of that tonight."

*And how will you judge me tonight? Will
you ever see me the same again?*

"See that plane down there?"

Maggie nodded, following the line of his
pointing finger.

"Well, there's something you should
know about."

Maggie placed one hand on her father's
shoulder and squeezed. "Dad, why don't
you tell us both at dinner tonight? If I don't
get home right now, we won't eat until midnight."

A reprieve. "Okay, it'll keep." *It's kept a
long time already.*

The sensation of Maggie lingered long
after she had left him alone on the park
bench. When she had asked to come
home, he'd been hesitant, loath to give up
his independence. He'd imagined being a
parent again, fretting about late hours and
bad company. Then he worried about her
disapproval at his own habits. The three
days a week she spent in Boston made a
nice compromise for both of them.

Now he couldn't imagine her leaving.
She would though, sooner or later. Some
new lover would come into her life and give

her what her old man couldn't. Of course, there was always the possibility he'd be the one to go first. With each year's passing, Joe saw his peer group fast diminishing or disappearing, like Judy, into the maw of old age.

The Hellcat rocked almost imperceptibly. A tiny flicker of light sparked from the sunlit water to a piece of metal somehow not corroded, catching his eye. Forty-nine years ago he'd taken that plane into the air. Climbed higher and higher, looking down on that peculiar Durante schnozz of land called Hawke's Cove and then across the vast expanse of open water beneath him. Forty-nine years ago he'd dropped out of the sky, into the water, and emerged Joe Green. His hands clenched reflexively at the memory of the stick between them. They ached, and he looked at them, surprised at the web of wrinkles that floated across the backs of his hands. Those hands had flown that plane, had milked countless cows, had held his children. Those old hands had been young when they touched the soft skin of Evangeline Worth's face.

Somewhere outside of Chicago there

was a marker at an empty grave. He imagined that it read simply: Spencer J. Buchanan 1915–1944. Died in Service to His Country. It would always be a lie.

Joe Green was born in 1944.

Twelve

Joe

I sit here on this park bench where I can see the hulk of the plane that brought me here. The midafternoon sun is warm on my neck, and for once I'm not cold. Over there I know that at least six people of my longtime acquaintance are running their errands on this Saturday afternoon. Going into stores I have patronized now for, what is it? Close to fifty years. In that little coffee shop my cronies share the afternoon paper and wonder what's keeping me. For ten years I was an elected selectman, working out of the only brick building in this town, the town hall with its clock imbedded above the front doors. A clock that stands still, that has always stood still. I sit here on this park bench, and my beautiful daughter is on her way to get the food she will feed to the son of the woman I have always loved.

Sometimes, when I let myself indulge in the solipsistic feast of memory, the overwhelming sensation is that of falling. All of my life, it seems, has been one fall after another. I fell into working for Sylvester Feeney. I fell into despair when Scott was killed. I fell from the sky. I fell in love. Some people plan their lives, or at least follow some outline. Not me. I simply fall.

Right now I feel as though I'm falling down a bottomless pit; there is no hope of knowing where I will land once Charlie Worth and Maggie Green make the inevitable connections. I should call them together and tell them how I came to be.

The ocean swells looked soft, welcoming, irresistible. It was my first flight since the accident. Accident. What a gracious word for a graceless event. It was my first flight after I shot down my own wingman in a moment of complete inattention. He shouldn't have been where he was. He shouldn't have crossed in front of me in the sun. He shouldn't have . . . but he was a kid, we used to say, still wet behind the ears. The war was old by that time, and the pilots they sent to us, in unending replacement, were nervous, untried. But I wasn't. I was the old man; gramps, they called me. Twenty-nine years old. Real old. I'm seventy-eight now, and I feel so less old than I did then. I was hardened, experienced and callous. I fired at the shape in front of me, my physical reactions so much more engaged than my cognitive. Act first, ask questions later.

I leveled out over the water of Hawke's Cove and did what I had been unwilling or unable to do the whole time I spent stateside recovering from my burns. I searched for my humanity. But I came up with the same thing. My initial reaction to my mistake was not regret, but anger. "Fuckin' idiot!" I screamed over the radio. Within seconds the Zero I had expected was behind me and I was hit. That's all I remembered as I flew over the open water beyond Hawke's Cove, tapping my oil gauge in growing concern that my pressure was down. Being angry.

I woke up in pain, and the physical pain was the only preoccupation I had. I didn't think of the kid or of my mistake until late one afternoon as I sat in the solarium of the hospital. My burns were nearly healed, relatively minor compared to so many of my fellow patients. My back was still tight with second-degree burns, but my hands were unbandaged and almost free of pain. At the end of the week I was due at Great Harbor for a few weeks of practice before heading back into action. As an experienced pilot, I was much too valuable to let sit at home for too long. It was April, but not like this year. Very rainy, cold. It was very warm in the solarium.

"Lieutenant Buchanan?" A man and a woman came towards me. He held a brown fedora in his hands, tense fingers clutching the brim until it curled. She wore a pale blue cloth coat, a tiny matching hat perched on a head of gray curls. They looked to be about my parents' ages, maybe their mid-fifties. They both wore the same expression of grief and high expectation. The man introduced himself, but I didn't catch his name. His voice was timorous, as if he had no air behind his words. The woman said nothing, but examined my face as if trying to memorize me.

It was too much of an effort for me to stand up, so I just offered my hand. They blinked hard at the sight of my scarred hands, the healed patches shiny against the unburned skin. He touched my hand gently, without gripping it. She made no move to touch me.

"You were with our son when he died."

I felt myself falling. "Your son?" I'd been with so many who had died. How was I to separate their son from all the others? What did they want of me?

"He was killed in the same mission you were wounded in."

Suddenly I realized which of the many boys they meant. The sense of falling spun into my gut until I folded my arms across my stomach and pressed against the nausea. I couldn't tell them anything.

"Will you tell us a little about how he died?" I realized they had no idea, no one had told them. For one brief, glorious, self-abrogating minute, I thought maybe I had been mistaken. Maybe I hadn't shot the boy down, maybe it was an illusion. As relieving as the thought was, I knew that it wasn't true. I had been through the enquiry, polite young military lawyers asking questions as I lay swaddled in gauze. I was absolved. So what did this pale, shaky couple want me to say?

"I'm so sorry for your loss."

"Was he brave?" The man spoke, his tremulous voice even lower than before.

I leaned towards him. "He died bravely."

"Thank you." This time the woman spoke, her voice strong, emphatic. "He was a good boy. He always treated his family well. We weren't happy that he chose flying. But he was headstrong and would do as he wanted." At this point a tear rolled down her soft, plump cheek.

"I'm so sorry." I couldn't look up at them, to make eye contact, knowing my culpability.

They left without another word, and I wondered what possible benefit seeing me could have been to them. I understand better now. Since Scott.

I took the Grumman F6F "Hellcat" out on that April morning to get some flight time in. I headed north then east, planning a leisurely circuit that would put Hawke's Cove beneath me. I could pick out the various headlands along the south shore. The little town looked like a Monopoly board laid out. The pastures were that first lush green of spring, outlined by rock wall fences. The woods showed up as a lighter green with new leaves coming, punctuated with dark pines. I remember admiring the view as I rose higher and higher, leveling off where the sun existed, glowing against the tops of the clouds, hidden from the groundlings below me.

When the mild Atlantic sun forced me to squint against it, I remembered the blinding Pacific sun. As I shaded my eyes and turned away from it, the April sun brought back the enormity of my sin. My sin was not so much the accident of killing the boy, but the fact I had not *regretted* it. I still could not think of his name. I had become so inured to death, to causing death, that I had turned into a monster. I had been corrupted by the war and the job they asked us to do. I was a Christian man, the son of an Episcopal priest, and lifetime choirboy. I made a point of attending the interdenoms as often as I could. I believed in Christ and forgiveness.

I started shaking up there in the April sky. Shaking with an ever-deepening fear that I had become so corrupted there was no hope. It hadn't occurred to me to ask for forgiveness, either from God or those parents, because I hadn't accepted my actions as sinful. If the Navy had exonerated me, it was inconsequential against the fact I had never even owned up to the sin.

My mind and my heart were racing, and at the same time I was paying attention to the gauges and dials, to the feel of the unfamiliar plane in my hands. What had I been thinking of when I shot him down? Adding to my score? Buchanan 39, Japs 0. My hands were beginning to sweat, and I could hear my own breath sounds.

The oil pressure dropped to zero, and I leaned forward to see the nose of the plane with its trail of black smoke. I laughed out loud. How perfect. God was in charge now. I would surely die with my sin on my heart.

I did all of the responsible things for a pilot in this position. Turned off the engine, radioed my location, attempted to glide towards those maternal-looking swells in the hope that I wouldn't explode into a million pieces on impact.

I did a pretty good job of it. The plane

floated long enough for me to get the raft out and inflate it and my vest. I was bleeding a little from where my head had hit the windscreen, but I wasn't even dizzy. I paddled a distance from the plane, dabbling her wingtips in the water like a child in a tub. Slowly she filled with water and disappeared beneath the waves.

The maternal waves were no longer comforting. The storm earlier in the week had blown out, but the waves still echoed its strength, and I had to keep paddling to prevent myself from being pulled out to sea. I could see land, a dark rim in the distance. It was already dusk, hastened on by the low clouds. I knew that within a few minutes no search planes would be able to spot me. A weak drizzle had begun, and I shivered. So, an instant death is too much to ask for, I thought. A fitting punishment. I pulled hard on the oars. As I pulled I prayed. "One more chance, please, God. One more chance to be human." The prayers became a litany against which I paddled until the pain in between my shoulders was like fire and the hope of survival was inconsequential.

I couldn't tell where I was. In the darkness all I knew was the rising and falling of the raft as I paddled. I couldn't tell if I was going in the same direction or changing with every wave. For all I knew I was going further and further out to sea. I couldn't fight the exhaustion anymore, and I know that I dozed even as I paddled. I suppose now it was the incoming tide that saved me. The sky had lightened imperceptibly, and the sound of waves breaking startled me out of my stupor. I made a nearly fatal mistake as I stood up to see if I could make out landfall. A wave caught the raft and flipped it over. I was tangled in its lines and forced underwater by the action of the wave. Thrashing, I found my knife and attempted to cut myself free of the lines. My frozen hand slipped, and I gashed the raft. As the air softened the buoyancy of the raft into a deadweight, I began to accept my death. Suddenly it was easier to die than to fight. Suddenly it seemed a better choice than to live knowing my guilt.

The human need to survive was stronger than my guilt. With numbed hands I found the line, and this time made a clean slice. My vest brought me back to the surface only to be battered by another wave. This one, though, brought me close enough to shore to feel sand beneath my feet.

I collapsed on the hard white sand of the beach. The name came to me then; the boy's name that had eluded me for weeks. Joe Green. As I slipped into a deep sleep, the memories became nightmarishly vivid. I remembered his face and his voice and the fact we called him Guiseppe Verdi as a joke. The last thing I said to him came to me as unconsciousness washed over me in a wave. "Hey, Guiseppe. I'll buy you a beer if you break your cherry on this run."

"You're on, Lieutenant. You owe me." He climbed into the cockpit with a jaunty wave made of sheer bravado. His voice, like his father's, was tremulous. The kid was scared. *You owe me.*

Spencer Buchanan fell into the sea. Joe Green climbed out.

The boom of someone's thumping bass startles me from my reverie. A black car with tinted windows races up Main Street, the stereo so loud it must deafen the car's occupants. The bench is getting a little hard on these old bones, but I am reluctant to leave. The Hellcat sits on her barge, her wings bobbing just like the last time I saw her. Signaling hello? Flights of fancy inappropriate to an old man.

I woke half a day later to brush the sand off my face and review my options. No. I never did. I simply knew I wasn't going back. I don't remember debating with myself about it. I crept off the sand and into the woods and found a new life. I found Vangie. The tumbledown barn with its stuck-open door seemed a perfect place to hide. I hid and I watched. There she was, standing on the back steps of her kitchen porch, staring off as if waiting for someone. I heard a sigh, a sound of contained unhappiness. Every night she'd do that. I'd watch from my hiding place and wonder who it was she sighed for. I stole food from her garbage pail. I stole her husband's clothes. And I'd listen to her melancholy, stealing her privacy.

During the day I kept to the woods, sometimes slipping into town to spend a dime for a loaf of day-old bread, buy my last packet of cigarettes. I had about fifteen dollars in my wallet when I crashed. I buried my uniform and the ID papers in my wallet, sticking my money in the pocket of John Worth's jeans. Some superstitious reluctance made me wrap my dogtags in my handkerchief and hide them in the barn, where I could retrieve them if I changed my mind about what I was doing. To prove who I really was, even if only to myself.

When Vangie offered me a job, I felt as though I had been reprieved. The Ruths sent me to her.

"You go see Mrs. Worth. She could do with some help. Don't let her tell you she doesn't." What wonderful old biddies they were, one brusque and the other mild.

"The barn needs work." Vangie seemed to be waiting for me. As if she'd planned on my coming.

Blanche DuBois said it best: "I have always depended on the kindness of strangers." Or something like that. It seems as though I have been dependent for most of my life on the silence of others.

Ernie Dubee looked the other way when I appeared in his town. He had every reason to be suspicious of a stranger in this small place, but something, some humanity in him, kept him from pursuing it with me. He's never asked. I've never told. We were the same, both kept here on this peninsula by the hand of God. The difference between us, he was born here and I was reborn.

I forged stolen baptismal records, giving the newborn Joe Green an identity; crying as I forged my father's signature, aware of my cruelty to my parents, equally certain I could not go back.

Sylvester Feeney must have had his doubts. Able-bodied young man shows up from nowhere. He never cared, Yankee enough to let a person keep his own counsel. As long as I gave him a day's work for a day's pay, Sylvester was happy. I liked him. I was sorry when he passed away, sitting on the seat of his old Harvester. I was sorrier that his kids sold the farm to developers.

Judy Frick certainly must have entertained notions about me. She'd fish around for answers. "Where you from, Joe Green?" asked out of the blue during a card game. "Right here, ma'am," I'd answer, right up until she went into the nursing home. "I belong right here."

The only indication I ever got from her that she knew, or at least thought she knew something about me, was the day she told me to marry Denise. "You can't spend your life waiting for someone who will not come back."

"I don't know what you mean."

"She's gone, Joe. And you'll never leave. You deserve a life, and Denise will make one with you. It might not be the one you wanted, but it's better than lonely bachelorhood."

If Judy Frick had divined my love for Vangie Worth, what else could she know? How did she know I'd never leave? Of course, Judy was wrong about making a life with Denise. I simply made her miserable. When Denise wanted to move off the peninsula she had lived on all of her life, I wouldn't. When she begged to take a vacation, wanted me to go with her to Boston, I couldn't. She had been so young when we got married; I'm sure she thought she would be able to cure Joe Green out of his never leaving Hawke's Cove. Judy was right about one thing. I never have set foot off this peninsula. I never left to see my son off to war. I never left to bring his body home. And I would not leave to save Denise's sanity. I suppose I didn't really think she was on the verge of a breakdown. In some ways I guess I never really knew her, not like a husband should know his wife. I thought she was just being selfish.

"Please, Joe. I can't stay here another minute with everyone touching me and weeping and telling me how sorry they are. And making me feel as if I did something wrong in letting Scott join up. As if I could have prevented him from going."

"Denise, they just want to help. They don't blame us. You have to understand that there are people in this town who feel as though he was their son too."

"Well, he wasn't, and they have no right to claim they know how I feel. No one does."

"Denise, that's not true." I should have touched her, pulled her close and rocked her, but I couldn't. Denise failed to recognize that Scott was my son too. The grief I felt had lodged itself firmly in my sternum and would not budge. I couldn't swallow.

Sometimes I couldn't speak for the pain. My wife crawled into bed and developed the first of her imaginary illnesses.

Judy. She was a great comfort to me. When Scott died, Judy bustled around us, organizing the food deliveries so that we didn't eat too much lasagna and not enough meat. She physically hauled Denise out of bed to dress for the funeral. She held me while I cried, as if I were her own.

"Joe, honey. I've been there before you. Go ahead, let it out. Never mind all that nonsense about men can't cry." She held me against her soft maternal breast, and I gave her the view of my grief I was unable to share with my wife.

"Do you want me to call Vangie?"

The sudden interjection of her name into the moment surprised me into pulling away from Judy. Oh, to have Vangie with me now, to share this horrible thing with her. To feel her comforting arms around me. The temptation was so great. In the end I shook my head; it would not have been fair to her to put her in that position. "I'll write to her, Judy. I don't want her to have to feel like she should be here."

"She'd come, you know."

I repeated, "Judy, I don't want to put her in an awkward position."

Judy nodded her head and handed me a tissue. "It needed asking."

I should abandon my pretense and go see Judy in Great Harbor before it's too late.

I sent a letter to Vangie filled with long sentences expressing my agony in a way I couldn't with anyone else. Deliberately, I sent it after the funeral so that she wouldn't have to struggle with deciding to come or not. It would have been more than I could have borne to have her within reach and not touch her. I don't mean sexually. That part of our passion was so unexplored that it seemed something I have imagined. No, I needed her loving touch, the touch she had given me when nursing my blisters, or coming up behind me as I milked. The touch we gave each other when words were useless.

Writing that letter, I knew that for all its single dimension of words on paper, I was far closer to Vangie Worth than I had ever been with my wife. Vangie knew everything about me. I kept nothing from her.

* * *

As I sit here on the park bench, I can see an osprey dangling above the harbor. What magnificent hawks they are. The Audubon people set up poles a few years back, trying to entice them away from using the telephone poles as nesting places. This one worked, and every year a pair settles in, adding to the debris from last year's nest. At that lecture I went to a couple of years ago the bird guy said that ospreys sometimes play house for a season before actually getting down to it. They build a nest and hunt and test each other's skills before making a commitment. A lot of folks in the parish hall chuckled, and the inevitable comparisions to human behavior came out. I look up at the osprey and imagine I know what his view is like.

The Hellcat bobs a little as the wind picks up. I'm getting a little cold. I usually am. I should drive the sad thoughts away and think only of the joys I have known because that little single-engine pile of rusted scrap metal crashed. I suppose I've reached the point in a man's life when he is forced to review the testimony and deliver a verdict. Was it a life well lived? Have

I done more good than harm? I wave to Craig Collison and chuckle to myself. Well, if I'm going to play *It's a Wonderful Life* I guess I should count Craig and his twin brother, Carl, fortunate I did fall into the sea. If I hadn't, well, maybe things would have turned out differently for them.

The very first time I saw Ernie Dubee was at the sand pit, him yelling at those two boys to take down the breeches buoy they'd rigged across the mouth of the thirty-foot-deep pit. I saw a man about my age, his authority tempered by a poorly hidden amusement. Even before I could speak, he saw me, and the amusement was gone and the authority more pronounced in the way he stood, his hands on his hips, the right hand just in front of the holstered weapon at his side.

"Mornin'," he said, and he might as well have said, "And who the hell are you?" In those days Ernie knew every soul occupying this peninsula.

"Hi." I came closer to him, my eyes wide open in what I hoped was friendly innocence. "I can see the attraction of this place for a boy."

"Suppose so."

"Joe Green." I gave him my name before he could ask. "I'm camping."

"This is town property."

"I'm not a vagrant, Chief." I was close enough now to read his badge. "I'm planning on staying here."

"What do you do?"

The most believable answer would have been, "I'm a Navy pilot, just discharged." But I didn't dare claim anything that might be fact checked. So I answered, "Between jobs right now. But I'm a good carpenter." I looked over to where the boys had nailed a turnbuckle to a tree. "I could take that down for you."

"Highway department'll take care of it."

I felt the rebuff but took no offense. "I'll be going, then."

"Green."

"Yes, sir." My formality quite reflexive.

"Go see Ruth Banks. Sometimes they need day labor."

"Thanks."

Less than a month later Ernie asked me to help him locate the boys, missing for half a day. I was nervous and wished Vangie hadn't been so quick to offer my services. I half knew he was using the opportunity to figure me out. We stopped by the sand pit first. Thank God. It was the sight of the broken wire snaking against the side of the pit and Pal's agitated whuffing in the backseat that alerted me.

"Pal, knock it off." Ernie climbed out of the police car and motioned to the dog to stay put.

"Chief, I think he senses something."

"Joe, he's no police dog. He thinks I'll take him for a walk."

"Ernie. Let him out."

With ill-concealed skepticism, Ernie ordered the dog out of the patrol car. In a flash the half-hound mongrel was down in the pit and snuffling along the newly exposed dirt, a darker orange against the yellow sand. I ran for a shovel in the highway department building, and Ernie ran towards the site of the landslide.

When I think back, the thing I remember best is Ernie and his big grin looking at me over the tops of the boys' heads, the boys squirming and coughing, but otherwise safe.

After delivering the boys home to their mother, yet another woman holding home together alone, Ernie took me to Linda's.

He eased himself down on the stool next to me and handed me a menu. "This is my treat. You earned your lunch."

"Look, don't make this bigger than it was. Besides, Pal's the one who deserves a treat."

Ernie folded the menu and stuck it back in the metal holder. He rubbed his knuckles along the side of his cheek, then across his lips. "Joe, I have to apologize. I really didn't think the boys were in any trouble. I brought you along in a not-so-subtle attempt to find out who you are." He didn't look at me when he admitted this, and his voice was discrete in the crowded coffee shop.

"I know." I folded my menu and replaced it. "So, what do you want to know?"

"I know enough."

I suppose I'll tell him now. Everyone else will know, and it's not fair my best friend hears it from someone else. It's inevitable that Charlie Worth will put these rather obvious pieces together.

Do I regret doing it? Deserting? That's the word, the one I avoid even to myself. *Desert.* On Veterans Day when we bow our heads to honor the brave lost, do I want to say, "Hey, I was there too!"? Except that I effectively removed myself from the ranks of the brave. No. A long time ago I stopped thinking about it. Except on that one day a year, when it is forced on me. When I was Scott's scoutmaster and we stood at attention during the sounding of taps in the little cemetery. That was hard. Long ago I justified my action to myself. I did my service. Over and over until I lost my humanity.

Oh, I do sometimes wonder what might have been had I gone back. If I had survived another tour. I once toyed with the idea of the priesthood, following in a two-generational tradition. My experience, though, had divorced me from ever feeling I could follow that path honestly. My liberal arts degree might have led me to teaching. Maybe I would have become a journalist like Charlie.

Well, no sense in going over what might have been. I was a milkman and every day gave absolution over broken bottles and late payments. I read a life's story into one bottle of milk, then two, then four, then back to one, all in twenty years of delivery.

Yeah, sometimes I wish I had my freedom. More so now than when I was young. I'd like to go with Ernie to Florida. Except that I've played this role of agoraphobic for so long I'm not certain I can leave. Like in a fairy tale, I can't break the enchantment I brought on myself.

But, if I did leave, I would go to Vangie.

I intended to go with Scott to the bus station. I went to the filling station and gassed up the car, checked the oil and the tire pressure. I ran a wet rag around the dusty interior and toyed with the idea of washing it. Scott always took care of the car, from the time he could earn a couple of bucks doing it for me. I see him now, all shaggy fair hair, dirty T-shirt hanging out over tattered bell-bottoms. In my mind's eye his sister comes from somewhere to my right, calling out in sibling mockery, "Can't get me!" Scott snaps the hose towards her, and she hops out of range only to come back for more. She adores her older brother. It is plain on her freckled face. She resembles me. I think Scott is his mother's child.

When Scott was born, I thought that I'd been forgiven. He looked at me with those muddy unfocused eyes and I was sure that I saw the face of a benevolent and forgiving God. Why, maybe he was the reason I'd made the decision I had. Maybe I had been intended all along to be this child's father. Oh, what a vain, ridiculous man I was.

If he was the reason I had deserted, he was also the real reason I married his mother. Denise. She was very pretty, very young, and I was susceptible.

"I don't mind, Joe. I want to love you." She kissed me hard, her tongue playing lightly over mine, her hand on mine to take it to her breast. The oldest trick in the book.

I don't blame her. I mean, for leaving me, or trapping me. The daughter of a fisherman and his common-law wife, she looked at me as security and stability. And maybe I looked at her the same way. Besides, she loved Hawke's Cove, and I never expected that she would want to leave.

After Denise told me she was pregnant and Judy told me to marry her, I began to tell myself that what had happened between Vangie and me was the result of being young, emotionally needy, and that both of us were sexually deprived. I tried hard to diminish in my heart what had happened. It would have worked. Time would have covered up the memory eventually, the distractions of everyday life soon do. Except that we wrote to one another, keeping what we had together alive through our words. We wouldn't let it go.

Denise couldn't compete. And she knew it.

After Scott was born, I wanted immediately to have another child. I wanted to repeat this unclouded happiness as soon as possible. Denise would have none of it. In her view, the whole experience had been horrifying. Heartburn and swollen legs, back labor and a long birth, were not worth it.

"Honey, not before you're ready, I promise." I held Scott in my arms and sang him the cradle songs I remembered hearing my mother sing to my little sisters. "Rock-a-bye baby, rock-a-bye." Oh, hush.

Maggie, product of accident, of faulty precautions, is making dinner for Vangie's son. The guys are coming out of Linda's. I should have been in there with them instead of dredging up the past like that old plane was dredged up. Both stink.

Scott washed the car before he left. Maggie, no longer freckled, brought him lemonade. At some point, just after he'd enlisted, he'd had all his fair curls cut off. He looked like a stranger. He didn't threaten his sister with a dousing, and for the first time I felt the conviction that he was to be my ultimate sacrifice. I had stolen a life and grown complacent. For years now I had forgotten who I was and how I had come to Hawke's Cove. I had a family, a job, and a community.

Tomorrow we would take Scott over the bridge to Great Harbor and put him on a bus. I would put him on a bus to his future. This immoral war would finish the job the other one began.

I leaned against the oak tree and gave over to this feeling of presentiment. Scott hosed off the soap from the old car and drank lemonade with the other hand. I had tried to talk him out of enlisting. His number was high enough he might never have been called. He was doing well at the state college; he didn't need to enlist.

"Dad, it's my decision. Just because you sat out your war . . ." He pulled himself back. When I think of this conversation, I only hear his voice. I could not look at him. I leaned against the oak tree. Once again, I was falling out of the sky.

We were a silent group, the four of us driving to Great Harbor. In some acknowledgment of his manhood, Scott sat in the front, his mother in back beside an uncharacteristically quiet Maggie. Even the sighting of a great blue heron over the marsh went uncommented on.

I had awakened with my parents on my mind. I remembered them taking me to the train station. My father stiff in his clerical collar, my mother dabbing gently at the already reddened skin of her eyes. The only comment my father had made was an offer to see about conscientious-objector status. I remember looking at him with what might have been contempt if I hadn't understood so well his motives. War was about death, but it was also, in that war, about saving humanity. My father allowed himself one selfish hope, and that only in passing.

"Thanks, Dad, but what I need to do is

take part and get this thing over with sooner." Stock patriotic reply, which came so easily to my lips.

This morning as I drove my son to the bus, I imagined what my life would have been like had I said, "Yeah, help me out, Dad."

As I drove around the bend in the road and straightened the car towards the causeway and the bridge, I felt the unrelenting weight of choice. The emotional weight became physical, and as the bridge to Great Harbor drew closer, I began to panic.

March 21, 1967

Dearest Vangie,

I could not take him across. I stopped the car and got out. Scott followed me, and Denise started raging from the backseat. "I can't go, son. I can't . . ." There was absolutely nothing I could say that would explain my behavior. I let them think it was the agoraphobia. I let them think I gave in to an old fear. My children have accepted that I don't leave Hawke's Cove. They have never asked why. Scott didn't ask me now, even as I abandoned him to his fate. I couldn't tell them that it was fear of being recognized. Fear that some cop would stop me and discover I have no driver's license. I have no identification. Nothing that tells people who I am. That I don't exist. Vangie, it really wasn't that. Not anymore. What I couldn't tell them was my deep con-viction that Scott was my sacrifice for living so well. I was Abraham and he was Isaac.

There, on the side of the road, Scott let me hug him close. "I'll be fine, Dad. I'll call. You just keep the kid out of my room."

He got into the driver's seat. I walked over to the window and took the last look of my son's face I would ever see. "I love you, Scott. I'm proud of you."

I don't know if I really said that. I sit here now and think that maybe if I had gone across, he would still be alive.

* * *

I sit here. An old man on a green park bench looking out over his past. I don't in-

dulge all that often. For a long time after I
ran away from Vangie's barn and down the
stone wall to the woods, I rehearsed each
tender memory so that I wouldn't forget. I
fairly wallowed in memories so recent they
hadn't yet hardened in my mind.

But life is relentless, and day-to-day living
a natural buffer between memory and reality.
Memories have crystalized, and new memories have joined them. Except for those of
my children, none have ever been so dear
to remember as those that evoke Vangie.

I don't know what I would have done if
she'd refused to write. If she had, rightfully
and understandably, said no. Leave me
alone.

August 30, 1967

Dearest Joe,

　　*How I long to hold you and take
some of your grief to myself. Just like
you did for me. Once I wondered if it
was better—or less awful—to lose a
child at birth or to war. Now I know. I
thank God every day Charlie is too
young for this evil war. Every day I see
the war protestors, hairy youth with*

placards and slogans, peace signs drawn on their cheeks and embroidered on their jeans. I flash them the peace sign, and they hand me flowers. Most of them are students, some even mine. Bright, articulate, and righteous. I don't think you should explain Scott's desire to sign up as anything to do with your own claim that you were 4-F. He was never ashamed of you. Scott simply chose a different path than student deferment and peace rallies. You have to be proud of him. Of his choice.

The sun is nearly down, and I'm cold now. But I sit here still, reluctant to leave my memories and enter the real world. I think that I'm glad Maggie ignored my wishes and invited this young man home. Vangie's son.

Thirteen
Charlie

Charlie found the nursing home in Great Harbor without any difficulty except that he passed the entrance twice, not believing that the imposing white mansion was actually a nursing home. The Seamen's Home had been the brainstorm of a developer who had foreseen the aging of America. Built in 1840 as a marine hospital, it had survived incarnations as a private school, a hotel, and, briefly, a private residence. Now the place had been turned back towards its original purpose, with its original name, offering assisted living on the first floor. The second and third floors represented increased degrees of skilled nursing, culminating in hospice care on the fourth floor.

As one's soul grew closer to heaven, one's physical reality got closer as well, as the receptionist told Charlie.

On the way Charlie had entertained himself with thoughts of Maggie, partly to close off the dread he always felt in going to a nursing home and partly because she was pleasant to think about. He liked her, liked her style and her wit. Liked the fact she laughed at his jokes without seeming to force herself. Especially, Charlie liked that they had a common bond already; after all, their parents knew each other, at least they did once. Charlie reprimanded himself. One lunch was hardly a fair sample.

When Charlie finally accepted that the big white house was in fact his destination, he was involuntarily drawn into making comparisons with his father's nursing home. A four-story brick building with the institutional atmosphere of a nineteenth-century mental hospital, St. Elizabeth's was clean and the care adequate, but the odor of depression filled the halls. The aides in their pathetically cheerful flowered uniforms made little effort to lighten the air. Mostly they worked their shifts and, in his view, did as little as possible beyond their basic job descriptions. Charlie always felt as if the overheated air weighed on him, slowing his own steps as he walked down the hallway. Aligned along that hallway, residents slumped in wheelchairs or geri-chairs, their white socks peeking out from under inadequate blankets. One always reached out to touch him as he walked by; several others moaned rhythmically, or cried out at the visions in their minds. If Dante had imagined a nursing home, St. Elizabeth's would have been it.

By contrast, this place was sweet-smell-ing; an open window overlooking Great Harbor's eponymous port let in the April afternoon. The receptionist, happily helpful, directed Charlie to Judy Frick's room.

Judy had been a resident in the assisted living unit since shortly after Ted died. Her only regret was having to live out the rest of her life in Great Harbor, but the water view from her patio was something she had never had before and great compen-sation to her during the warm months. A couple of heart attacks had slowed only her body down, not her spirit, and she still doled out advice and opinion to her visitors.

"Mrs. Frick?"

"Charlie Worth. Come in!"

Charlie bent down and kissed the papery cheek, letting her hold his hand as if he were her child. "You remember me, then?"

"Charlie, I admit you've grown up a little since I saw you last, but you haven't changed. You still look like your father."

The Fricks had come to Boston every couple of years, although a little less frequently in the last decade. He hadn't seen them the last time they'd come, when Ted had been to Brigham and Women's for a hip operation and Judy had stayed with his parents. This was before his father's first stroke. Did he really look like his father?

"Besides, my boy, I may be ninety-two, but I haven't lost my marbles yet."

Then why had his mother made that gesture, leading him to think maybe Judy wouldn't be of any help? Inexplicable.

"Your mother told me you might come by. Chasing some mystery."

"I never told her I was . . ." Charlie let the thought die along with a flicker of annoyance. "So she told you I'm trying to locate the pilot of the Hellcat."

"She said you were assigned a wild-goose chase."

Charlie smiled and shook his head. "Well, nonetheless, may I ask you a few questions?"

"Shoot."

"How easy would it have been for a man to show up in Hawke's Cove and fit in?"

"Easy enough."

"I thought New Englanders were supposed to be crusty."

"You're a New Englander. Except that you're a reporter. We keep to ourselves, right? I see the skepticism in your eyes, thinking, 'Not really.' We're nosy. Well, we fuss over everyone's problems if they can't keep their problems to themselves. I mean, a man works hard, causes no one any trouble, keeps his own counsel, no one faults him for it. We might wonder, but we don't ask. That's how it could be done. We don't ask."

"So you think that this guy actually did come ashore and stay."

"The ultimate wash ashore. Ha. No. I don't." Judy got up and fussed a bit with her African violet. "If such a thing happened, I'm sure that he would have kept going." She pinched three dead leaves from the plant.

"According to the Navy report, there was a brief investigation following the pilot's disappearance because a young nurse claimed to have seen him. In Hawke's Cove. The report was inconclusive, but the pilot, Spencer Buchanan, was deemed AWOL. Pretty serious offense for wartime."

"Spencer Buchanan." Judy dropped the dead leaves into the wastebasket. "Nice name. Sounds Irish."

"But doesn't ring a bell."

"Charlie, if you were a deserter, would you use your real name?"

"I'd certainly pick something easy to remember." Charlie watched Judy's lips as they compressed. "Something like John Smith or, maybe, Joe Green."

Judy straightened up and faced Charlie. "Would you like some tea? They'll bring me a pot if I ask for it."

"I have a photo; would you look at it?"

Judy took the eight-by-eleven black-and-white copy of the missing pilot, a studio portrait of an unsmiling young man, in full dress uniform to the carefully placed hat on his head. Judy pushed her plastic-framed glasses with their stylish bent bows back up her nose and held the picture out, then towards the light coming from the patio doors. "How old-fashioned he looks. How young."

"Do you recognize him?"

"No."

Fourteen

Judy

Anyone with eyes in his head could see that they were in love. The way they looked at each other, all moony-eyed. Not that I'm sayin' they did anything wrong. No. Just that they were both young, healthy, and desperately alone.

I'm also not sayin' that I know for sure that Joe Green is the AWOL pilot. But he did just sort of show up, never spoke of his war experience, and, except for those scars on his back, was pretty fit. Vangie showed up with scars too. It took me a long time to figure her out, but I knew that there was something eatin' at her.

Anyway, I'll never forget the day we met. Ted'd been doin' work up to Bailey's Farm for a few weeks, so I knew she was there. Remember her as a skinny kid too. She and her cousins. Anyway, we back into each other at the magazine rack in the Rexall. Funny how it is. If we hadn't literally bumped into each other, we might never have become friends. Course, Vangie was, well, not young enough to be my daughter, but pretty much in need of mothering. I was forty-five then. Well into middle age. Course nowadays they've pushed middle age up some. *I'm* still middle-aged according to these baby boomers unwilling to grow up.

But then, my girls were still teenagers, boy crazy and all the time fussing with their hair, moanin' they didn't have the right shoes or the proper sweaters. They were at the age of not wanting a mother around. We'd lost Teddy early in the war. He would have been twenty-three in 1944. Lord God, he'd be seventy-two now if he'd a lived. But, by the time I met Vangie, he'd been gone for three years and I could pay attention to her worries because my own had played out. I had arrived on the shores of acceptance. Clearly, Vangie Worth was still drowning. I couldn't figure her out. She acted as if she'd lost her husband, grievin' before the fact.

Course, eventually it all came out. What she really grieved for.

When Joe Green appeared . . . yeah, that's exactly what he did, appeared . . . everyone kinda took to him. Quiet, polite without being smarmy about it. I think he appealed to every woman who had a son gone. Even the Ruths, those old childless biddies took a shine to him, and suspicious old Ernie Dubee gave him the benefit of the doubt.

Oh, yeah. Joe and Vangie, it was as plain as the nose on your face that they were in love. And fightin' it! We'd get together, me and Ted, Ernie, Vangie and Joe, and play cards. We all got a little silly sometimes, but those two. My goodness, they'd trade barbs across the table. She'd needle him about the mess he'd make comin' in from the cows; he'd fire back with complaints about her cookin'. They'd laugh as if the real meaning behind their words was a private code.

When she finally broke her silence about her dead baby, Joe nursed her like she was sick. Gave her too much whiskey and put her to bed. Sat there all day, he told me, just watching to make sure she was breathing. I know he didn't realize just how much he was telling me. That he was watching her out of love. She scared him. Her grief scared him.

"Judy, you've got to come talk with her. I don't know what to do. I'm so afraid she'll think that she needs to go back . . ." Joe finally left a sleeping Vangie to find me. When I saw his face, I thought that someone had died. "What should I do?"

"Honey, I'll come out tomorrow and talk with her. You go back and make sure she's okay." I called after him, "Joe. She'll be fine. She's been holding this back and poisoning herself with it. Get her to talk."

"I will."

I was never so surprised than when he comes back up my porch steps and puts his arms around me and gives me this big thank you hug. "She'll be fine, Joe. Now go." I was a little embarrassed.

I always felt a little guilty, later, I mean, when my initial reaction to John's disappearance was *at least she has Joe.* I didn't know John then, and it seemed natural that Vangie would end up with Joe. Funny how it is, you just link people. Abbott and Costello, Tracy and Hepburn. Joe and Vangie. It seems to me that you go against nature when you try to link up the wrong people. Like I did to Joe and Denise. Yes. I take full responsibility. Course, she's the one who got pregnant. And he's the fool who fell for it.

In my own defense I still believe that he needed to settle down and find a home. He couldn't keep living in Syl Feeney's spare room. Denise was a Cover. Born and bred, even if it was a little to the wrong side of the blanket. Such a snob she turned out to be. Think her . . . you know what . . . didn't smell.

Joe came to me that day too. The day Denise sprang her delicate condition on him. Myself, I was a little doubtful, seen ten-month babies as well as eight-month. Still, he never said he loved her. But I thought, well, this is God's hand. Vangie's home and settled and living the life she chose long before Joe Green arrived. She'll never come back, and he ain't leavin'. Most men would've left Hawke's Cove by this time. The postwar boom was in full swing, jobs everywhere, a lot more interesting and better paid ones than as Syl Feeney's milkman. He wasn't going to, though. I knew it even if Denise didn't.

Well, water under the bridge.

So now Vangie's son is in town and asking questions. Nice young man, though he's not so young as they were then. Joe's daughter, Maggie, comes and sees me now and again. Aunt Judy, she calls me. Could be my granddaughter. Smart girl. A nurse.

I wonder if Joe is the pilot. We talked a little bit about war when Scott joined up. Joe was beside himself. That would have been the time to tell me if he'd ever been in active duty. Said not a word about himself, only fretted about the boy.

"It's hard to send one's son to a war which is so . . ." Joe raised his hands in a half shrug. ". . . wrong. Misguided, inexplicable? Maybe if I could see the sense in it, the valor, I would understand his rationale. But, Judy, it's not even as if he believes the government is right and his peer group is wrong. He seems just to like the idea of being a Marine."

"Then, be proud of him."

" 'The Few, the Proud,' etc. What bullshit. Sorry." Joe pulled at his beard, which he'd let grow a little longer with the styles in those days. His hair was still mostly dark brown, although the gray was more obvious, it seemed to me, as soon as Scott signed up.

In our war, the whole population got into being at war. We did without; we saved bacon grease. We accepted our war-imposed limitations with grace and patriotism. The Vietnam War inspired none of that. It never involved the country; that was their mistake. The government waged an undeclared war and let the populace go pound tar. No wonder the kids protested. Joe said that. He thought a lot about it. Then Scott was killed and I thought Joe Green needed Vangie.

He needed her because they had this thing between them that I knew hadn't died because of time and distance. Joe admitted to me he heard from her; she told me they wrote. I told them both news about the other because I never lost touch. Vangie'd be hungry for news of Joe. But she wouldn't look at pictures. Said she wanted to remember him exactly as he was.

He said the same thing.

When I told Vangie that Joe was getting married, I saw her go pale. Then she smiled and agreed with me it was the best thing for him. She was pregnant then—with Julie, I think. "He'll be a wonderful husband." That's what she said, but she couldn't hide the hard swallow she took before she said it.

What do people want? Of course she couldn't've abandoned John Worth. It wasn't that she didn't love him. He was her husband, and in those days that was that. And, of course, Joe was too good a man to ask her to.

There were times, though, over the years when I think she might have done it. Left John. He wasn't easy. No, he wasn't a wife beater or a cheat. Just difficult. She told me. She always claimed being a POW had hurt him in ways that couldn't be explained. Wouldn't shut the bedroom door except when they had relations. All her adult life Vangie's had a light on in the hallway. She told me they left it on long after the kids had grown and gone. Still uses it, even though John's in the home. Well, that wasn't what made him difficult, wanting a night-light like a child. She called it his darkness. Wouldn't talk; kids made him nervous. Wouldn't ever come to Hawke's Cove. That, probably more than anything, bothered her. Not that I think she'd have ever really come. She just wanted to know she could.

John Worth really hated it. The Cove. The farmhouse. Vangie explained that he wanted to start his own firm, they needed the cash. But, I think he had some sixth sense about the place and getting rid of it exorcised whatever demon it held for him.

I think that was the hardest news I ever brought Joe. "Vangie's selling the farm." I was going to suggest he buy it, but the look on Joe's face stopped me.

"Sell Bailey's? That can't be her idea."

"John's starting his own business."

"I see." Joe sucked in a lungful of air and let it hiss out slowly, a pressure cooker. "Jesus." Without another word he got up from my porch rocker and walked home. I didn't see him for a long time after that. Joe had his dark side too. But he kept it pretty well hidden. Denise got pregnant with Maggie not long afterwards. I half believed that some secretly held hope had been demolished and Maggie was his second attempt at making a life with Denise.

Denise was well on her way to becoming a hypochondriac by this time. Every time I saw her, she listed her aches and pains like an old woman. I think Joe Green supported Dr. Richardson single-handed with Denise's complaints. Trouble was she was a victim of her own designs. How could she expect a man in love with another woman to love her? It certainly wouldn't be kindled with whining.

Oh, yes. Denise knew about Vangie. Oh, nothing concrete, nothing she could get alimony with. Yet. Eventually. She just knew, as a woman does, that his heart was not hers. She saw his eyes light up when I gave him some news. I saw her jaw clench.

"Judy, can you do me a favor?" Joe always had time for a cup of coffee, pausing on his route to keep me company.

"Sure, what?" I don't know what I expected, probably to baby-sit.

"I think it's best if you don't mention Vangie in front of Denise."

I'll say this for him, he was sensitive, kind. He might have told her, "Mind your business, woman." But he wasn't the type. He chose instead to work harder to keep Denise unawares. Being a man, he thought that if she didn't hear about Vangie, she'd forget about her. Ha.

Fifteen

Charlie

"Mom?"

"Charlie, hello. How's your project going?" Charlie could hear the water from the kitchen sink running. "Did you see Judy?"

"Yes. Yes I did."

"How is she?"

"Pretty good, actually. She's a little frail, but her mind's clear." Charlie thought he heard a little "humph" over the staticky connection. He stood very still on the porch of the Seaview Bed and Breakfast and hushed the hum in his cell phone. "She sends her love."

Leaving the Seamen's Home, Charlie thought about asking his mother if she maybe wanted to move Dad here. He played with the idea a little, balancing the pros and cons as he always did with any question. Pro: good food, nice surroundings, odorless, lovely view. Con: no one lived here. How would Mom come every day? The cons evolved into a daydream, and before he could govern his imagination, Charlie had Vangie uprooted from her home of fifty years and ensconced in Hawke's Cove, where he would be a good son and visit her every weekend. Charlie unabashedly allowed himself to imagine Maggie as a prominent feature in his daydream. He liked her, this athletic, rather matter-of-fact woman. It had been a long time since he'd met anyone who interested him beyond one shared meal. Not that he was a snob or fussy. Too much effort had to go into peeling away the layers of someone else to get to the substance, too much effort had to go into protecting one's own layers to make casual commitment rewarding. Only twice had he liked a woman enough to let her get past his protective bonhomie. The first time was when he was a student at BU, but graduation had sent them in opposite directions and the relationship had not survived distance. The second time, only two years ago, had ended when she balked at a deeper commitment. He'd been hurt and now worked hard at resisting the urge to go through the effort ever again.

Until today. Maggie Green had chipped a little at his resistance.

As he settled his car into his assigned parking spot behind the B and B, Charlie pulled his thoughts back into line.

They reared up again as he spoke to his mother. "Mom, how come you never brought us here?"

There was no immediate answer. Then, "I wanted to, Charlie. Very much. But I couldn't." Charlie's phone was suddenly perfectly clear, and the note of old pain carried over the airwaves like a descant.

"Why not?"

"Don't be a nudge." The pain was replaced by annoyance. Subject dead.

"I met a fan of yours."

"Of mine? Who?"

"Maggie Green." When she didn't say anything, Charlie added, "Joe Green's daughter."

"I know whose daughter she is. I didn't know she was a fan."

"Has all of your poetry books and still keeps the poem you wrote for her over her bed."

"Is she living in Hawke's Cove now?"

"Part-time. With her dad. I'm having dinner with them tonight."

"With Joe?"

"Are you all right, Mom? You sound funny." Charlie moved away from the porch post, and the hum distorted what she said next. He asked her to repeat it.

"Okay, Mom. No problem." He filed her request in his mind and then broached the subject he'd intended to discuss all along. "I showed Judy the photo of the missing pilot, Spencer Buchanan."

"Did she know him?"

"She said no, but I think she was lying. She said something else which would indicate she did recognize him. 'How young he looks.' "

The hum increased, but Charlie thought he heard his mother chuckle.

"Mom. I've got nothing concrete, but I've got a pretty good hunch Joe Green is the guy. Am I right?"

"How would I know?"

"Jesus. Is the entire older generation in on this masquerade?"

"Mind your mouth."

"Mom. Steve West says the photo looks like his son, Scott."

"What does Maggie say?"

"I haven't shown it to her yet. I'm bringing it tonight."

There was a long silence, and Charlie wondered if his phone had quit. "Mom?"

"Please don't."

"So, I'm right, aren't I?"

He could see her in his mind's eye, one hand over her mouth, the other gripping the receiver, maybe standing there with her eyes closed against the decision to tell him or not.

"Charlie. Let it rest. Let us all rest with our secrets. What good, except for a five-paragraph story, is this thing to you?"

Charlie sighed and couldn't answer.

Sixteen

Vangie

April 18, 1993

Dearest Joe,

By the time you get this letter you will have met Charlie. I'm taking the coward's path here, not having called to warn you. Letting nature take its course, as it were. I thought about it, about calling. I called directory assistance and got your number. Wrote it right here in my old address book, listing it as casually as any other. When I go through my book, I can see stages of life listed there. The pediatrician, a dentist long since retired, dormitory phones, and the kids' ever-

*changing and ever-increasing tele-
phone numbers. Despite the cruel at-
trition of age and death, I have never
erased anyone. Looking for my cousin
Fran's number in California, I see the
Sunderlands' old three-digit written
there in faded fountain pen. Remember how we used to have to ask for
a number: "Six-oh-three, Sally." No
secrets in a town controlled by an operator.*

*I am writing this before the events
that effect us will occur, so feel a little
presumptuous, or maybe more like
someone staring hard into the future.
I have spent the last few days looking
hard into the past. I have read the
chronicle of our relationship, my diary
and your letters. Ebb and flow. We
have felt both a rising and a falling of
our need for one another, like the
ocean tides. The early letters were still
passionate, powerfully felt, driven by
a mutual need to preserve the new—
forbidden—love. As time went on our
love solidified into trust. Whatever
happened, whatever we did, we had
each other. Never absent in thought*

and heart. *Eventually, just as if we had lived our lives together, we achieved that quiet friendship of complete understanding. But, I have always missed your touch.*

So now I sit here, staring out at the empty bird feeder in the backyard and watching disappointed jaybirds, thinking of what you will tell Charlie and Maggie. I think you will tell them the truth. And, by telling them your truth, you will tell them mine. I guarantee you, the fact of our relationship will far outweigh anything you might tell them about how you became Joe Green. Parents aren't supposed to have been young and known passion. However, Charlie has fumbled enough through his amatory life to eventually become sympathetic. I think. It will be easier, I hope, for Maggie to understand you.

Joe, the one thing I have never told you is that once I very nearly came to you. I enclose here that letter, the one I wrote but never sent because for a long time after the event, I wasn't reconciled to its conclusion. I sent another one instead, I remember it being very chatty and bland. Your next letter after it asked what was wrong. I had to let a whole month go by before I could answer that letter. By that time I had regained my equi- librium and my grip on the life we both agreed to live. The only reason I send it to you now is because I would hide nothing from you.

And I might yet come.

July 17, 1968

Dearest Joe,

I nearly came to you today. I got as far as the bridge and I stopped. All I had to do was cross that single- lane wooden bridge to change our lives irrevocably. For a few hours I imagined that I didn't care about any- thing but joining my life with yours. Do you realize that not once in all these years have we ever discussed changing our minds?

How do I tell you this story without showing myself the impulsive, angry, unpleasant woman I am in midlife? The one benefit of an epistolary relationship like ours is that we get to self-edit, allowing only the parts we want revealed to show. I write that and know that isn't true. I know we have been successful in showing our warts to each other. And loving each other despite them. Otherwise we couldn't depend on the truth of our letters.

Throughout all these years I have believed you to be out there for me, a lifeline should I need one. It has been implied any number of ways in your letters. I very nearly took hold of that lifeline today and hauled myself ashore.

Where you and I have always been circumspect is in our portrayal of our spouses. You read in "Dear Abby" all about men who tell their lovers how bad their wives are, and vice versa. Justifying an infidelity. You and I have never fallen into that trap, though we both suffer from contentious marriages. Clever, we lay hints as groundwork. I know you are unhappy with

Denise. There, I've said it. Your unhappiness shows in those tightly con-
structed sentences that leave her out
of your life.

John and I are often at odds: he is
critical; I am stubborn. We argue
mostly about the children, his hours,
my housekeeping. My hours. Minor,
petty, adult gripiness. We are seldom
cruel, often silent. What touches off a
skirmish from an innocuous state-
ment? Today he simply complained
he didn't have an ironed shirt. I was
in the middle of a stanza. He often
does that, makes a comment on
something undone while I'm stealing
a little time to write.

In my anger I snatched the shirt in
his hands and in so doing knocked
my jar full of sea glass onto the floor.
It smashed, and bits of green and
white glass skittered in every direction. Pieces you had helped me to
collect. Rare blue and, rarer still, rose-
colored glass flew under the desk and
into the carpet and across the room.
The lovely rounded edges of glass
worn frosty by the sea mingled with

the shards of clear, ordinary glass from the jar. I looked down and wondered how I would ever separate them.

John and I looked at each other, and it seemed as though if one word was spoken, too many would be said. I grabbed my keys and purse and walked out of my study and out of the house. I hurried, desperate not to hear his voice calling me back. Desperate to leave before Charlie woke up, before Julie dropped in or Amanda called, drawing me back into my role as mother and wife. I drove away from my life, certain I meant to stay away. When I pointed the car northeast, I knew that I was going to you.

I tried to think only of our past, of those months on Bailey's Farm when you and I danced around our feelings, pretending to ourselves that we felt only friendship. I wanted to be angry enough at John to justify this desertion. My desertion. Instead I grew angry at you.

You never let me make the choice, Joe. You made it for me, and I resent it.

But, we both know it was the right choice. By the time I got to the bridge, I knew that I couldn't cross it.

I have never hated my life enough to change course. Even during the bad times, I have kept true to that decision. As have you. Neither of us has crossed the border.

Sometimes life is one shattered illusion after another, and it is the illusion of ourselves that is the most fragile. As long as we stay apart, we can depend on the purity of our illusions. I will never pick up your dirty laundry; you will never see my sagging breasts. Our relationship is immune to the mundane realities of a physical presence. We have not grown old and crabby nor has the precious fact of our love been lost in the frets and annoyances of life lived together. We can hold it like a jewel, our ordinary lives a foil around it.

Seventeen

Joe

Joe stared at the face in the bathroom mirror. Fifteen or twenty years ago he saw his father's face in this mirror. Recently, though, it was his grandfather who stared out at him over the sink. Like his grandfather, he had most of his hair and all of his teeth, and he was pleased enough with himself that he carried maybe only twenty pounds more than he did as a young man.

Yet, so little remained of the smooth-faced young pilot who had crawled onto the beach. Only the deep blue of his eyes was the same, but when he smiled, the creases laid there by decades of outdoor work served to camouflage the young man behind them. Joe smiled again at his image; he had nothing to fear from a fifty-year-old photograph.

Joe could hear voices downstairs. That slightly forced volume of new acquaintances, polite phrasing. A little laughter. He waited until he heard the coat closet door shut.

At some point this afternoon Joe had stopped being nervous—at least about being found out. He admitted a little excited nervousness at meeting Charlie Worth properly. He knew him well already. He'd watched him grow up through Vangie's letters. Known about his successes, and failures. His love life and his peripatetic career. Knew his mother saw Charlie as gentle, funny, a good man. Joe knew that Charlie was Vangie's son, and there was so much he wanted to ask him. Did she still wear her hair long, gathered into a loose twist against the back of her head? Did she still like to play cribbage, and was she any better at counting up? Did she ever talk about those times? About him?

Joe hesitated at the top of the stairs, his right hand touching the top of the banister, stroking it, taking an unconscious comfort in the solidity of it.

Joe heard Maggie calling him.

They were in the kitchen, where Charlie was uncorking the bottle of Chianti he'd brought. The mingled odors of lasagna and homemade bread lay as a backdrop to the scene. As Joe came into the small room, Charlie offered him a glass of wine and then his hand. Joe took one, then the other. "Welcome, Mr. Worth." Joe winced, thinking his response to Maggie's introduction was a little too drawing-room farce. "I'm so glad you found us."

"Well, if Maggie hadn't dropped her purse . . ."

"Hey. I was going to call you anyway." Maggie lifted her glass towards the doorway. "Let's go sit."

"I think your investigation would have led you to us in any case."

"Yes, you're right. You've been on my list of people to talk to."

Joe nodded and led the way back to the living room. He waited to see which chair Charlie would take, then sat in the Boston rocker near the cold fireplace. "So what have you learned?" He lifted the Chianti to his lips, using the action to cover his sudden anxiety.

"Not as much as I had hoped. Well, actually, I never expected to find anything. It was a lark, come here and take a look. Write a nice little quasi-travel piece with the Hellcat as the center."

"But something changed."

"Maybe." Charlie licked his lips.

It had rained that long, cold night. At some point the wind had risen and with it the seas. When the raft tumbled him out, he had panicked and slashed the rubber raft in trying to free himself. Tangled in the lines, numb and frightened, Joe had given himself up to death until the waves, which had nearly drowned him, left him on shore. Charlie's equivocation was like that April water so long ago.

Maggie shared the couch with Charlie, leaning with her elbows on her knees, uncommitted to relaxing next to him just yet. They bumped hands as they both reached for the dip, apologizing with a smile. "So what have you heard?"

"It's less what I have heard, and more

what I'm just guessing at. Nothing really. Nothing substantiable."

"Dad, you were going to tell me something about the plane this afternoon. What was it?"

Pretending to struggle a little getting salsa on a chip, Joe didn't answer.

"Dad? Do you know something about the crash?"

The dip slipped off the chip, and Joe put a soggy nacho in his mouth. "Oh, no. I really don't. I was going to tell you about the efficiency of the Hellcat in war."

Mercifully, the oven buzzer sounded, and Maggie excused herself, leaving Joe and Charlie to poke around for a new topic. "So, ever fish?"

Charlie shook his head. "Not really. My dad took me trout fishing a few times when I was a kid." He set his empty glass on a coaster and raised his forefinger at Joe. "You're the one."

Joe felt his fingertips grow cold. "The one?"

"Yes, in the snapshot of two guys and a line of fish."

Joe hoped his guilty relief didn't show. "Ernie Dubee and me. I remember your mother taking that snapshot. She still has it?"

"I don't know. I expect she does. I remember it in a box of a million others."

"How is your mother?" *Don't tell me about her age or infirmities; just tell me she is well and happy.*

"Sassy as ever."

It was the perfect response, and Joe laughed with joy. Now he could say her name out loud. "Vangie and I worked hard on that farm. Did she ever tell you?" *What did she say about me?*

"Yeah. Every now and then she'd get started. You featured prominently in a lot of her stories."

Joe felt the cold leave his fingertips and a light warmth touch his cheeks. "Did I?"

Maggie came into the living room to call the two men in to dinner. In an old-fashioned gesture, Charlie offered his arm to Maggie. "She always made this place sound so magical. I still don't know why she never came back."

Joe followed them into the dining room, grateful they couldn't see his face and know that he knew the answer.

Eighteen

Vangie

The new marbled black-and-white notebook had an inviting heft to it. It was exactly the kind Vangie had used—one hundred pages, wide-ruled—for years. It was a little exciting, a new notebook, one hundred blank pages to fill with internal dialogue, private thoughts, random imaginings. Usually Vangie scratched out new poems in these hardcovered books. Today she began a new journal.

April 18, 1993

After I went to the nursing home this afternoon, I went out and bought this notebook. I probably have half a dozen like it at home, but each one has some false start in it, or has been cannibalized for poems. I was once a keen journal keeper. Since then I have been a sporadic one, my days too filled and my nights too weary to write. My public time spent on fulfilling obligations and tasks. My poems and my letters to Joe taking up all my private energy, nothing left for reflection, or repetition in journal form. I should have kept copies. I'm sure that my whole life has been mapped out in those letters to Joe. As his life has been for me. Does he remember half of what he's written to me? An autobiography for my eyes only.

It's eight o'clock. By this time Joe and Charlie have met. Joe's daughter will serve them some neutral meal, and Charlie will be extravagantly grateful. They don't know Charlie's subtlety. He will interview them without their knowing it. Ask questions that don't seem important, then piece together the whole. I will suck the marrow from his visit when he comes home. I will ask direct questions and know that Joe is still Joe. I will not be subtle. It is possible, by the time

Charlie sees me next, that he will know everything.

When I bought this new journal, I felt a little silly. What have I got to record except the exceedingly routine patterns of old age? Today is mild. I watched *Oprah.* I ate a Swanson's dinner because I hate cooking for myself. My hip doesn't hurt today. But a journal is a recording of thoughts, emotions, memories, and I am filled with those.

After shopping, I came home and wrote to Joe. I mailed the letter on the way to the nursing home. As I have done a thousand times before, I tipped the postbox door open and dropped in a letter to my best friend. Somehow, today, the very act of mailing the letter was high drama. It is the first time we face the possibility of including others in our secrets. Is the game up?

The nursing home today seemed particularly pungent. A thin layer of cleaning solvent rode the breeze as the aides pushed past me, linen carts piled high with draw sheets and diapers of their ancient babies. John has a new roommate. He is also a stroke patient, but his mind is clearly involved. He moans a single note incessantly. I've only seen visitors twice since he's been there. Even though it was a little past noon, John wasn't up yet. The place is often short-handed on weekends. We've been there long enough now that I help myself to supplies and so got a bowl of warm water and towels. Sometimes I think that they count on my being there and thus don't worry about getting John up. He doesn't acknowledge my presence these days. Yet, he is as cooperative as he can be with one side immobile. I shave him as best I can; his beard is weakened by age and a few whiskers along his cheeks are easy to get. I make a monkey face at him to get him to draw his upper lip down, but he doesn't react, so I gently take my thumb and pull his lip into firmness, then lift his chin to catch the few hairs there. I wash his hands and slip a clean pajama top on.

All the time I am caring for my husband, I am thinking of Joe Green. When we were young and John was making love to me, I thought of Joe. I would think, Joe touched me thus, and thus; John does not. In the middle of making love, I was unfaithful. Where Joe's touch electrified me, John's was mechanical. Three times in twelve hours Joe and I made love. I could bring to mind every stroke of his hand and the very taste of his tongue. I could remember the heat radiating from us, the pulsing heartbeats. I lay in my husband's arms year after year remembering what it was like to be passionately engaged in the act, instead of going along for the ride. It was only fair, I told myself. If I had come home to pick up our lives again, at the very least I wouldn't feel guilty for remembering.

Now I touch my husband's treacherous body, the body that has robbed him of his usefulness without robbing him of his mind, and think of Joe meeting our son. I am certain that John has forgotten that I ever knew anyone named Joe Green.

Sometimes I wish that I could forget.

Every decision I have made, every private thought, every move has been held against the backdrop of Joe's existence. Like a guardian angel, my imagined Joe smiles down on me. There has always been this little piece of me that belonged exclusively to him, making it impossible for me to be wholly John's. Maybe if I could have closed that chapter in my life instead of rereading it, I could have been a better wife. John deserved my full commitment.

That day I went to the veterans' hospital to see John for the first time, I was shaking with nerves. October had turned chilly overnight in prelude to winter. I remember that I hoped my trembling would be seen as the shivers by those riding the train with me.

I didn't know what to expect from John. I really didn't even know how badly injured he was, or even if he'd been injured. He was a casualty. But no one had said wounded. I didn't know what to expect from myself. So much had happened. To both of us.

Everything that mattered in my life at that moment was tied up in the greeting we gave one another. If I flinched when he touched me, the game was over.

The VA hospital was potent with the scent of disinfectant. The ward I was directed to seemed endless; narrow iron beds flanked the walls. Men with unspeakable wounds called out lewd greetings at me as I walked through the gauntlet of hospital beds. Why was he so far away? Orderlies and nurses kept their eyes away from me, looking only at their grisly work. I was beginning to panic. Had I walked by him, not recognized my husband? Was he so badly wounded he had become one of these gauze-wrapped creatures?

"John! John Worth!" I inhaled the taste of the hospital, wanting to cover my mouth and nose against it. The men in the beds began calling after me in imitation, "Oh, John! Johnny! Your girlfriend's here!" I couldn't yell back at them. Maybe their wives hadn't seen them yet either. Maybe their wives wouldn't recognize them.

Lost among the acres of cots, John lay somewhere in this place. He was waiting for me to find him. It seemed the cruelest taunt to make me search for him here, now, after all the waiting and not knowing.

"Mrs. Worth?" An orderly touched my elbow. "Your husband is in Ward Three. This is the amputee ward. He's not a surgical case."

I think I could have collapsed into this white-coated stranger's arms had he not had hold of my elbows. "Thank you. How do I get there?"

He was a gentleman and led me across the hall to the double doors of Ward Three.

"Wait. What kind of injuries do these people have?"

The young man touched my elbow again. "Shock cases mostly." He pushed the left-hand double door open for me. "Guys on their way home. Go in, Mrs. Worth. You'll find him. He's waiting for you."

Today we sat in the dim solarium, too many of my thoughts on the past. John sat quietly, as he always does, as he always has. Reading all of my journal and most of Joe's letters, I have cast myself backwards into emotions I had numbed with living realities.

That day I went to find John in the VA hospital, I was still alive with feelings I thought would never dull. Would I never be done with grieving? For Molly. Then the missing John. Now Joe.

Now I know that some grieving happens before the real death. Every day I grieve a little for John, missing the husband who opened his arms to me from his hospital bed so many years ago. So very happy to see me. I sat on his bed and held this skinny, frightened man, so haggard and thin that I might not have recognized him had he not been watching for me. We gripped each other and wept. I wept a little for the fact that the woman John held was not the same woman he had left behind. No longer the woman he thought I was.

"Evangeline, you will never know how you kept me from giving up. Knowing I had you, had you to come home to, I kept going when it would have been easier to die."

I wept because for the rest of my life I would have to pretend to be that woman.

He came back from the war a defeated man. Those months in a German concentration camp had reduced him in ways that went deeper than the physical changes. He needed constant reassurance, needed, in those first few months, to know I was there in the house with him at all times. Or, if I went out, exactly when he could expect me back. He needed my devotion. I loved and cared for him through all those months of regeneration, but I thought of Joe and missed him horribly. Sometimes all I wanted was a few minutes to indulge myself in thoughts of those days. I would invent a need to run to the store just so I could think of a conversation or a moment, to study it for clues to our love as I walked.

John would say I seemed distracted, was I upset about anything? I'd settle my happy face back on and just say I was worried about him.

There is so much I haven't recorded. Events and occasions that were every bit as important as those seven months in Hawke's Cove. My whole life.

The aide brought in John's lunch tray, setting it on the tray table but leaving it covered, assuming I would feed him. I ask her to help me move him out of bed so that he can eat his lunch in a chair. She shrugs, on the verge of telling me she doesn't have time, but I start pulling him forward before she can say no. Some of these girls are condescending to me. "If you need help, you just call, Mrs. Worth." Others are glum, like this one. Overworked, underpaid. She should be glad she's got a job. There's one who manages to treat me like I'm not a patient. Cindy. She always brings me up to date on John's life when I'm not around, how he slept and if they've changed any medications. She treats me like I'm still a member of society. The trouble with being elderly is that people here think I'm a resident even though I'm dressed and wearing shoes. One young man on the reception desk downstairs even asked me where I was going when I left the other day. The nerve. How presumptuous. How I hate being old. When I reread that line in my journal about admiring Mrs. Grace, wondering if there was ever anything in her long life she regretted, I realized that I am the same age she was then. She's probably been dead for fifty years. I can still kneel at the Communion rail. I feel the eyes of the young staring at my back, wondering if I will be able to get up. I embarrass them; I am their future. And no, there is nothing I regret.

"Will you regret this?"

"No. Never."

Today they gave John brown stuff. Because of his uncertain swallowing, he is on a "mechanical" diet. Everything is whorled in a blender, making piles of green, brown, or yellow-white paste for him to chew. Occasionally I slip him some real food, soft, like pie or meat loaf. This is relatively new. In the beginning I just cut everything up very small. Piece by piece he ate, sometimes taking an hour until all the food was icy and the pleasure he might have taken from it long gone. The mush is at least warm.

"Oh, boy. Steak," I tell him, and he opens his mouth like a little wrinkled bird, sucking the mass off the spoon. I wipe his mouth with a moist cloth and untie the bib around his neck. I have shoved the tray table away, never sure how soon it will be removed. Someone has turned on the television for his roommate and the blare is intrusive, but masks the incessant moan. My husband sits mute, his useless hand in his lap, the other resting on the chair arm. He is held upright by a posey. He doesn't look at me, though I know he is happy I am there. I've adjusted the blinds to let in what sun eases itself between the buildings. I can see where I've missed a spot in shaving him.

I am antsy. Simply knowing that Charlie and Joe are in the same town has made me crazy with a blend of curiosity and dread. I imagine them meeting like fencers, *en garde.* Or, better, I force a fantastical dream of the two of them falling into one another's arms as reunited strangers. An invisible bond recognized between them. *Me.*

It is now eight-fifteen. Certainly they are at the same table.

Nineteen

Joe

"Then Vangie says, 'Drink it?' " Joe leaned back in his chair. He loved telling Charlie and Maggie about the whiskey pit. "I wonder if that booze is still there in the root cellar. No one but summer people or renters have used the place since . . . since it went out of your family's hands. No one's been in it in years."

Charlie sat forward, comfortable enough with Maggie and her father to lean his elbows on the table. "Could I see it?"

"The scotch?"

"No, the farm. Bailey's Farm."

"Sure. When?"

"I'm leaving tomorrow."

"Why not go out on your way home?"

"Will you show it to me, Joe?"

Joe nodded. "Sure. About nine?"

It was quite late. They had never left the dining room, content to keep the cluttered table under their elbows. Maggie had outdone herself, completing their dinner with a simple dessert of vanilla ice cream and California strawberries.

"Maggie, that was wonderful. I hope that I can do the same for you when you're in town."

"Is that a date?"

"Could be. How does your schedule look?"

Joe stood up and began collecting the dessert dishes, brushing aside Charlie's offer of help. He wanted to give Mags and Charlie enough privacy to complete this date business without his supervision. He carefully rinsed the glass bowls, edging a filigree of ice cream off the rim with his thumb. What will Vangie think, their children dating? She'd think it was something out of Shakespeare or a Greek comedy. Joe played a little with possibilities and found himself chuckling out loud.

"What's so funny, Dad?"

"Oh, Maggie, life is full of sweet irony." Handing her the dish towel, he pretended to need the bathroom.

Twenty

Charlie

"I really like your father." Charlie took the wet pan from Maggie and rubbed the damp dish towel around the inside. "He's a great guy."

"Well, I'd like to meet your mother. Beyond the fact I'm one of her fans, I mean. Because she's an old family friend."

"You know, the next time your father comes to see you, we should get everyone together."

"Oh, Charlie. That's not possible."

"Why?"

"My dad's an agoraphobic. He never leaves Hawke's Cove."

"How long has he been like that?"

"Forever. As far as I know he's never ever left. Not even as far as Great Harbor."

"Really." Charlie set the dried dish on the kitchen table. "I thought agoraphobics couldn't leave their homes."

"No. Not always. Those are severe cases. Dad's just this side of eccentric."

"So he was born here?"

Maggie swished the sponge around the inside of a serving dish. "No. But he's lived here all his adult life. I know that much."

Too many pieces were falling into place for Charlie. He stood behind Maggie at the sink and kept silent for a minute. Maggie's hair was loose and fell with a slight curve just at the point where her shoulder blades moved beneath her soft lambswool top.

"I'd still like to meet your mother."

"She'd love to meet you, Maggie. I'll bring you by before we go to dinner on the twenty-fifth. Okay?"

"Great. I'd love that."

Charlie flopped the dish towel around the inside of the bowl. "Funny, don't you think, how she never came back."

"I don't think so." Maggie fished around in the dishwater for the last pan. "I think it makes perfect sense."

"How so?"

"Charlie, hasn't it ever occurred to you that they were two adult people living in the same house under difficult circumstances. And that, well . . . fill in the blanks."

"No, Maggie. My mother was a married woman. A war bride and devoted to my father." Charlie shook his head in rejection of the notion, all the while letting it sift down to where he knew he'd always wonder.

"Who was, as you've said, missing."

"Maggie, I really don't think anything happened."

"Charlie, I'm not suggesting malfeasance, just the logical culmination of a deep friendship."

"So, why didn't they keep in touch?"

"They have, Charlie. They've been writing to each other for years."

"How do you know?"

"My mother found her letters to my father."

Charlie felt a strange watery feeling in his intestines. "Love letters?"

Maggie sighed and took the dish towel away from Charlie. "Loving enough that she left him." Maggie turned back to the sink. "Charlie, I'm sorry. Dad doesn't even know that I'm aware of it. And, I'm really just guessing. I don't know for sure. Only that Mom found some letters, and it was their last big argument."

"Maggie, I don't know what to say."

"Don't say anything. My mother would have left my father anyway. She just needed one good reason." Maggie let the water run out of the sink and dried her hands on a paper towel. "I have to make a phone call. Why don't you go sit with Dad a minute. Unless you're ready to leave?"

"No." Charlie was still thinking about what she'd said. "No, I'm not ready to go." As he walked by her, Charlie impulsively touched Maggie's cheek with his fingertips, making her blush a little. Evidently, for Maggie, other pieces had fallen in place.

Joe was sitting outside on the porch. *"Shhh."* He held one finger to his lips. "Listen, Charlie." Charlie had already picked out the distant sound of a bell buoy marking the channel more than a mile away. The random rhythm of the hammer striking the bell reached them, the sound unobstructed by gentle hills and stubby trees.

"Your mother used to call that her lullaby bell. She'd count between chimes until she fell asleep. On a calm night, like this, she could get to ten, maybe fifteen."

"She wrote a poem about a bell buoy." Charlie sat on the porch rail, facing Joe Green in his porch rocker.

". . . Sing to me of faraway places . . . where my love might be . . ."

Charlie smiled. "Yeah, something like that."

". . . And lulled, I'll dream of a time . . . when he will sing to me."

Charlie had scarcely considered his mother's work, and if he had thought at all of this poem, he would have attributed the inspiration behind it to his father's time away in the war. Now, looking at Joe Green, Charlie wondered if he'd be wrong.

Twenty-one

Joe

Dearest Vangie,

I have just seen your son out to his car. Well, not exactly. I shook his hand at the doorway and let Maggie walk out with him alone. She stood a long time by the car, and I worried that he was telling her something. But, she came back into the house, all private smiles, and kissed me good night. She hasn't done that in a long time. I may be deluding myself, but there's a certain spark between them. I am absolutely certain I do not imagine it.

You are anxious to know whether or not I told them the story. I have not. I'm not sure if you approve or not. Charlie is indeed hunting down Spencer Buchanan, but he is desperately considerate and never asked a question I couldn't answer honestly. We actually veered away from the topic early on in the evening and never got back to it. He never even produced the photo he's been showing around town. Claimed to have left it in the B and B. Thus, I am certain he is on to me.

I told them stories, Vangie. I told them about fixing the barn and finding the scotch, about the cows and the Fourth of July. I pulled out stories about the Ruths and the Sunderlands. I probably numbed them with my old man's recollections. Purified by the refiner's fire of discretion. I told them all kinds of things except that I am he whom Charlie seeks. I told them everything important to me except that you and I . . . we are, well, what we are to each other.

Imagine my joy at speaking your name out loud. Imagine the frisson of pleasure at hearing your words through your son's voice. I asked him more questions than he asked me.

I overheard Maggie telling Charlie about my "agoraphobia." Something occurred to me then, something that had never crossed my mind before.

If it hadn't been for you, I might have given up this reclusive life. I might have given myself up and taken my punishment and gotten on with my life. But I stayed here in Hawke's Cove because I never gave up hope that someday you would come back.

Twenty-two
Vangie

April 19, 1993

After church I sat with John for a longer time than usual. Because they had been so slow in getting him up, I didn't want them to put him back in bed for a nap too soon. His whole life is spent getting up and going back to bed, punctuated by meals and my visits. Because the TV was so loud, I wheeled him into the solarium. What a misnomer. What sun manages to come through those dirty windows is cowardly. I should move him out of here. Except that it is so close to home I can walk. Would he even know the difference, one place or another?

When he had the first stroke, we worked

together to bring him back to normal. Hours of physical therapy and speech therapy. We were in this together. A team whose only goal was to regain the dignity he lost when he tumbled to the floor in his office. We always said he was lucky it happened there. Lucky Missy was bringing in files just before leaving for the day. Oh, yes, we looked on the bright side.

I refused to baby him, and some of our friends thought I was harsh. John understood what I was doing and knew I wouldn't let him give up. One night he reached over and touched my breast. Words were still difficult for him, but there was no need to speak. I wish I could say that it was wonderful, that the act of love made everything better. Truth is, I was glad when it was over. John, though, was renewed by success. By the end of that horrible year, he was back at work, and I was happy to take on a third class at the college.

The second stroke stole that back and then some. By the third I knew I could not care for him at home any longer. I'd let the home health care workers take care of him so I could at least keep one class, but the guilt and effort were too much for me, and for the first time I felt I needed help. Why am I writing this down now? For posterity so that my children, who supported my decision, can see that I hated it, but knew it was the right one. It wasn't just that I didn't want to give up my career; it was for the good of both of us.

John was a good provider and wise investor, and I have no trouble paying for this place. He has protected me from worrying about it. But now I have to provide loving care for him and protect him from the indignity of this place.

The sunlight shifted around and found its way into the solarium through a clean patch in the clouded window, leaving a puddled brightness on the floor, shimmering with shadows of wind-shaken trees. Leaf buds, like pickled cauliflowers, give weight to the maple trees.

I pulled my chair in front of John and leaned towards him, placing my hands on his bony knees.

"It's been all right, hasn't it, John? Has it been what you hoped for?" His face betrayed no emotion, but his eyes began to water. "I mean our life together; have I been a good wife?"

With effort, John placed his good left hand on mine resting on his knee. His hand is soft and papery. His good hand squeezes mine, and he nods.

Twenty-three

Joe

Joe hurried to get to Bailey's Farm before Charlie did. He wanted a few minutes on his own to get past the changes that others had wrought on the place and winnow out the memories he knew would flourish at the sight of things that had not been altered.

The most obvious change was the loss of the winter pasture to scrub oak and pines. Nearly filled in, the old stone wall barely visible from the driveway. Joe shook his head and then reprimanded himself for it. He hadn't been back since the day he'd driven the three cows across the winter pasture and across the neighboring fields to Sylvester Feeney's place. It had felt like he was driving himself away.

Parking the truck in the place where the old carport once stood, Joe got out and assessed the yard, taking a moment to reconcile his memories with the reality. It was almost as if he hadn't been gone. The place had been left derelict, abandoned by the last owners against back taxes or a contested will, Joe couldn't recall which. It had been long enough that the most recent coat of paint had weathered off. The screening of the back porch was ripped open, and the shutters on the kitchen window hung askew. Someone had added aluminum gutters, but the weight of the decade's worth of leaves and grit had buckled them. Leaving it till last in his survey, Joe finally looked at the barn. He smiled, tugged at his cropped beard, and then let himself grin in self-satisfaction. His foundation work had survived. One door was open, and Joe went over to it and gave it a gentle push. After fifty years, the doors were still plumb. The door swung easily to meet its mate.

When Charlie pulled up to the house, Joe was sitting on the back porch steps. He stood up as Charlie got out of the car, flourishing the keys he'd gotten from the real estate agent.

"Shall we go in?" Charlie held the screen door open.

Joe hesitated a little. Charlie saw his hesitation and put out a hand to steady him.

He knew exactly what he'd write to Vangie. "You wouldn't believe how unchanged it all is. It was modernized in the fifties, deserted in the seventies, and now the old place has regressed back to the forties. The linoleum in the kitchen is a different pattern, but cracked in the same places. The old combination range is gone, replaced with a white Glenwood gas stove, and there's central heat now. A silver radiator sits in testimony to someone's ambition to live there year round. What must have been new wallpaper thirty years ago is faded into a pale yellow nearly the same shade as the kitchen always was. Ditto the blue paint in the parlor. Of course, everything seems smaller than memory. And empty. No voices echo."

Charlie had brought breakfast in a paper bag. He and Joe leaned against the porcelain sink that had replaced the soapstone one of memory and sipped lukewarm black coffee out of paper cups and ate home-made sugar doughnuts from Linda's Restaurant.

"Want to look around?" Joe brushed crumbs from his shirt and put the lid back on his coffee.

Charlie led the way, still munching a doughnut. They wandered around the first floor, then up to the second.

Joe said nothing to Charlie, pointed nothing out. He let Vangie's son take in the old empty house without annotation.

"Well, I can see why Dad had no use for the place. Yet, at the same time, I can see why Mom did. Yin and yang." They were back in the kitchen. "Can we look at the barn?"

"Sure." Joe left his coffee cup on the counter.

The stalls were cluttered with junk, cob-webs hung thick above their heads. But the light was the same. The dust motes swirling as the two men moved through the aisle towards the ladder to the loft.

"It looks just like it did the first time I

saw it." Joe kicked at a pile of newspapers. "Full of junk and swallow nests."

"Tell me about coming here, Joe."

"Well, your mother wanted to get this barn straightened up. She was alone, and I needed a job."

"No. I mean about coming to Hawke's Cove. Tell me about coming here."

Joe grasped the rungs of the ladder and hauled himself up, easing himself to the loft floor. He was mildly pleased with how easy it had been for him to still get up there. "Come up here, Charlie."

Charlie set his coffee cup on the pile of newspapers and followed Joe up.

The loft was empty. A thin layer of old straw covered the boards, but everything else was gone. The loft doors were closed. Joe stood leaning against a massive joist. "Why do you ask, Charlie? What do you want to know?"

"Joe, I want to show you something. Come back down." Charlie went back down the ladder and out the open barn door.

Joe heard Charlie's car door open and then slam shut. He held his breath, hoping to hear the sound of the engine but only heard the screak of the screen door.

It was harder to descend the ladder.

Charlie held a glossy photo of Spencer Buchanan. "I had one of the guys at MIT play around with the pilot's photo. I realized no one would recognize the guy in a 1942 photo, so I had him computer-age the image. This is what Spencer Buchanan would look like if he had survived and was alive in 1993. If he'd spent most of his life working outside. If he hadn't died in a plane crash."

Charlie handed Joe a computerized image of himself.

"When did you get this?"

"Last night. Before I came to dinner. They faxed it to me."

"Have you said anything to Maggie?"

"No."

"Thank you."

"You should tell her, Joe. She needs to know."

"She'll know soon enough."

"No, Joe. I'm not writing this story. I can't."

Joe felt himself sag against the sink.

"You don't have to protect me. I can take my lumps."

"No. Some things are meant to stay undiscovered. Not like the scotch."

Through the kitchen window they could both see Maggie's car pull up beside Charlie's.

"I'll tell Maggie." Joe handed the copy back to Charlie. "Can I tell you too?"

Charlie slipped the copy into his file folder and shook his head. "No. I don't need to know." He went to the back door to open it for Maggie. With his hand on the latch, he turned back to Joe. "Just tell me one thing, Joe."

Standing there on the back steps, Joe Green nodded. "Sure."

"Did my mother know?"

Dear Vangie,

. . . What could I say? Everything that has defined my life suddenly condensed into one word: yes or no. The guilt, the shame, and the love I feel for you. Charlie was asking for all of it.

I am by nature a runner. I run from the painful things in life. I ran away from the truth that I killed that boy. I ran away the day you knew John was alive. By failing to cross the bridge, I ran away from my son. I wanted to run away from Charlie. But, Vangie, I'm too old and there's nowhere left to go.

I ran from you that day not because I didn't want you to have to choose, but because I was afraid you wouldn't choose me.

Twenty-four

Vangie

July 27, 1994

From where I sit, a little trapped by the old Adirondack chair, I can see the path to the cove. If I block out the new addition, I can almost cast myself back to my grandmother's time. The teenage voices laughing this morning were not mine and my cousins', but my grandchildren's. The adult voices through the kitchen window admonishing them to hurry and get dressed, not my grandmother's, but my daughters' voices, anxious with the momentous occasion of their only brother's wedding.

The path to the beach is still sandy. I haven't tried to follow it, except in memory.

It winds down along the pasture and through the trees that seem exactly the same, no taller and no more bent over than I recall. It splices the duck pond, brackish on one side and fresh on the other. Up and over the dune and there you are, Hawke's Cove to the left and Dwight's Cove to the right, their headlands scalloped along the shoreline. Charlie tells me that he's found out the cove wasn't named for some pre-revolutionary family named Hawke, but for the osprey that lived here in abundance then. Who knew? Inconsistent Yankee spelling.

They say that, with all the recycling, there is very little sea glass left to gather anymore. That what you find is mostly white or brown. I would like to walk the beach again and see if this is true. John swept up my sea glass and threw it away. He thought he was doing me a favor, cleaning up my broken jar. Maybe I'll attempt to get down there later, after I've rested and recorded these events. Maybe one of my granddaughters will come with me.

When Charlie brought Maggie home that first time, I was nonplussed. Even though I had expected them, I had not expected her to look so much like Joe. How Joe must have looked at forty. Charlie offered to let me see the computer photo, but I wouldn't.

They bought Bailey's Farm together. Maggie and Charlie. They've brought it back to life; beyond the new paint and repairs, they have filled it with unabashed love. Even when I am watching them, their fingers touch, they glance at each other as if needing constant renewal from the source. I watch with a jealousy they cannot imagine.

I like to think that Maggie and Charlie fell in love right here, at Bailey's Farm when she met them that afternoon. I like to think that the spirits of the long ago Joe and Vangie breezed through them and opened their eyes to one another. Full circle. That they might finish what we never could.

Charlie relayed my message to Joe. And Charlie relayed one back to me when he got home that Sunday. "Mom, he told me to take your hand like this . . . and tell you that for him, too, not a day goes by he doesn't think of you."

* * *

I knew his voice the minute I heard it. He called me that afternoon, just after Charlie had gone home. I knew it was Joe, even though the slight raspiness of age laces his soft voice. "Vangie."

"Joe," I answer, and hear the age in my own.

We are not the same people, but it doesn't seem to matter. The first call has undone the self-inflicted prohibition against calls. We talk often; embarrassingly high phone bills are now part of my life. Words, once the province of our correspondence, flow from us. We are reluctant to hang up, always something more to say. At first we spent a lot of time reminiscing. That didn't last long; there were too many other things of interest to discuss. Politics and movies and opinion.

Then, when it became obvious our children were "getting serious," it was the future we reviewed. We both admitted an unreasoning fear they'd break it off and we'd be on opposite sides of a fence. But they didn't.

Yet, we have never met face-to-face.

It would have been easy; I could have

gone any time with Charlie. But John began to fail. I couldn't leave. I have long since forgiven myself for the infidelity of the body; I could not, in these last months, commit the infidelity of the mind. When there was no comfort left for him, except being with him, to be absent from John would be unforgivable. For the same reason, Joe did not come. He would have broken out of this prison of his own choosing to be with me, but I would not let him. I owed John that much. Even after John died last month, I could not fly off to meet Joe. There was so much to take care of. It would have been somehow disloyal to be so precipitous.

When we talk on the phone, we see ourselves as we are, but imagine each other young. I am so nervous about seeing him, not about the changes time has made in him, but in me. Before I came out here in the yard to wait, I stood in front of the pier glass in my grandmother's bedroom and stared hard at the old lady reflected there. I stared long enough that the soft edges hardened and she stood up taller, her hair darkened, and her eyes grew sharp. I stared at my reflection until the real Vangie looked back at me, the Vangie Joe Green will expect.

Everyone has gone to the rehearsal. Because it is Maggie's second and because this is a late marriage for Charlie, the whole thing will be simple, uncluttered by the trappings of youthful marriage. Still, they need to practice. In my role as matriarch, I need no rehearsal, and am infinitely glad for the few hours alone. Here.

Someone will come back to take me to the big family dinner in Great Harbor's fanciest restaurant. Denise will not be there, bitterly angry at Maggie for loving my son. Maggie says, never mind. Eventually she'll get over it. I admire Maggie's courage, but I'm not sure she understands the magnitude or the reason behind Denise's presumably unreasoning dislike.

No one has said if Joe will come, if this event is significant enough for him to abandon his exile. He still hasn't left the Cove. Despite, as he puts it, the weight of a lifelong lie having been removed. I didn't ask him when we spoke last night. I called a few minutes after I arrived at Bailey's Farm with Julie and her family. Things were pretty chaotic, and we only spoke for a minute.

Our first local call, Joe kidded. While everyone bustled around bringing in luggage, we spoke of inconsequentials. I told him the trip was fine, very different coming all the way by car. Can you believe it, the bridge is now two lanes! Yes, the house is coming along nicely. Stopped in Great Harbor to see Judy, still going strong!

Then, when left suddenly alone in the kitchen, "I can't wait to see you." Kids. We behave like kids.

By the time we got into Hawke's Cove last night, it was too late and, even in July, too dark to see much. I was up early this morning to get a good look. I think I felt as much excitement about seeing my house as I do thinking about seeing Joe. The two are inextricable in my heart. I was so afraid Charlie and Maggie had changed the place so much it would bear no resemblance to my memory. Charlie assured me over and over that they had kept the "integrity" of the place, and he was as good as his word. Except for the addition, of course. They've enlarged the kitchen into one of those "great rooms," which serve as living room and dining room and gathering place. Above it, two more bedrooms. Joe's room is gone, absorbed into the new plan. It is not without perfect irony that I approve of the remodeling. Essentially the same remodeling John wanted to do and I refused to have done, our first wedge.

Charlie led me to my old room, my grandmother's room. It's clean and fresh and just the same as I remember it, except that the old spool bed is long gone and the new one is bigger and an unremarkable pine. As I lay there last night, I could hear the bell buoy on the shoals ringing out its erratic warning. The sea was calm, the chiming spaced out in long intervals. I lay awake a long time.

The sun is hot today. I am like a snake, soaking in the warmth and taking pleasure in it. There are clothes on the line, barely moving in the light air. I promised Amanda I'd take them in before I join them for dinner.

I tiptoed out of the house at dawn, anxious to stand alone in my yard and see the changes time has brought. Not many, not really. The tree line and the rise of the pasture effectively block out the new houses I know to be there. The winter pasture, as Joe warned me, has reverted to woodlot. My garden is all lawn now, not even a depression to mark its location. How many yards of topsoil must that have taken? I wonder.

Pulling my housecoat belt tighter and glad of my sneakers, I went into the barn. No bovine perfume lingers behind. Only cars and their particular odors, garage, not barn. I dodge an oil patch instead of a cowpat. But the ladder is still there. The wood rung beneath my hand is smooth from wear, from generations of farmers climbing up and down to feed their stock. From children's bare feet, racing up to play hide-and-seek. Joe, sheltering there in the loft against his nightmare. My foot, as I come down the ladder towards the rest of my life.

I wonder if I could still climb up there. I am wondering this still when I hear Julia calling everyone to breakfast.

I like to think this is the same Adirondack chair in which my grandmother presided over us. Sitting here in her floppy hat, her afternoon cocktail in one hand, long cigarette in the other. Grand dame. Matriarch. Me. Except for the hat. I amuse myself with such fantasies. Blame it on the poetic soul.

Maggie sought me out after breakfast. Took me by the arm and gently walked out with me, ostensibly to have a prenuptial chat with her mother-in-law-to-be. Pretending to want the lowdown on her intended's bad habits. They've been living together in their new Beacon Hill flat, so I think she pretty much has his bad habits figured out. However, I went along with her ruse, and we came out to these chairs.

"Hope this weather lasts through tomorrow."

"Oh, Maggie, it will. You and Charlie don't need to worry. Look, not a mare's tail in sight. Red sky last night too."

"Vangie, I really love him."

I smiled at her. "I know you do, honey. And he loves you very much. You've been the find of his life."

She licked her lips, dry with nerves. "Vangie, for all these years you've been the only person to know who my father really was."

"No, Maggie. You knew. Maybe not his

name, but you know perfectly well who he is."

"Point taken." Maggie sat forward on the edge of the green chair, hands clasped together like a child at prayer. "May I ask you something?"

I wondered what tipped her off, what clue had tweaked her instincts. "Go ahead."

"You and my father were lovers."

"That's not a question."

Maggie said nothing.

"Will my answer change your opinion of your father?"

"No."

"Of me?"

She hesitated, then smiled. I am still amazed to see her father's smile on her lips. "No."

"Yes. For one . . . beautiful . . . night. The next morning I learned that John had been found."

"Oh, Vangie." Maggie reached across the space that divided us and gathered my hands in hers.

"Consider it the luckiest break in your life. If things had played out differently, you and Charlie would have been siblings."

Maggie's laugh, like her smile, recalls her father.

After she leaves me sitting here, I think that I have misspoken. What we had has certainly lasted more than that one beautiful night.

Epilogue

Hawke's Cove—1994

I must have dozed. The light has changed. My journal is upside down on the ground beside my chair, my pen beneath it. I lean forward to pick it up, and that's when I see him. A dark-haired man, coming up the path with a young man's stride. I think, *How odd, he's still wearing John's clothes.* As he gets closer I see that, of course, he isn't. Plaid shirt and black Dockers, recent vintage. I have mistaken a baseball cap for dark hair. As Joe gets closer, I edge my way out of the deep Adirondack chair and stand up to meet him. There is an exquisite moment when we both pause, just far enough away from each other that the work of time is muted.

"You are as lovely as I remember." Joe touches my face with gentle fingertips.

We kiss in the way of old friends, then stand a long time just holding each other. The body never forgets, and his scent is as familiar to me as if I had breathed it in every day of my life. There seems to be nothing left to say, as if the letters have said it all for us and now we need only to hold each other. To be together.

It is so temporary. We have no idea how much time is left to us. Tomorrow we will see our children married and we will dance together at their wedding. We will toast their future with seventy-five-year-old scotch.

For us, it will have to be enough.